love

awaits

to

unleash

in

one so

splendid   ;

a

soul caught in a

mirror

palindrome

hannah

a novel
by Michael Bailey

Published by Written Backwards
www.nettirw.com

ISBN: 978-1-7355981-3-0 / Hardback Edition
ISBN: 978-1-7327244-0-2 / Paperback Edition

"… perhaps all the dragons of our lives are princesses who are only waiting to see us once beautiful and brave. Perhaps everything terrible is in its deepest being something helpless that wants help from us."

– Rainer Maria Rilke

palindrome

hannah

PART ONE

reflections

pu llup i fi pu llup

[reversed, but not entirely]

1

THE MIRROR

A pale sky slowly darkened to a violet-and-crimson–smeared mess bleeding through the flat line of clouds along the horizon. Aeron sat on a park bench, a faint, coolish breeze fanning his face as he waited for his virtual work shift to end. Admiring the violent beauty of the sky, he felt a strange and new respect for life, though he still felt the shock of what had happened. Suicide had taken a lot out of him.

As the sun edged down toward the horizon, the breeze on his skin cooling, bad images shuddered through his mind. The scene hit him like a nightmare. Aeron saw a mirror, stippled with flesh and streaked with dark blood—his own—running down the sink.

A new reflection showed in this dream mirror, not the image that had been staring at him earlier, but an image of his wife and son staring in horror at the grim sight on the floor. Karen covered her mouth and gagged, forcing down a retch and then gasping for breath; she looked away. Matty, their soon-to-be eight-year-old son, stared, immobile, wanting to look away but fixated on the lifeless form lying gracelessly at his feet, its head blown open on one side.

High-pitched double beeps came from the body on the floor. Aeron's corpse ... *beeping?*

The darkening crimson on the mirror became a dark sky as he jerked a little, startled back into now. Another pair of beeps jolted him again, this time beside him on the bench ... his wrist. It was the sound of his own watch. The timer he had set for six o'clock had gone off, reminding him that it was time to leave the park and go home.

He slid into the 1969 MG coupe as the sun slipped below the shimmering horizon. He shut the door and was reminded of the hammer clicking onto the first empty chamber. The second chamber, also empty, clicked in his mind as he fastened his belt. He pulled the choke and turned the key, pulled the light switch, and flipped the defrost. Condensation dissipated as a clear spot slowly grew at the bottom of the window. Aeron rubbed his hands together and blew into them, waiting for the old car to heat up.

He pushed the choke back in, and the engine settled into a low, familiar growl. By now the windshield was clear. The back window, on the other hand, was not. He had learned to live with this over the years, knowing that if he popped open the two side windows in the back, the air current would soon clear things up. With a grind and an audible clank, he found the car's long-suffering first gear and sped out of the parking lot. The MG backfired once, as if to remind him of the gunshot that had blown a hole in the bathroom wall. He chuckled at the thought, glossing over the fact that he had almost done himself in.

Ten minutes passed and Aeron pulled in to a Home Depot. It took forty-five minutes to get home from work, but the park was just a few miles from the house. He had time to kill—and some important business to take care of.

He waved to a man standing by the store entrance, witnessing to passersby that "God is in town." The grimy, obviously homeless proselyte smiled to him as he passed, and said, "Bless you, my child." His matted shoulder-length hair looked right for Jesus; his sandals housed a pair of dirty, hobbitesque feet.

The store reminded him of an airport: people herding down the rows and buying things they didn't need, all the while crowding and bumping into one another without care. Hundreds of mirrors covered the walls.

Knowing Karen would want something with a light wooden trim to match the bathroom, he settled on the perfect replacement: a medium-size oval mirror much like its predecessor. He searched for it on the shelves below, not caring about price. He was in luck: one left. He grabbed the box by the plastic bands that bound it, and lugged it to the nearest register. The box seemed heavy to his weakened body and was awkwardly shaped, making it feel like twice its twenty pounds. He took out his checkbook and smiled, pleased to have found the perfect mirror.

"Hello, how are you doing today?" asked the woman behind the register in a perky but fake tone. It was no doubt part of her job to ask. Her name badge read JULIE.

He thought for a while about his life before replying.

"Actually Julie, I'm doing surprisingly well."

"Is this a gift?"

She was curious, but he didn't know why.

"A replacement. I broke our last one," Aeron said.

He had shot it, in fact.

The amount flashed on the monitor as she scanned the barcode on the box. The price was a number palindrome.

"That will be eighty-seven seventy-eight," she said.

Aeron signed the check and handed it to her.

"Is there anything else I can help you with?"

She brushed the blonde hair out of her eyes and rested a hand on her waist. She was wearing a pair of tight, low-cut jeans, and a loosely worn orange smock. As she bent sideways to move the mirror, the beginning of a black tattoo dragon peeked out near her pierced navel. It looked too good to be fake, at least the part he could see.

Sure, Julie. As a matter of fact, there is something you could help me with: you could get me a time machine and warp me back to last week, before this most terrible episode of ...

He moved his gaze from her tattoo to her face—he had been caught staring.

"No, this will be all."

There was something about her.

Aeron handed her the check.

She handed him the receipt, avoided eye contact, and rang up another customer. She was short, cute, and fit, curving in all the right places, but also kind of rebellious, which wasn't a bad thing. And Aeron was married, so there ended the fantasy.

In the reflection of the glass doors, he noticed her smile as he walked out.

During the drive home, he thought of Karen, their son Matty, and black dragon tattoos. He also thought of the new mirror and what kind of reflection it would behold.

And then he remembered the letter and the rose.

2

A FEW DAYS PRIOR

When Karen finally awoke, she opened her eyes and let them into his. Her skin was soft, her touch gentle. Her limber, smooth fingers grazed across his scruffy cheeks as she peered into his soul. The picture Aeron took right then with his mind would last forever, a picture of perfect bliss. It would later be the picture that saved his life. It was late Saturday morning, four days before he first pulled the trigger—the beginning of the four dreadful days leading to his suicide attempt.

The weather was strange. It was warm and bright, yet there was a heavy downpour as dark clouds floated past. They loved sleeping in on the weekends after a long night of passionate lovemaking. It had been a long time, six months exactly, and the months of bitter arguing had almost led them to a disastrous breakup. Last night was their makeup night. He could still feel the heat of the candles at the headboard. They had flickered through the dark and danced off the walls so gently. He could feel her skin rocking against his, warm and smooth like the skimpy silk she wore.

Her eyes were dilated and still had a wanting look. Her fingers moved over his lips. Aeron leaned over and put his lips to hers softly. Karen wore a black silk bra and panties, barely covered by her open nightie. Just as he began to slip the right side of her gown off her shoulder, he heard a gentle rapping on the bedroom door. He imagined a raven perched on the door as he covered them both with the comforter.

Instead of *nevermore* came the gentle voice of Matty.

"Mom? Dad? Can I watch cartoons?"

"Of course you can, honey," Karen said. "Just keep it down."

Matty's feet shuffled down the hall.

"Okay," he said, fading.

Aeron pictured his son running down the stairs, rounding the hall and rushing into the living room, where he'd grab all three remotes and skillfully work the complex television system.

His eyes met with Karen's again. Both smiled rapturously as they got out of bed to begin the day. Karen stood next to Aeron in her underwear, brushing her teeth in front of the bathroom mirror. He got out the shaving cream, squirted out a thick, blue-white layer on his palm, and slapped it on his face. She laughed and then they both burst into laughter.

The bathroom was warm from the hot shafts of sunlight that permeated through the curtains in dust-revealing beams. The plain white ceramic tiles that he had lain the year before felt pleasantly cold to his feet, but then he shuddered seeing the walls with their awful off-white, brown-flower wallpaper (probably there since the house was originally built). There was still plenty to do in the way of remodeling.

He continued shaving, looking at Karen's reflection, still in awe of her beauty: perfect face, perfect body, and perfect soul. He felt the razor catch and pull against his face—Karen had probably stolen it to use on her legs a few dozen times—so he grabbed another from the drawer, all the while paying full attention to her lovely form reflected in the his-and-her sink. He fumbled with the bare blade as he continued to stare, getting more aroused by the second. But suddenly he felt fear, along with something foreign, enter his body.

The look in Karen's face transformed from cute to horrified. She was looking at Aeron's hand.

He broke his fixation on her beauty and looked down at the blood welling up from his palm. He slung the bleeding hand into the air, spattering the mirror with streaking drops of blood.

Karen responded frantically, searching for a washcloth. Aeron looked back into the mirror and felt the chill of dread run through his spine as blood ran down into the sink. An uncomfortable, distant but familiar feeling filled his heart as something dark and deep inside wished it were his wrists instead of his palm. Cold, terrified. Karen wrapped a white towel around the cut hand, and he pressed hard to cut off the circulation. If only he could stanch the mental pain as easily.

They were out of the emergency room by noon. Twelve stitches later, Aeron's hand, though throbbing, was mostly repaired. Three veins in his palm had been sliced along with some non-recoverable nerve endings. The deep cut spanned from the thumb joint to the base of the ring finger. Dr. Edalb Deggar gave Aeron codeine to keep the pain to a minimum. In heavily accented English he also hinted that it might be prudent to stop using old-fashioned single-blade razors and switch to something more modern and safer.

As the doctor blathered about his hand situation, Aeron replayed the unwanted images of the blood on the mirror. It haunted and perplexed his mind. Karen was attentive, nodding in agreement with the doctor like a bobble-head car ornament.

They left the hospital and Aeron managed to file the gruesome images away in a small pocket hidden deep in his mind. The automatic doors welcomed them to a bright and clear sky. The rain had stopped. Smells of ozone filled the air, wet wood and wet ground, the air fresh and crisp.

They headed to the store as they had originally planned. Matty had stayed at the neighbors' playing with Billy, one of his friends from school. Karen had figured he'd enjoy playing cowboys and Indians and caking himself in mud much more than spending the morning at the hospital. His school had banned the game a few years back, about the same time Crayola stopped producing Indian-red crayons, but it was still Matty's favorite game.

His absence gave them the opportunity to plan for his birthday party. He was an unusual almost-eight-year-old boy, so it made it hard to shop for him. He never wanted much.

They browsed through the Wal-Mart toy department searching for gift ideas. They had already given Matty a cowboys-and-Indians party with cake, party favors and the works last year, so anything on that theme was out. Karen didn't want to get him a toy gun, not with all the school shootings lately. It seemed every year there were more and more.

On their way past the Lego sets, Aeron stopped at an air rifle display. Karen kept walking, unaware that he had stopped. She was still in full conversation with him. Aeron stood at the display case, his eyes wide.

Give him a gun.

There he stood with his eyes glued to the same Daisy rifle he had played with as a child. Besides the new plastic stock and pump, which were once wooden, it was identical. It would be the perfect gift for Matty. It featured the same black steel barrel with sites at both ends for targeting. He remembered his rifle and how much fun he had with it when he was little. He remembered the window he once shot, his mother scolding him.

Then he remembered her real gun.

Give him your gun, the Colt.

He shivered and thought more of his mother and the little green army men: heads popping off some, round craters in others. Matty would have fun with a rifle. He snapped back to reality and quickstepped to catch up with Karen.

Karen said, "Honey, you're sweating."

Aeron hadn't noticed, but his shirt was soaked.

"Probably reacting to the medicine or something."

Aeron knew he wasn't reacting to the medicine. Something else was wrong. When they got home, he immediately went to the bathroom to run some cool water on his face.

He turned the water off and grabbed the hand towel. It was still crusted with dried shaving cream. He dried his face, and as he moved the towel away, the mirror streaked with the blood from his hand. His pulse raced. The blood was fresh blood, not dried, as if it had just gotten there. This was dark red, fresh, and frightening. He raised the towel to the mirror and filled the cloth with red streaks.

He jumped when Karen appeared next to his reflection.

"Aeron?"

"Yeah, I was washing off"—he glanced down at the clean white towel in his hands and finished in confusion—"my face."

Blood was gone from both the mirror and the towel.

Not feeling quite himself, confused at the delusions, Aeron blamed the medication for his hallucinations.

They spent the rest of the day relaxing, just the two of them.

Matty had called to see if he could spend the night at Billy's. His room was clean and his toys were away; he could definitely spend the night. He always came home tired after staying at Billy's, but he always had fun.

Aeron decided to go to bed early and Karen joined him—it had been a stressful day. Karen fell asleep first.

It must be the medication.
Reality sank into a short but deep sleep.

The dream started off like any other: confusing and bizarre. Aeron stiffly looked upward to Matty, who was in his room playing with a bucket of plastic army men. He couldn't remember ever buying his son army men. Aeron tried to move but couldn't, his entire body paralyzed. He felt no heartbeat and took not one breath. His eyes were burning but had no eyelids to blink with; all he could do was move them, so he looked at his son. Matty a giant. Aeron the size of a bug and looking up from the floor at his son's massive body. Aeron's arms were frozen above his head and holding a rifle. The wound on his hand was again open, dripping blood down his arm and onto the floor. He turned his eyes downward to his feet and found they were bound together by some strange green substance. He was surrounded by a moat of his blood. His legs, arms, body, and even the gun he was holding were green. Aeron was a green army man toy. The only thing about him not green was the blood flowing down his arm. Blood flowed from his hand and there was nothing he could do about it. He tried yelling out to Matty, but Aeron was mouthless. He watched as Matty placed a few more army men next to him and wondered if they were just toys. Matty reached in to his closet to grab something when Aeron woke up.

He sat up, damp with sweat, and glanced at the clock: 1134. He looked at his hands and feet and was relieved not to see green plastic. Karen sensed his movements; she awoke instantly, offering comfort. She somehow always knew what he needed, and what he needed now was companionship and a hand to hold. For the rest of the night Aeron remained attached to his wife, and slept without dreaming.

3

FALLING

When he woke up, Karen was still holding his hand. With his free hand he gently released the tight grip she had kept throughout the night. Without stirring her, he rolled to the side and headed to the shower. He turned once to admire her as she slept, delighted to see the tender and mild expression on her face.

Aeron avoided the mirror and slid open the glass shower door, reached in and turned the knob, waited for hot water. He leaned against the sink, reflecting on the dream.

It had already become hazy. He recalled being immobile and Matty messing with something in the closet, but that was about it. A headache was emerging.

Maybe he was reaching for someone who really loves him.

"I love him!" Aeron said out loud, and instantly checked to see if he had disturbed Karen. She was asleep.

He wasn't reaching for you.

Aeron blotted out the thought and checked the temperature of the water, slipped off his boxers and stepped into the shower. The dull bang of the closing door startled him. The floor like wet, packed mud. Cold air wafted through the open window and around the curtain and it was refreshing.

The hot water ran down him in a steady flow. His skin tingled with gooseflesh and relaxed. A throb in his injured hand grew to a sting as water passed under the bandage and penetrated the wound.

He grabbed the body wash and then caught a peculiar mark on the glass door. He did a double take before recognizing the familiar funnel-shaped divot. Hair on his arms stood upright, the tingling returned. The body wash fell and the liquid oozed out.

(bleeding)

He moved his eyes from the shower door to the floor and then back again, only to find the glass unblemished. He felt the frosted glass in disbelief. For minutes his eyes fastened to the spot where the chip had been, waiting for it to magically reappear.

His heart pounded.

(pushing)

His eyes widened.

(opening)

Movement formed behind the glass.

(trying to find a way through)

Barely visible through the steam-frosted glass, the shape crept slowly to the handle of the shower door.

The door whooshed open. Karen offered a smile as she stood there naked, and then she stepped in to join him.

He pulled her body next to his.

"You're ... *cold*," she said.

They held one another, water raining over them, holding on like parting lovers at the end of a sad movie.

Tears hidden by the shower rolled down Aeron's cheeks and over Karen's back.

The weekend seemed like it had just started, yet it was coming to a close. After the event in the shower, Karen thought that they should go to church. They hardly ever went to church; in fact, they hadn't gone for almost a year.

"Are the Sonics playing?"

"We're *going*."

Ever since they moved to Seattle, Aeron had taken a liking to basketball. The company he worked for had moved to Washington, and luckily, Karen had relatives in the small town of Brenden. The neighborhood was friendly, which made the move easier. On weekends, children could be seen playing in the park, sometimes trailing red wagons and such.

Karen wore a tight black dress, almost too sexy for church. She had to remind Aeron to finish getting dressed when he stopped to admire her slipping it on.

Aeron dressed in black chinos and a gray button-down, long-sleeved shirt Karen had ironed earlier. She dropped a pair of black shoes at his feet and returned a moment later with a dark crimson tie, her favorite. Aeron put on his shoes and stood facing the full-length mirror in the bedroom. He closed his eyes and tied the tie, knowing that the mirror would only confuse him. He opened his eyes, looked at his reflection, and snugged it around his neck.

Tighter.

Aeron ignored the uninvited thought.

Tie it around the banister down the hall and jump!

His body froze, eyes fixed on the red tie against the light gray shirt. A headache pierced behind his watery eyes.

"Can I wear a different tie?"

"That one's fine. Ready?"

She walked out from the bathroom.

The searing headache instantly left as he turned to her.

"Will you drive?"

"Yes, please. I don't want you driving. You think after church we can go somewhere to eat? Someplace we can sit down? We haven't had a nice dinner out in some time."

"Where were you thinking?" he asked.

Karen had expensive tastes.

"How about—"

"Better idea," she interrupted. "Why don't we get something to go and have a nice, relaxing meal at the park? We'll take the MG. Matty can sit in the back or on your lap."

"What about church?"

"*Nice try*," she said, not amused. "We'll go *after* church. We can play on the swings and Matty on the monkey bars."

Sometimes Karen could be such a kid. Sometimes he could. He followed her down the hall and downstairs to the living room. It must have taken Matty only a few minutes to get ready, because by the time they were downstairs, he was watching television, remotes arrayed around him.

They packed into the car like clowns in a circus act. Karen sat in the driver's seat, and Matty buckled in with Aeron in the passenger's seat. She turned the key, but the engine didn't catch. Aeron snapped at her, reminding her about the choke. It wasn't like him at all to react such a way, and her look told him that.

His mind wandered like a lost child as he instantly sank into a mist of confusion, drifting into daydream.

The mist turned into thick coastal fog, obscuring Aeron's view. He felt faint as he moved in a slow, rocking rhythm. The fog cleared, and he realized he was drifting alone in a skiff, heading to sea. On the shore stood Karen, Matty, and Aeron's soulless body. All were staring back, expressionless, waving goodbye as he headed farther from shore.

Their faces were empty.

They hate me.

Aeron waved back to them, sat in the boat, and looked up into the dark sky; instead of stars, there was a shadowy depiction of a crucified Jesus and an old man in a beard—he guessed was God—standing next to Aeron's dead mother. God was looking to his son, crying. Aeron's mother was looking to God, crying.

They once loved me.

Aeron then glanced down at his watch, which for some reason was upside down, and read a mirrored image of 11:34. When he looked back up, the tableau was gone. The shore was too far away to see his family.

They are gone.

Again the master of his body and mind, he grabbed the oar at his feet, but the harder he rowed, the farther he drifted from shore. It was useless.

There's something I can do.

The oar in his hand was now his Colt .38.

Aeron gasped for breath, which caused Karen to scream. Swerving in her fright, she just missed a garbage truck in the oncoming lane. Tires squealed and the truck's blaring horn faded behind them.

"What are you doing? You scared the hell out of me!"

The mist cleared and Aeron came back to reality.

"It's nothing."

"Wrong answer."

"It's nothing, really."

"Either you tell me what's going on or I turn this car around and take you to Dr. Stun. He seems to be the only one who can pry anything out of you. You never talk to me, Aeron. He—"

He was the shrink.

"I don't like Dr. Stun," Matty added.

"We're not going to see him. It's the medication again," Aeron said, knowing he had forgotten to take the pills. The mere mention of the marriage counselor made him uneasy. "He said there would be side effects."

For a moment he wondered which doctor he was referring to: the physician or the shrink.

"Side effects or not, you're scaring me," she said, shaken by it all. "Keep this up and you can sleep on the couch."

Aeron had slept on the couch the night their problems first came to a head.

They fell into a kind of silence that only happened when they wanted to stop the arguing.

Aeron's hands left sweaty imprints on his pants. He wrapped them around his son, who was silent and distant. Aeron wondered what he was dreaming about.

Living alone with Mom.

Karen wouldn't even look in his direction, so he stared absentmindedly ahead, trying not to sleep.

Matty yawned as they pulled into the church parking lot, which made Aeron yawn, which made Karen yawn—a chain-linked tiredness. Silently they headed to the entrance and were met by the Johnsons, who were painfully cheery.

"Well, hello, there. How are the Stevensons this fine and dandy day?" asked What's-his-name Johnson.

He probably wore his Sunday best seven days a week and lived his entire life to serve his god.

Fuck off!

"And how's little Matthew doing?" Margaret Johnson asked as though talking to a kitten. She said his name like a bible reference. Marge, as she liked to be called, had a Carol Brady kind of hairdo and a cloying personality to match. Her yellow curtain of a dress—she had obviously made herself—enshrouded her arms and chest and stretched down to her shoes. In fact, the only skin showing on Mrs. Johnson was on her face, neck, and hands.

After a nudge Matty said, "I'm doing okay. After church we're going to go to the park to play on the monkey bars."

"Is that right?" Marge said, as though something about it were vaguely sinful. "You can sit in our pew in the front row if you wish. There's surely plenty of room."

"Sounds *great!*" Aeron said enthusiastically, knowing they'd sit in the back. "See you inside, then."

Aeron smiled and acted as though there were something more do at the car, politely getting rid of them. After the Johnsons entered the building, Aeron led his family inside. Something pushed him back at the door—a sharp, dizzying pain; he nearly fainted as thoughts cluttered his mind.

Think strength can be found in a place where they bow to a torture device? Go ahead and drink the blood of the man who gave his life; you should give yours in return.

He thought of the dream in the car and wept.

Bad thoughts vanished the moment he stepped inside. His mind became lucid; the pain gone. It felt as though he had stepped through a magical door. Tears welled. He feigned a yawn and wiped them away.

Karen spotted the Johnsons first. She grabbed Matty's arm and motioned to an empty pew in the back.

Aeron sat amazed at how clear and uncluttered his mind had become. He felt great, the same as the day before when Karen had stared into his eyes, wanting him, the black silk and her touch, the wanting smile. He had to quickly return his attention to the pastor to keep from getting aroused in church, which *had* to be a sin. The melodic choir reverberated through the sanctuary.

Following the song, the pastor talked about the crucifixion and the atonement. Aeron glanced at the cross hanging over the pulpit and wondered why it was there. He wondered why his denomination, along with so many others, portrayed the cross as its logo, wondered whether, if Jesus had been shot instead of nailed to the cross, if a giant gun would hang in its place, or a bullet perhaps. He wondered if people would wear silver gun necklaces holding black Bibles with gun silhouettes on their covers.

Everyone drank of the blood and ate of the body—in this case grape juice and tasteless, unsalted crackers—and sang a few more songs, and the preacher preached, and then finally it was over. The Johnsons waved goodbye, so he waved back, smiled a real smile.

Their faces resembled the faces in the dream: empty.

And then it all came rushing back in. His mind clouded and a painful headache returned behind the eyes. Everything around him turned into an unimportant blur.

Matty's kid's meal ironically came with a plastic gun from a recent movie promotion. He ate half his cheeseburger, gave his mom and dad each a hug, and ran to the playground a few yards away. Karen still wouldn't talk to him. And she didn't eat any of her meal; she just sat on the bench next to him, sipping her soda and staring into space. Aeron tried reasoning, but she wanted nothing of it and wouldn't even look at him. He was invisible.

Both were mad and in love.

They had fought in the past; one of which required counseling. Most of their struggles were over stupid things: not calling when working late, not putting things away, leaving lights on in the house—simple things that often fueled larger fights, which sometimes lead to makeup sex.

This was not one of those fights.

She's ignoring me.

"Why are you ignoring me?" Aeron asked, breaking the silence and speaking his thoughts with a note of irritation.

"Why don't you start acting normal for a change, and maybe I'll consider it." Karen said.

She doesn't understand.

"You don't understand."

"You never give me the chance, Aeron. And don't blame it on the medication. I saw the pills on the counter. The seal wasn't even broken."

Karen glanced in Matty's direction. He was still playing on the monkey bars, disjointed from his parents.

"Are you having trouble at work? What is it?"

"Let me get through this, by myself."

Leave me alone.

"Just ... let me get through this," he repeated.

"If you want to get through this by yourself—whatever this is you're going through—then I'll stay out of it. I love you, Aeron. I'll take Matty and spend the week at my mother's. You can stay home by yourself. It's not a problem."

It was a problem.

She would rather be alone.

"You're just going to pack up and leave?"

"Whatever it takes to have you back to how you were two

days ago." Her voice cracked and tears filled her face. "We were finally fixing things, Aeron. Look what you're doing to us."

I am the problem.

"If that's what you want."

He was angry with himself more than anything.

"I'll leave tonight, then. You can call me when you're back to your old self," she said evenly. "I'll tell Mom you're going away on a job or something and that you didn't want me and Matty alone in the house."

Matty played on the monkey bars, unaware.

They both held back tears, knowing they loved each other more than anything, yet baffled about how to fix things. Something unseen kept tearing away at Aeron's feelings, putting words into his mouth, which spread cancerously. Self-esteem faded further and further from his grasp.

He reached for Karen, but Matty sprang out of nowhere and shouted, "*Bang!* You're *dead*, Daddy."

The plastic gun pointed in Aeron's face.

They both jumped—Aeron, from fear; Karen, from his fear. Aeron's eyes watered and burned. Pain shot through his head like a bullet, as if he had really been shot.

"Matthew Jordan Stevenson! What did I say about toy guns?"

She took the gun away and threw it in the trashcan.

"Sorry," he said to the ground, hoping for forgiveness.

"Just don't do it again, okay, baby?"

Despite Aeron's active mind, the drive home was silent. He felt bad about the conversation at the park. And Karen was set on taking Matty away and leaving Aeron on his own.

You need to find yourself again, she had said, *like last time.*

Karen packed a suitcase for her and another for Matty as

soon as they were home.

"Daddy's not going because he has to work."

Daddy really did have to work, just not for two straight days and nights.

Aeron saw them both out to the car.

Karen whispered in his ear, "I'm here for you."

She gave him a kiss before rolling up the window of her Audi. She was only going thirty-six miles away, and only for a few days, yet it felt as though she and Matty were driving away forever.

Never had he felt so alone.

They waved to him like they had in the dream.

Aeron sat on the porch for over an hour, hoping the car would pull back into the driveway. The exhausted sun collapsed behind the mountains in a glorious crimson sunset. Black shadows from the mountains stretched toward him as the sun submerged.

Stars appeared; their glimmer reminded him of Karen's lovely gray eyes, of the silver plastic gun.

He sank, like the sun, into a dark place.

Bang! You're dead, *Daddy.*

4

ALONE

Through the long night, he had tossed and twisted in a tangle of blankets. The *Brenden Daily* hitting the front porch startled him. It was Monday morning and the alarm clock sounded at 7:00, which was enough to startle him again. His body refused to come around after a night of fitful sleep; he recursively dipped back into dreamland between confrontations with the snooze button. Voices from the morning radio show spoke of failed relationships, of all things, but he heard only snippets.

He reached for Karen, only to find her cold pillow.

Not once could he remember sleeping alone, without Karen at his side, not until these last few months. Not once before then had they gone to bed upset at each other.

In one of his dreams, a young boy and his father fed seagulls on a beach. Aeron as a boy, he knew, because the boy was faceless. He was never able to see his own face in dreams. But why was he feeding the birds? And why was his father encouraging him. And then he remembered. It wasn't bread, but broken pieces of Alka-Seltzer he was throwing into the wind. The gullible birds devoured them. One flapped its wings and swallowed a piece, and another bird landed and took the piece next to it. The birds swooped down and fought over the pieces as if taking sacrament, and one by one they convulsed in the air and came crashing down onto the sand, dead from burst bellies. His father stood next to him, laughing.

In what seemed like seconds, the radio was on again. The clock read 7:09. His nine minutes had flown by. Radio hosts were blabbering about gun control laws. Fighting to wake up, he reached past the Colt .38 on the headboard and hit Snooze.

His eyes opened when the radio boomed again—7:18—and he hit the clock hard, as if the blow might broaden the nine-minute snooze function a little. It probably would have hurt his hand if he hadn't been so tired.

Fading out again, he curled up in a fetal position in the center of the bed, too fatigued to dream. Aeron slept, but restlessly, and then the harsh ring of the telephone ended his efforts. Lying on his back, he glanced at the clock, which read *hE I I*.

Startled, he turned it right side up: *I I ЗЧ*.

Who would be calling?

The time on the clock clicked in his mind, and anxiety filled his body as he remembered it was Monday morning, the start of the workweek. He must have turned the alarm completely off—or had broken it—the last time he hit the snooze button. The phone rang again, and he wondered how long it had been ringing. He jumped up, pulling on a pair of jeans in the process.

Please don't be work.

He knocked over the phone and had to grab for it on the floor after stumbling across the room, half in his pants.

"Hello?" he said, fumbling to get the phone.

A seagull stared blankly at him from the windowsill.

"Aeron, there you are. This is Sam." The voice sounded worried. "I've been trying to reach you the last two hours."

He heard his cell phone vibrating on the coffee table down the stairs. It rattled for a moment more, then stopped.

Sam was the receptionist at Pollard Networking, his employer. If she were calling, it meant the bosses weren't happy. A fist-size knot filled his solar plexus as he raced for an excuse: *Flat tire, have the flu, kid's home sick …*

"Just wonderin' where you were. We thought you mighta

taken the day off since the Pollards took a week off for vacation and all."

Aeron had completely forgotten they were going to be gone. A sigh of relief instantly flushed out the adrenaline. Aeron could tell Sam anything and she'd believe it. He thought up an excuse.

"Hey, Sam. Didn't they tell you I was sick? I got the bug that's been going around." It was a lie, but it would work.

"Didn't *who* tell me?" she asked, as if wondering whether she had been told but had forgotten.

"Um, Jack. I called him last night and left a message that I was sick and would be out for the next few days." As the words came out, Aeron felt evil and cunning, but he could use this time off to get his act together. It made him feel less guilty, anyway. He continued, subtly adding a fake wheeze behind his voice: "He said you could move my schedule around." The lies flowed out of his mouth like a river.

"Oh, here it is, silly me. It's on a sticky on my monitor: 'Aeron is out sick.'" She lied, as easily as he had. Sam had pulled favors for him in the past, but on this one she was oblivious. "Well, get some rest and get better, Aeron." She was probably trying to find a note or a message. "And I'll see you Wednesday if everything goes well."

Aeron added a rasp to his voice. "Okay. I'll be sleeping most of the day, so if you call, leave a message."

That would easily cover him if he decided to go out.

"Will do," she said.

She ended the call before he could respond.

The seagull was still perched on the windowsill.

Stupid birds.

They were everywhere in Seattle.

Shoot it, like the army men.

He ignored the thought, moved downstairs and sat on the far left side of the couch. Karen normally sat on his right. He realized his sad freedom and moved to the center, spread his legs wide, and let his hands rest on the empty space to his sides. He missed Karen holding his hand.

When his cell phone vibrated again, he turned it off.

He pressed the red power button on the first of the remotes and the television hummed on. The screen slowly focused: a black–and-white-speckled mess of static. "Snow White in a snowstorm," he used to say as a kid. The television hummed off. A book would be better anyway.

He browsed the thriller and suspense novels, the strange books of David Mitchell, some Palahniuk, and older books with stories by Poe. Nothing was appealing. He skimmed over a full shelf of King. He skimmed a selection of depressing novels: *Where the Red Fern Grows*—no. *Watership Down*—no. *Jonathan Livingston Seagull*—hell no! He needed something uplifting to read, not literature written to depress the soul—or frighten it, for that matter.

With nothing to watch and nothing to read, he sat back on the couch and nearly crushed the cat. She rolled on her back, purring. Alex was a longhaired Siamese-Manx mix with dark blue eyes like Aeron's. Sometimes she'd stare at him from down the hall after he tucked Matty into bed, and her eyes would glow.

"Hey, there, Alex," Aeron said in a childish voice, rubbing her belly. "What are you up to?"

No response.

"What should we do today? Can't watch television. The cable's out … nothing to read that I haven't already. I could read you *Jonathan Livingston Seagull*. Sound good?"

He was talking to a cat.

Pitiful.

Self-esteem fell to the floor like a man shot in the chest. He felt like a fungus living off the dead, growing to a more pitiful and disgracing larger fungus.

Fuck my pathetic life.

The newspaper was at least waiting for him, he remembered. It was something to do, at least. Opening the front door, he found it lying centered and parallel with the outlines of the welcome mat, which was quite remarkable figuring the paper had been thrown.

CHILD RETURNS FROM THE DEAD. That was the cover.

"Local resident, 13, found dead in mortuary display coffin."

All he could think about as he read the headline was how poor news had become. Lately, it seemed, he could find more credited stories in tabloids than in the paper. Despite that, he read on:

> "Paramedics arrived after local police, acting on an anonymous tip, discovered the body. The boy was found clinging to life, and was given CPR by one Officer Milton on duty at the time. The boy (name withheld), died before paramedics arrived on the scene. However, they were able to resuscitate him before reaching the hospital. He is in stable condition but is expected to experience mild to severe brain damage from oxygen deprivation."
>
> – More on page A8

One page was enough, one paragraph, really. Disgusted by the tabloidesque *Brenden Daily*, Aeron dropped it back to the mat where it was welcomed—according to mat's message—and ventured back to the living room couch. Alex jumped onto his returning lap. He felt yet another headache forming and tried to ignore it, but it continued to pester.

Go away!

Alex bolted and sliced Aeron's legs with her claws. She hissed and growled as she ran in an animal fright down the hall. Aeron grabbed at his stinging legs but thought nothing more of it. Everything was focused on the headache, which grew blindingly painful. A flash of light, and the pain was gone, along with reality.

This cannot be possible. This cannot be happening.

Aeron's hand throbbed as blood ran easily down his green arm connected to the green rifle, which connected to his other green arm, all of which were held firmly above his head. His non-closable eyes stung. His legs were bound again with green plastic substance, and again his son stood above him, enormous, lining a procession of little green army men.

All like Aeron.

He was in the selfsame dream as before.

Usually at the point of realizing one is in a dream, the dreamer immediately awakens and forgets, in a moment or soon after, the content of the dream. Aeron however, knew he was dreaming and couldn't get out of it, and was unable to shout because his mouth was bound with plastic.

Matty placed the other figures. Some had bazookas; some held radios; others had handguns or rifles. After lining up four or five, he set one next to Aeron. From so far away, it seemed smaller than the other soldiers. Aeron's eyes strained in its direction after Matty set it down, and he noticed that the short soldier's head was missing—completely gone, with jagged edges of plastic at the neckline. No blood, no pain, just a broken toy. He looked up at his own injured hand; it throbbed and gushed blood. He wished then that he were a toy, and glanced at Matty. He had finished lining up his army men. As in the previous dream, Matty went to the closet and opened its sliding door.

As he reached inside, shouting erupted from down the hall. His own voice arguing with Karen, words indecipherable. Matty with hands covering his ears, humming to muffle the noise. He sat quietly, rocking until the arguing faded.

After all was quiet, Matty removed his hands from his ears. He reached into the closet and pulled out a pellet gun. It was still in its box and had a bright red bow on the outside. Matty tipped the box and dumped the contents.

Matty stroked the smooth black metal and wood-grain plastic, found the pump action, and pumped it ten times. Each pump more strenuous than the last. Tucking the stock against his shoulder, he sighted down the barrel at the rank of army men on the floor. He made a clicking noise with his tongue and pretended to shoot each one from across the room.

Two of the frozen green figures stood to Aeron's right, three to his left. They were lined up, as if before a firing squad.

Click.

Click.

Matty stopped when he got to his dad, and waited a thoughtful moment before making his best gunshot impression. He bent over to Aeron's green figurine.

The flick from Matty's finger was like that of a cannon blasting through Aeron's head. On his back, his head pounding, he peered at the five soldiers still standing around him.

Matty returned to the firing line and finished off the rest of the soldiers.

Click.

    Click.

        Click.

For what seemed hours, Aeron lay motionless on the carpet, head aching, arms aching from holding the rifle.

As time dragged on, the pain grew worse. He squeezed his eyes shut and pressed both hands to the sides of his head, trying to ease the pain, hoping to wake up.

Feeling his hands against his temples, Aeron realized he was no longer lying on the floor, no longer a toy, no longer in a dream, but lying awkwardly on the couch with a colossal headache, back in the all-too-real world.

Aeron felt drained and used, as if he had been tossed to an unsuspecting seagull and had destroyed it from within.

According to the clock, he had wasted the entire day in sleep. It was tomorrow already.

5

AWAKE

The darkest hours, after the moon had set, were the worst. Faint
creaks of the house settling sounded like gunshots, tormenting
Aeron's mind into imagining strange horrors. Coyotes yipping
at the moon turned into evil spirits lurking outside. Spiders
formed on the walls. The evergreen bough drumming against
the bedroom window became imperceptible footsteps down the
hall. Light through the cracked door sparked questions: *The hall
light—was it on before? The door to the room—was it always open?* Soft
moonlight and mysterious shadows cast dreary images onto the
walls. Waking to these imagined horrors, Aeron long-awaited
the morning's arrival.

Still shaking from the dream, he sat in the big, lonely bed,
listening to the creaks of the house.

Alex sat upright at the end of the bed, glaring at the half-
open door. Her ears perked to every whispery noise. A faint
crack, like that of a breaking plastic spoon, came from down
the stairs. Her left ear moved downward in response. Aeron's
eyes followed. A creak in the ceiling moved her right ear slightly
upward. A thin ruff of hair stood upright along her spine, registering her unease and causing Aeron's to build. He watched her
movements, hoping she could sense that which he couldn't. Her
presence kept him from losing what little equilibrium he had
and simply covering his eyes like a child and whimpering. Just as
he began to relax a bit, Alex shot off the bed and slunk out the
door, low to the ground, and bounded down the hall.

The room was darker than it had been when he first woke.
He tried several times to return to sleep, but something kept

him wide awake and unsettled, and now, with the cat gone, he had to face his fears alone. The sound of a plastic dish spinning edgewise startled him before he realized it was Alex finishing her food.

He closed his eyes, then immediately shot them open again. He peered ahead at the dresser, then to the darkness behind the open bathroom door, then to the window to assure himself that he was alone. The half-closed mini-blinds let in thin bars of moonlight; its dull illumination revealed outlines of objects in the room: the squat, rectangular dresser, the round wall clock, the bulk of the television, the man standing in the corner.

Blinking hard, he eventually decided it was a stack of laundry on a chair. His thumping heart seemed to have trouble registering the fact.

Aeron slowly moved his way to the window, peered out at the globe of the moon, and then closed the mini-blinds. This further darkened the room, but forced away the gloomy shadows. Turning around, he felt his way past the television and groped ahead. The groaning of the door hinge filled the house as he cautiously pressed it closed. Next to the door was the pile of clothing that had startled him. He flattened the stack of shirts and pants by stomping them to the ground. Gazing once more across the room, he went to the bathroom to run cool water on his face.

The mirror, it faced him.

A yawn forced his eyes closed and his mouth open. The lights refused to turn on. He flipped the switch rapidly before looking to the alarm clock. The clock face was black.

Leaning with his head down and hand braced against the glass, he remembered the flashlight under the sink. He bent down, took it from behind the cabinet doors, turned it on, and looked into the mirror. The fright made his fingertips ache with adrenaline.

Karen stood behind him. Her reflection held a gun to the back of his head. The nickel-plated Colt .38 reflected the rays of the flashlight in an unsettling display. Karen had a determined look in her eyes, like that of a predator.

Aeron stood petrified, breathless.

She stood steadfast, calm.

Sweat droplets crawled down the small of his back. He finally managed a breath and slowly turned around, a slow and unsteady about-face, expecting a gun barrel to his nose.

Karen was nowhere to be found. Stupefied, he looked around the room in disbelief. Finally, he shook it off, delusional but alone.

Looking at the mirror a second time, he realized he was wrong. Matty stood in Karen's place, pointing the same gun up to the back of Aeron's head. The youngster held the same deliberate glare.

Aeron reached behind him, but there was nothing there.

He closed his eyes, grabbed a bottle of painkillers on the sink, struggled with the child safety cap, and downed a couple of pills dry. The pain and confusion refused to cease, so he swallowed a handful more. The room spun crazily around him.

Without looking into the mirror ahead, eyes still closed, Aeron turned the cold-water knob on the sink until steady water flowed. He cupped a double handful and splashed it on his face.

The water was tepid and thick like milk.

He opened his eyes and quickly shut them, for the face in the mirror was a bloody mess. In the sink below, a warm, scarlet flow gushed from the faucet. Shaking, nauseated, he spun around and grabbed a towel to wipe his face. He pulled the towel away and it was clean.

The mirror: no Karen, no Matty, no blood.

Aeron staggered out of the bathroom and onto the bed, plopping down, bottle of pills in hand. The tablets scattered across the carpet; the plastic bottle's rattle reminded him vaguely of a maraca.

He took another couple of pills.

Don't stop.

He threw the bottle across the room and spit out the bitter tablets still in his mouth. How many had he taken?

Not enough.

He rolled over and covered his ears.

There are less painful ways.

Aeron rolled around on the bed, smothering himself with the pillows to block out the voice in his head explaining the various scenarios for killing oneself.

Hanging: too much trouble with preparation; gruesome to the finder (but aren't they all?); if the neck fails to snap, it could be a long and painful death; a shower rod or railing could break, leaving one crippled but alive.

Jumping: a publicity stunt for those wanting attention more than death; the whole way down to think of the impact; a chore to find a tall enough ledge to jump from; one had to find a way *to* that ledge.

Overdosing: long and possibly painful; someone usually comes to the rescue and pumps your stomach; hard to find a strong enough medication; street drugs are undependable.

Slitting: painful and slow; more of a self-mutilation than a self-destruction; so much blood to look at before dying.

Gun to the head ...

Unburying his face, Aeron looked to the revolver, in easy

reach on the nightstand. He ran his fingers across its cold, silvery-sleek surface. He lifted the revolver in his hands, felt its heft, and the thought echoed:

Gun to the head: *quick, painless, effortless, efficient, dignified.* He thought of an addendum to this list: *gruesome, messy, shallow, heartless, and brainless.* He cringed at the irony of the last in his list and put the gun away.

Awake and staring into the darkness, and eyeing from time to time the gap under the door, Aeron waited for the rising sun as the night dragged on ever so slowly. Morning felt like an eternity away as the minutes took hours and the hours took days to pass.

Sleep never came, but morning did.

He slouched against the sink, exhausted from the long night. Rain rapped against the bathroom window as he peered out at the sad, uncertain sky. The early light pierced his sore and reddening eyes. They appeared deep-set, the skin around them dark and slack. It was warm and humid in the room, so he cracked the window and let in cool air. The crisp early-morning breeze was refreshing. Unsure when he had last checked the power, Aeron flipped the bathroom light switch—the power was back on.

All this while avoiding the mirror.

For a while he sat on the couch where Matty normally would sit and flipped through channels, not really paying much attention to what was on. All the shows were boring—mostly infomercials. His eyes were heavy. He was too tired to sleep. He would cry if it did not require so much effort.

The television assaulted his eyes. Aeron eventually gave in and turned it off in disgust. Then he put on a CD and cranked it up as loud as he could without blowing the speakers. The melo-dramatic lyrics of Staind were unfavorable to Alex, who rested on the couch, looking at him with puzzled bewilderment. Aeron wondered what cats thought about music and how it sounded to them. He turned down the volume after seeing her ears drawn back in displeasure.

For the entire afternoon, Aeron sat nearly immobile, getting up every hour or so to change discs, all sad and depressing and loud.

The gun: how it could hurt; how it could heal.

Tears filled his burning eyes.

At a quarter to five, the phone rang.

"This is Aeron," he said, clearing his throat.

"It's Sam again," she said, as if he couldn't figure out who she was by the voice. "Feeling better?"

"Not really. What do you want?"

"The Pollards haven't left and aren't happy about you taking off sick. I tried coverin' for you. Their plans got a little jumbled, so they couldn't catch a flight out. They'd have come in yester-day—and we all thought they'd left since they didn't ring in—but they just stayed at the airport all day trying to get another flight. They're planning to leave tomorrow now."

Aeron suddenly hated the twangy voice. He remembered why he hated country music so much.

"They came in a few minutes ago and blabbered on about how everyone's always sick around here and how everything falls apart whenever they leave. Then they got on my case about scheduling. They kept rantin' about everything." It sounded more like -thang. "Sometimes they're like three-year-olds the way they try to impress each other and sound important. They're gone now, though, thank the lord. They want me to schedule an early Monday meeting next week. Probably a pep talk." She acted out a credible impression of Mr. Pollard: *Alone we can only score a basket; as a team we can win.* "You know how they are."

"Tell them they can *suck it* the next time they call in!"

Aeron hung up, shaking with rage.

He picked up the phone and dialed the office.

"You know I won't tell them that," Sam replied the second she answered the phone. "Get well, if you *are* sick. I'll talk to you later." And then she hung up.

The phone rang seconds later.

"That *was* you, right?" Sam asked.

"Yeah." he said, and hung up.

It was then Aeron realized how much he hated his job, not to mention his employers. They had started friendly but soon turned into money-hungry monsters as the company grew over the years. Then he thought of the impossibility of leaving his job and how arduous it would be to start fresh again. He was stuck.

Aeron lay with his face to the ceiling and his back to the floor as his sickness grew and he continued to dive deep into an abyss of worthlessness. Aeron was alone, awake, and tired of life; ready and wanting to end it all.

6

THE LETTER AND THE ROSE

The clock on the wall told him that time was frozen. It was a ten-dollar garage-sale clock they had picked up when he and Karen first decided to move in together—a cheap piece of rubbish they had never managed to replace. The minute hand was stuck at a minute before the seven; the stubby hour hand precisely between eleven and twelve. 11:34 once again.

Aeron let two hours pass.

The hands on the wall clock were frozen. He blinked, and it was 1:34. He blinked again, and it was back to 11:34.

Squinting to decipher the barely legible numerals, he peered at his watch. It was 1:34 in the morning. The batteries must have run dry in the wall clock—dry like his eyes. It didn't matter to Aeron what time it was; nothing mattered anymore.

It was time to write. He took a pen and three sheets of paper from the desk drawer and sat down at the kitchen table. Not knowing what to write, for his mind was a mess, he doodled.

He drew the ground with grass all around and flowers. Then he drew a tree with a simple trunk and a fluffy marshmallow top, like something a child would draw. He added a cloud to the sky and another and another, each one drawn with less effort. Soon the sky was a giant mass of poorly drawn clouds, like those that filled his head. Next came violent, burning flames in great, jagged strokes.

He threw the drawing into the wastebasket and cried. His eyes had somehow found a few more tears to bleed out. With a hand on his brow and the other gripping the pen, after only the slightest of hesitation, Aeron wrote:

Karen,

My love for you will never die, unlike my cadaver of a body and unlike my dismal soul, which both lie before you in this mess and whose ghastly images will perhaps forever disturb your mind as you remember me. For that, I am sorry. Push these images out with forbiddance, ban their revisit and let only jovial memories and picturesque images of our life together fill your mind always. I hope that despite the transgression of ending life prematurely, I am still allowed the opportunity of taking your love with me.

The time we have spent together was a utopian paradise, which I now ask for you to hold in your heart tightly as you did when I was still around and able to share it. Continue to love me, despite what I have done to ease my torture. Do not hate me for that. What I have gone through and what I have endured this last week was a minimal speck of dust in comparison to the mass confusion that has agonized my soul from childhood to adulthood, tearing me apart inside. It must be incomprehensible to those not in my shoes, and you along with others may suppose I took the effortless way out by pulling the trigger and ending it all, but know that it was not me I was aiming at. I had to kill the demon inside, and through my body was the only way.

Hold onto our trophy of love that is Matty, and raise him as our son, as we had envisioned long before his birth. He is the symbol of our love and is a reminder of our greatest accomplishment together. He is both the embodiment and the cornerstone of our family. Tell him what you will about my death, but let him know he was one of the two people I loved most. Help him to understand that for the interrupted fatherhood, which I cut short, I am forever sorry.

Please try to understand my sickness. Even if you never empathize, know that it wasn't you, it wasn't me, and it wasn't us that led to this. It was the sickness living inside, which I held within for so long. The sickness would rise; the madness of clouded confusion would fill my head to the point of hysteria; the images of my reflections would suddenly, violently change to a blood-sickening fright and all I could do was play the part.

Memories of the past and visions of the forthcoming flashed through my mind. Driving me mad. Unwanted thoughts and ideas. My entire life consisted of this, but to a lesser extent. And for that, I am not sorry, but infuriated with unparalleled rage at my inescapable lack of control! I love the both of you so much. It is incomprehensible.

With your love held within, forever …

Writing such a piece required Aeron to tap into both his sense of love and his state of utter depression. Aeron was certain that if this were the letter to be found at his death, it would be the perfect letter for his passing, and its words would fully capture the violent sickness living within, his deepest love and sorrow for those he would be leaving behind and, most importantly, their absence of any responsibility in his destruction.

Tears daubed the words as he read the letter.

Aeron signed his name, the paper tearing slightly. Head buried in folded arms, he mourned quietly over the letter, physically weak and psychologically fatigued.

Hours passed and he found himself in the garden clipping a single black-skirted crimson rose from one of the rose bushes out front. Karen's favorite. He never gave flowers as a token of love. He had always felt that gifts given with the deepest of love should last only as long as the love of the expressed affection. A flower or bouquets of flowers, were gifts of temporary love, which should last only as long as the flowers. Such gifts were suited for someone sick or mourning, or for saying sorry. With the falling of the flower petals, so falls the affection. A gift to express eternal love—such a gift should last forever.

Aeron placed the letter on Karen's pillow, with the flower on top. The flower, his final gift to her; it resembled a last, temporary gift of love.

Without hesitation, Aeron reached over to the middle of the headboard and grabbed the nickel-plated revolver. After loading a single round, he staggered to the bathroom to face the mirror, and to kill the man trying to break through from the other side.

7

A NEW REFLECTION

He stood looking in the bathroom mirror, talking to himself, with the cold barrel of a gun pointed at his right temple—left, according to the man staring back. This man was unfamiliar—not a friend, not an enemy, just an unfamiliar face that taunted his actions.

Who are you?

Aeron gazed deeply into his eyes and, like a deer in headlights, the image stared back. He was a stranger who was weeping, crying, and terribly hurt. He couldn't know what it was like to be in such emotional pain. This man was different and in need of help. This he could tell from the look of desperation.

He reached out to the man in the mirror, and a quick needle of pain rushed into his head, directly behind the eyes—the beginnings of another agonizing headache. The image blurred.

"Why are you doing this?"

Aeron's true thoughts and feelings were so heavily blocked that he had no recollection of what had driven him to this madness.

Let me through, said the man in the mirror.

"No," he told the reflection.

I'm already through. I can squeeze the trigger.

Click.

The hammer fell to an empty chamber.

Aeron cried out. He had lost all control.

In the mirror: a stranger holding the gun to his head, the cold barrel pressed hard against his temple, the hands shaking violently. With the gun pointed at the floor, his reflection spun the cylinder with its single live round and put the muzzle back to Aeron's head.

Aeron wanted to live.

"Matty's turning eight next week," he told the stranger. "He's a great kid and we're getting him something special. Karen and I ... Karen ... she's so beautiful; she's an angel ... we're going to get him a bike," he stuttered. "I'll teach him to ride."

You should teach him to pull the fucking trigger.

Click.

The hammer struck on another empty chamber. Aeron's body quivered. His reflection barely gripped the gun, almost dropped it. He held it with the tips of his fingers. The stranger was gone.

Reflected by the mirror, flash: a scared boy in a box, holding a lighter and clawing his way out of someplace dark; flash: an elderly man reaching out to a woman next to him, closing her eyes with his fingertips; flash: a girl carving a crooked smile into a jack-o'-lantern over a spread of newspapers, a single tear running down her cheek; flash: a tree in a park with kids jumping out of its fiery limbs; flash: Aeron smashing a new mirror with his fists and forearms, his face breaking apart as the shards fall; flash, a familiar woman staring through the glass, a black dragon across her stomach, sharp claws at her navel, a tail disappearing below her waistline; flash, the gun firing in silence.

The mirror transformed into clear glass—a window with white and yellow flower-patterned curtains, a funnel-shaped chip in the glass. It was the window looking out onto the front yard of his childhood home. The chip was the result of an accident long ago. He had only meant to shoot the little green army men displayed in pretend battles. He had loved and cherished that air rifle; then his mother took it away. After the window incident, she swore never to have toy guns around the house. She was afraid that next time it might be a brother or a sister instead of the glass. She also decided to lock the real gun inside the family safe—the same Colt revolver that Aeron now gripped in his hand.

Another flash and a stab of pain as the vision of the window disappeared. Reality sank back into place uneasily, as if it might flee again in an eye blink. He searched in vain for the chip in the glass that was there seconds before, then squeezed his eyes shut, trying to end the hammer blows of the headache, the hammer falls of the revolver, the movement in the glass.

The mirror face returned, his reflection on its surface.

Aeron ransacked his mind for thoughts to help pull the gun away. He thought of Karen and smiled.

A few days ago, she was lustfully staring into his soul.

Now, the man in the mirror with his red glowing eyes.

His hand reaching through, taking control.

Trembling, ever so gently.

The man in the mirror.

Finger on the trigger.

The blast echoed through the house as pieces from the mirror fell to the floor. Outside, birds stopped chirping; children stopped playing; the mild breeze stopped wafting through the bathroom window. It was as if the entire world had heard the blast send the mesh of Aeron Stevenson's mind through his skull and onto the wall, and everyone in the world had stopped to listen.

A cacophony of noise filled Aeron's head, and then silence as he crumpled to the floor. His entire life played through his mind the moment he sprayed it onto the bathroom wall.

8

THE OTHER SIDE OF THE GLASS

Dreaming? Dead?

Is this what it's like to die, to end your life and be put right back where it ended? No pearly gates, no hot flames, no God and no prince of darkness? Has suicide channeled me to an end worse than a Hell? Where's the blood? Where are the brain flecks and bits of skull that should be spattered across the wall? Why do I not see the back half of my head on the wall, ceiling, and floor?

He felt for the crater but found only the back of his head and a fistful of sweaty hair, which he had to make sure wasn't blood.

He laughed, the deep, bellowing kind, as he looked up and saw not a bloody mess, but a shattered mirror. During the struggle with his conscience, in his torment and confusion, he had shot the man in the mirror instead of himself. When the gun fired, he had fallen to the floor in a faint.

Aeron rubbed his elbows and sat on the floor in a mess of broken glass, alternating between tears and maniacal laughter.

He was alive.

The mirror was gone.

The man in the mirror …

Aeron's watch beeped.

Karen and Matty would be home soon.

He used one of the towels and cleaned the bathroom floor as best as he could, being careful with the sharp glass, but cutting his palms despite his caution. If need be, he could explain that he had slipped and fallen against the mirror. Karen would believe it. She loved him.

Unsure what to do with the gun, he reached past the forgotten letter and red rose he had placed on Karen's pillow, and moved the gun back into the case on the nightstand. Any moment they would be home. He couldn't drive back to work, and he couldn't stay home. Karen and Matty had it in their minds that he was at work.

After taking a moment to compose himself, he drove to Canford Park to pass some time and collect his thoughts. He pondered his dreams and pushed away the thought of surviving three rounds of suicide roulette.

At the park, he tried to forget everything as he waited for the sunset to finish bleeding out.

PART TWO

pumpkin carving

niΨon anomhmata mh monan oΨin

[wash the sins not only the face]

1

WATCHING

A dim sliver of moon hung just above the high-rises, with Venus caught on its horns. Not much else got through the reddish-brown smog ceiling that glowed in the city lights. The late-winter sun had dipped behind the buildings, ending his dreary day.

Done at Stratton Publishing for the day, Tayson Pierce headed for the watering hole down the block. It was Friday night and time to drink, time to have fun.

Some went to bars to release a little stress with a scotch on the rocks; Tayson went for soda and the social interaction. Hard drinks relaxed or emboldened other men, but for him the soda was merely a prop, something physical to have in front of him while he small-talked with bar hoppers. Tonight, however, he was here for one person in particular: his wife, to catch her with another man.

A strawberry blonde, who looked only seventeen or eighteen, pulled out the stool next to him and straddled it like a horse. The slender brunette who had sat there moments ago had not stayed long enough even to warm the seat. And the one before her, the heavy one with the crooked mouth, had sat down, listened to him utter the most repugnant syllable in the English language, and jumped to her feet and fled the bar.

The young girl waved a five at the bartender and shouted over the noise, "Shot of Jack."

"Can I see the dragon's tail?" Tayson said with a smile after a quick glance in her direction.

No response.

The kid tilted her head back and downed the shot like water.

She waved another five and the bartender poured her another, sloshing a bit on the counter, swiping it up with the rag in his other hand. The girl adjusted her cutoff jean shorts and shifted in her seat. The halter-top revealed a pierced navel and toned abdominal muscles. Flip-flops dangled from her painted toes, with the heels barely touching the floor.

Tayson flashed her a ten the way some men might wave money at a dancer in strip club.

"So how's the dancing nowadays? Did you learn to cock your head back like that in the private rooms?"

He took a sip of his drink—Diet Coke, wedge of lime.

No response as she knocked back the second shot.

"Why a dragon?"

"Ten bucks," she said without looking at him.

"Only ten? Cheap date. I would have guessed fifteen."

She was hot, but she held no interest for Tayson; he was done with women for a while.

"To see the dragon. I don't fuck for money."

"I don't, either," he said and laughed. "You know why they call that area of women a *waste?*"

He pointed at the tattoo to the left of her navel.

Not even a suppressed smirk on any of the faces near enough to overhear, but Tayson enjoyed it nonetheless.

She had apparently heard the pun before.

"Twenty bucks," she said, upping the ante.

Tayson reached for his wallet, flipped through a few receipts and bills, pulled out a twenty, and slid it across the bar to see what she would do.

She snatched the bill and stuffed it in a tight front pocket. The teenager—or so he had guessed—looked around, but no one was watching. She unbuttoned and then pulled down the left side of her shorts, along with part of a black silk thong, far past her crotch, revealing her smooth inner thigh, where the tail of a black dragon tattoo lay coiled. The girl buttoned up as the bartender turned in their direction.

"You look too young to be in here."

"You don't seem to mind. One of my IDs says twenty-one, the other says eighteen. You can probably guess which one is real. I don't get carded, though."

"What color's your baby?" Tayson asked out of the blue, not at all aroused by the view he had purchased.

She pointed to her shot glass and slid another five on the table. It was suddenly filled. It was strange that she hadn't started a tab. Three drinks, all paid for separately.

"She's white, but color doesn't matter. How'd you know? You following me or something?"

"Stretch marks. Was she worth the money?"

"I said I don't fuck for money!"

Several patrons turned their heads in her direction.

"She's three now. Her dad," she said and paused dramatically with tears welling under her eyes, "he was twenty-three. At least that's what his license said. I stole his wallet."

"Were you crying when he raped you?" he said, puncturing her heart with unwelcome memories.

"It wasn't rape," she said under a breath, her cheeks trembling, the fingers around her shot glass shaking.

"You were fifteen; he was twenty-three. Did it hurt?"

Her only response was wiping tears, drying her eyes.

"What—you enjoyed it or something?"

Tayson swallowed another straw-full of soda.

The poor kid—both in purse and in spirit—gave him a heartbreaking look. Reflections of canned lights danced like firelight in her eyes, twinkling in the tears.

"What kind of person are you? No, you're not a person. You are a hellish, morbid asshole! Where do you get off talking to me like I'm shit? Where's your heart? Where's your cold, detached, black heart, so I can stomp the shit out of it and smash it to a flat, black pile of crap?"

The words never rose above a whisper, each one cracking with a sick, sullen sadness as she took her stand.

"Here's your money back, you sick, twisted prick!"

She reached into her pocket and removed the twenty Tayson had paid for his peek. She dropped it in his glass.

As the saddened teenager slumped away, Tayson lifted his glass and took another sip; not feeling anything remotely kin to remorse. His sip ended in a final, silent slurp as he swallowed the last of his soda.

He cringed as his throat recanted the watered-down, money-flavored drink. After tweezing the twenty from the ice, he pushed the damp bill across the bar and signaled the barman to keep his cheap drinks coming.

Depending on the drinks he ordered, a guy could go through a twenty in a matter of minutes at a bar. Tayson, though, could make a ten last the night, but he only wanted to stay long enough to see his wife. He was waiting for her.

A few drinks and about an hour later, another woman sat next to him. She was middle-aged, slightly heavy with thick makeup and tight clothes that squeezed out rolls of pink flesh around her arms, thighs and midsection. Dimples dented her cheeks and the backs of her thick knees. The straps of her tall purple high heels ringed her ankles tightly and probably pain-fully. Her left heel was taped to the sole with duct tape; the right pierced a square of clutching toilet paper. Her crimp-curled red hair clashed with the yellow tank top and matching shorts.

"What's your name, honey?" she asked Tayson as she turned in her seat toward him.

He briefly pondered whether the chair or the load atop it had made the crude noise as her seat swiveled.

"Slim," he said to the mirror ahead of them.

She tried to meet his eyes in the reflection, but Tayson averted them to his glass.

"*Slim.* That a nickname or your real name, sweetie?" she asked as she attempted a second time to break the ice.

"It's an avoidance," he said dryly.

Tayson looked over her shoulder.

"What are you drinking? Can I buy you a drink?"

"It would take a lot more than that for me—"

He didn't finish his sentence, not wanting to subject himself to the mental image of his own reply. It was unusual for a woman to throw him pickup lines. Such an unfamiliar scenario threw him off his game. He normally wouldn't let a conversation reach flirtation before turning a woman off like a light switch while he exposed his meanness.

Once he had stumbled into a gay bar by mistake. He had a lot of fun that night. Men walked away distressed, some in tears, some sexually confused. Some left furious. Tayson loved treating them like insignificant objects, as he was now treating this garish woman. He continued to look past her, toward the other end of the bar.

Jackie had arrived.

Tayson didn't want Jackie to see him, though he wanted to see her. And who could see anything around the tightly wrapped whale that blocked his view? He wanted this woman gone, and fast.

"Let me put it out there on a plate. What would it take for me to get into bed with you tonight?" she asked with a bluntness born of desperation.

"A very large crane," he said.

He had composed his punchline halfway through her lead-in for the unplanned and self-degrading joke. He was a pro at giving the greatest offense with the fewest words. He could twist anything one said into an insult that came flying back.

She splashed her martini in his face, and either she or the chair made another funny noise as she got to her feet and stormed out.

Another woman quickly took her place, for the bar was busy that night. She was small and he could see around her—a plus. She slouched somberly on her stool. Her look held an exhausted air, as if she had spent the day counterfeiting smiles. She ordered a screwdriver and lit up a cigarette.

Tayson hacked a fake cough in her direction. He hacked louder a second time, but she continued smoking, with the remnant of a fake smile on her face. It would probably remain there indefinitely.

"Excuse me," Tayson said in his third attempt to rid himself of her smoke. He finished with a charade of putting out an imaginary cigarette in the nonexistent ashtray he held in his other hand.

She put her real one out in a crystal ashtray.

"Sorry," she said and fanned away the smoke.

The smoke was obscuring his view of Jackie.

"Don't be sorry," he responded. "I just wanted to see if you would do it. *I* smoke. But not that menthol crap."

She rolled her eyes. "I'd be pissed if that were my last. These are expensive. Luckily, I seldom smoke." She started to introduce herself, holding out her hand. "Hi, I'm—"

"On your period," he mumbled.

"—Angela."

He left her hand solitary but introduced himself.

"I'm Jason," he lied.

Tayson never gave out his real identity, nor let anyone see him walk to his car, which had probably saved his Porsche from getting keyed and his tires slashed a few times. His car was one of the few things he actually cared for. The apartment, the money, the wife—all were accessories, and all were meaningless now.

Angela drew her hand back, and then sat in an awkward and uncomfortable silence, probably wondering how he knew she was on the rag. She was wearing a rather short skirt and her hand disappeared. She waited a few moments before brushing her fingers beneath her nose, sniffing discreetly as she scratched a fake itch.

"Fresh Country Breeze, I believe that is the scent. That's what Tampax calls it, anyway," he said blandly. "At least you're not in that *pre-* stage. My wife can be such a bitch before she bleeds. You would think something that bleeds for five days would eventually die. Not her."

It was the first time he had poured out his thoughts in a long while. The content was unbelievably rude, but the marriage counselor couldn't even get this kind of progress with him.

Angela looked at him, sipping her drink, the last wisp of smile replaced by a look of both confusion and curiosity. She was calm and for some reason didn't leave.

"Actually, it's Fresh Mountain Mist, but close. What are you, some kind of specialist, or psychologist, or do you just work for Tampax or something? A pad tester, perhaps?"

Tayson decided to let her continue by refusing to answer right away. He was insulted, and he loved it.

"Do you just go around sniffing other people?"

The last person to ever insult him this well was his wife. That was back when he still loved her, when he knew where she was and what she was doing. He would have been aroused by the abuse if it weren't for Jackie. The impotence was her fault.

She sat at the far table, across the room, about thirty feet away, with the man who had entered with her.

"Wild guess," he explained. "Guys have noses. And feminine products all smell the same, and they *do* smell. We notice these things. You walk down the feminine product aisle at the grocery store and you can't avoid smelling it. They all have their Fresh Mountain Mist kind of scents, and all ultimately smell the same. They don't have the right descriptions, though. If they did, they'd call it 'Sex Repellent Breeze' or something like that."

Tayson thought he had noticed Jackie looking in his direction, so he shrugged down on his stool to make sure his face was behind Angela's comely figure.

"They do smell," she said. "What do you do, other than your secret life of pad-scent detection?"

He rose back in his seat ever so slightly, so that his eyes were in line with his wife again. Jackie was back to flirting with her date. At least, Tayson thought it was a date. She never seemed to be with the same guy twice. This was the seventh time Tayson had spied on her. This was the seventh different man.

"I work at a publishing house. Editing, copyrights and so-on."

He tried not to let it seem too obvious that he was not looking only at her.

"What kind of works?"

"Mostly short stories, anthologies, novels, poetry collections—sometimes even screenplay manuscripts, but not very
often. Every once in a great while, magazines will outsource
to us for editing, but only when short-staffed. We're a little
expensive, but we're also the best." He had no idea why he was
telling her this. He knew he was the best. Why would she need
to know?

"Anyone I would recognize?"

"You read a lot?"

"To tell you the truth, the last thing I remember reading was
The Scarlet Letter, and maybe *Fahrenheit 451*."

He gave her a questioning look.

"I read the Cliff Notes. And it was in high school, years ago.
I don't like to read at all. I find it boring. But I'm not saying *you're*
boring, since you work at a publishing house."

Knowing Angela was uncomfortable (and for once he actually cared), Tayson was going to change the subject when he
noticed a change in the view behind her.

Jackie and her date were gone.

2

THE OTHER SIDE OF THE BAR

I knew he was watching me. His eyes were hanging just above the woman's head in front of him, through the smoke and all the way across the room, staring at me. The smoke was thick throughout the bar, and there were a lot of people crowding the place tonight, lots of noise. You had to practically yell to the person in front of you to be heard, or to the waiter to get a drink. We would have sat at the bar, but that's where Tayson was with some floozy.

I sat as far away as possible, but still in view. I knew he would be here. I wanted him to see me with someone new again, to confuse him. He was slouching lower now, trying to hide behind his human shield, as if invisible, probably chatting away about nothing important, as usual. Or maybe he was ripping her a new asshole. Tayson could be such a dick sometimes. He either ignored you by talking about himself, or talked down to you. I made sure to ignore him so he wouldn't think I saw him watching.

He was good, but I was better.

Our drinks arrived and I drank all but a few sips of my rum and Coke. My pathetic date, if you could call him one, took a swig of his bourbon and made an awful face as he forced it down, his eyes squinting. I think his name was Nathan. My seventh.

Whoever he was, he wasn't a drinker. It was most likely one of his first drinks ever. He couldn't have been more than twenty-two, almost out of college and looking to hook up. Not a party man in college, by any means. He was going to one of those schools of technology, like they advertise on television during the day, for the unemployed to see while they're watching reruns of Oprah. He was only a few weeks before graduating with an Associate's and a Cisco certification of some kind, and was working for a network service company. At least that's what he told me as we broke the ice.

I wasn't paying much attention and couldn't care less what he had to say. I was busy thinking of those before him.

The first was hardest. It was always difficult starting something new. Like a new job, a new school, a new religion, or a new diet, it was difficult to adapt to and required a lot of patience. This was definitely a new way of life for me. The hardest part was sneaking around behind Tayson's back. It felt wrong, but also felt good.

To fulfill deep-down urges felt good.

The next two were the easiest. They were the stupidest of them all, education-wise—probably no older than nineteen or twenty and just out of school. If they ever graduated at all, it was a miracle.

I never went below eighteen—that was way too young.

The fourth almost got me caught. He was strong and also the closest resemblance to my father, and by far the oldest at thirty-seven.

By the last two, I had grown accustomed to the scene and knew exactly what to do. I was a pro. The path had been set out by then.

I looked at Nathan and smiled, acting as if I were listening. As we drank, Nathan continued to babble about computers and where the Internet was going, while I ignored him and pretended to care. Tayson wasn't looking, so I dragged my date out, and we sped off through the alley, down the side streets, and then to the freeway going south. Soon he had his head in my lap.

Tayson had somehow managed to follow us, but I was able to lose him after a few turns. Well, it may have been him. If it was, he didn't know the neighborhood as well and would have needed to backtrack to find his way home. He never had a good sense of direction—or erection, for that matter. The impotent loser would be home and asleep in bed by the time I got home. He always was.

3

Tayson had left the bar at ten-thirty; just moments after his wife had left with another man. He had tried following them from a safe distance, and managed to for quite some time, until he lost them down one of the side streets. It looked as though they were headed to Brenden, but he wasn't positive.

It was almost pitch black in the living room, where he now sat with his feet propped on a footstool. His eyes had attuned to his dark environment in the last long hours, and he could see almost as if it were day. Anyone entering the room would see only darkness. With his fingers sunk deep in the armrests of his black leather chair, Tayson awaited his wife's return, eager to hear her excuses, eager to see the surprised look on her face when he busted her. He stared at the front door across the room, his eyes burning in rage.

He imagined them glowing like red embers.

Any moment, his cheating wife would unlock the door, enter the house, place her keys on the table by the door and try to sneak upstairs and slide into bed. He had envisioned the scene each time he waited for her, imagining every detail: the sound of the door-knob rattling as she struggled in darkness to unlock the door; the soft rattling of keys placed on the table; the door clicking shut; the deadbolt sliding home; the sound of each step as she moved up the stairs. This time he would not be waiting for her in bed. This time he would watch her in the dark.

Sick to his stomach, Tayson didn't know what he'd be capable of doing if she confessed. He was even a little scared of himself in that regard. Would he just leave quietly? Would he break her spine? He didn't know.

Why isn't she home yet?

He pictures her in a strange bed with a strange man, both of which are beneath his wife. He sees her exposed body covered in sweat, legs open and hugging the stranger, body bending loosely to their sexual rhythm. For some reason, he pictures her facing away from her lover, toward Tayson, as if he is paying to watch them in some sick voyeuristic show. She stares, her eyes stabbing into his heart with malicious glee.

Any moment now.

He pictures her unlocking the door and sneaking in. He waits, surprises her. She shrieks and whips around, swings, misses, and he throws her to the floor. Her body lifts six inches from the entryway before he pummels it back down. Her spine cracks against the tile. He pictures his fantasy and it is cut short with the approach of a car, the low rumbling of her Mercedes and the crunching of gravel under tires.

Jackie's home.

He listened as she set the parking brake. The door opened and made a tone until she removed the key from the ignition. Her feet hit the driveway, and the car door closed ever so quietly. He heard everything.

Keys jingled at the door as she searched for the right one in the darkness and the thought of this made him smile, for Tayson had left the porch light off for her. After a few moments, the doorknob twisted. His eyes were glued to the door, though he sat motionless and in total darkness. The door swung open.

She finally entered. Tayson saw everything.

His view was clear; his mission wasn't.

Jackie used her heels to push off her boots. They looked caked with mud, but he couldn't tell for certain.

She slipped her coat off silently and hung it in the entry closet. She kept the door slightly ajar for light, but received little. Reaching for her boots, she accidentally knocked one over with a dull thud. Jackie stood upright, listening for Tayson to stir upstairs.

I'm right here, love.

She glanced around in all directions, squinting, trying to take in the shapes of the room. He knew she couldn't see anything more than a few feet in front of her because she kept reaching out, using her fingers as guides, feeling walls.

She stared straight at him a few times. It would be easy for her to turn on a single light and expose him, but this, Tayson knew, she would never do. She had never turned on a light in the past.

He watched as she placed her keys on the table by the door and barely heard the door shut. She was good. She felt her way up the doorjamb and locked the deadbolt without making noise.

Tayson's heartbeat quickened.

He rose from his chair and slowly crept toward her, his socks muffling every footfall. He came within twenty feet and paused. She had no idea he was even in the room. Fifteen feet. Ten feet. Five. He was close enough to reach out and touch her.

Jackie turned around, facing him. She looked hard around the black house, right past him.

There was no light source of any kind—Tayson had made sure by closing every curtain and hiding every splinter of light.

Tayson's darkest desire was to reach out, grab her by the neck, kick her feet out from under her, and force her to the ground. He wanted so much to pin her with his knees, make her tell him what she had been doing. He would break as many bones as necessary.

Never had he been this mad.

He brushed the back of his hand across a few stray hairs near the nape of her neck and then stepped back. Tayson wanted her to know how he felt and to know what he was capable of doing, even though he was unsure of these things.

She turned in his direction briefly but still was unaware of his presence as she looked into the void.

Instead of heading up the stairs as usual, Jackie headed toward the kitchen.

He was ready at any moment to pounce. When she stepped, he stepped, mocking her, yet minimizing the chance of a telltale creak. One wrong move and she would know he was there.

Tayson leaned against the entryway as she entered the kitchen. Jackie felt her way around edges of the tile counter-top, moving past the sink, past the knives, past the stove and dishwasher, finally stopping at the refrigerator. And then he remembered the one light he had forgotten—the refrigerator light. She was supposed to enter the house and sneak upstairs as she always did, not stop for a bite on the way.

Jackie opened a cupboard and got a glass.

Tayson's heart raced. Moments before, he had felt capable of ripping her cold heart from her chest; now he wasn't so sure. If she opened the door of the fridge and turned, she would see him. He wanted to step around the entryway and hide, but his feet wouldn't move. If she saw him, he would either wet his pants or rush her and thrash her into hamburger—he was not sure which.

She opened the refrigerator door, flooding the kitchen in light, and time seemed to stop.

She wore dark gray pocketed pants and a skintight black tank top. The front and side of her tank top and waistline of her pants were stained as if she had spilled an entire glass of wine. Tayson was too nervous about being discovered to look any closer. If she turned, she would see him standing there, completely exposed.

How can she not sense my presence?

Jackie filled her glass from the water filter inside, still facing the open fridge, tilted her head back and drank the entire glass. She did it again before closing the door and plunging the room back into darkness.

His eyes took a few seconds to readjust; he watched her place the glass on the counter. She had not turned his way.

Tayson's suspicions about her recent whereabouts grew more concerned. He sorted and combined the facts, as he had in bed so many times before. She was home late and sneaking into the house as usual. Another *different* guy—he had seen that much at the bar. Her clothes were stained. Why? What were they stained with, and why so badly? Wine? And why so thirsty?

Sex makes you thirsty.

Tayson stepped backward to the rhythm of her footfalls as she approached. He headed for the stairs and stopped halfway up. The house was too new for the steps to creak.

Jackie continued past the stairs and started shedding clothes on her way to the laundry room. More of a closet than a room, really. She pulled open the small folding doors, revealing the over-under washer and dryer. A white laundry basket rested on top. She peeled off her tank top and crumpled it into a small wad and dropped it on the floor. All he could see from this distance was her outline. No bra, but that was normal for her. Next, the pants. She unbuttoned them slowly, wriggled them off, and kicked them free. She hadn't worn underwear, or at least hadn't kept them. He felt a fist clench in the pit of his stomach.

She then bent over and collected the bundle of clothes, tossed them into the basket, folded the doors shut, and turned in his direction.

As she came up the stairs, Tayson silently climbed the last few steps and slipped into bed. Closing his eyes, he breathed in and out evenly, feigning sleep.

She entered the room. Tayson heard everything: every footfall, every rustle of bedclothes. Soon she was lying next to him, on her back, inches away. His body was still cold from staying downstairs for so long in just his boxers. Warmth radiated from her.

The room stayed quiet. Jackie remained motionless for perhaps fifteen minutes before doing a fake stretch and wrapping her arms and legs around Tayson's body as if she were restless, convinced he was asleep. He could feel her warm, bare body around his, and the cold heart, beating rapidly in double time to his.

It took her nearly an hour to unwind and fall asleep.

Certain that she was asleep and not faking, as he was, Tayson rolled her light body off him. She slid gracefully onto her back, her chin tilted upward.

He watched her for a long time, studied her face. What had he done to cause her to stray? Why so many men, of such varying ages and stature?

Thoughts and questions strayed to less practical thoughts and questions, then to unrealistic fantasies as he stood on the edge of a dream world.

4

BLACK HOME

The power must have been out because the house sat in an abyss of total darkness as I drove up into the driveway. Power couldn't be out though; the entire street was as lit up as usual, with its string of streetlamps shining like a strand of white Christmas lights. But something was wrong. My bulb was out. My bulb is never out.

Streetlights in front of the homes were on, but little glass triangles lay scattered below the light post in front of my house, broken by something—or someone.

The porch light was out, too, which was odd. The rest of the lights throughout the house were also out, but that was normal for it being so late—probably two, maybe three in the morning. Not that I cared. All I cared about was waking up in the morning and leaving the house before Tayson's alarm went off.

It had been a long and tiring adventure in the dark, and cold; the dead field we had walked through was swamped from collected rain. The wet, heavy air was stuck to my clothes, which were nearly dripping. I could barely feel my fingers and toes. The boots had helped, but they were muddy as sin. I could not believe the mess I had made of my shirt. Hopefully, it wouldn't be ruined.

Tayson would be deep in sleep and dreaming of sex. We had not had any for who knows how long and sleep was his only way of getting it. I had my ways. Everything was fine when we first got together, but he turned into a limper. When Viagra didn't help, he started blaming me.

I don't think I ever *really* loved him.

Somehow we had managed to stay together, but that's because we both made good money. That's what marriage is all about anyway—gathering in holy matri*money*. It probably kept us together in our "burning" love for each other. Oh, how I would love to burn Tayson and take his money. I'd burn him alive, right there in bed.

Money, the green fire that burns us all.

It was great staying out nights, satisfying my mixed-emotion clusterfuck of a libido. It was my way of getting back at the world, my way of getting back at my father for all the ways he hurt me and hurt my mother. He's dead now, but he will haunt me forever. Not a day passes without me thinking of my father, the reason for my new addiction.

I remember it clearly, like it happened yesterday, or even today.

Halloween morning, when it first started. I was dressed all in white as an angel, carving the pumpkin on the newspaper-covered floor, sawing out eyes and a mouth with a dull, orange paring knife. I had cut round eyes into the pumpkin, and a mouth that grinned devilishly from ear to ear, seeds and veins dangling out where teeth should have been. Mom was dead, so it was my first time carving a pumpkin by myself. I was lost without her and was getting pumpkin guts all over my costume. And then I was on the floor as my sad jack-o'-lantern stared sadistically at me while I suffocated under my father.

I was seven.

Older now, I continue carving pumpkins. Who wouldn't enjoy that? I make my own rules and play my own games.

I listened for Tayson up the stairs, but heard nothing, although hairs on neck prickled. I peered into the black to assure myself I was alone. A creepy feeling.

The countertops in the kitchen were barely visible, but they led me in. Tayson was a light sleeper; even the faintest of lights would wake him, so I kept the lights off, took a glass from the cupboard, and finally found some light in the refrigerator.

After a few drinks, I went to the laundry room and peeled out of my clothes. They were filthy.

Naked, I walked upstairs to join my "husband."

Tayson's body was arid like a corpse when I joined him in bed, but unfortunately was breathing, so he wasn't dead. I wrapped my body around his and it felt dirty and wrong, like spooning with my father. I hated pretending to love him.

5

GARBAGE

When he woke up the next morning, Tayson was relieved to see
that his love—an ironic title now that he thought about it—had
already left for her work. Her job started an hour before his. His
only concerns were whether she was going to work *for* someone
or to work *on* someone, and what sort of "job" she would be
engaged in. He brushed the unwanted images out of his head as
he took a shower and dressed. He had less than ten minutes to
investigate and gather clues before going to his own job.

He first checked the laundry downstairs, for he had seen her
in stained clothes last night and had watched her toss them into
the laundry. Jackie was trying to hide something, and he knew
it. The clothes were in the dryer, its cycle complete. He pulled
from it the tight, shapely outfit she had worn; even dry, it barely
made a handful in his fist. He stretched the material apart to see
if he could find any stain remnants—nothing.

Tayson continued to search through the laundry, as well as
the rest of the house, but found nothing. The boots were even
missing. He found traces of foxtails or wheat in the closet, but
that didn't mean anything. He searched the entire downstairs
before looking at his watch, noticing he had only a few minutes
more to look around.

The box of condoms in the bathroom was unopened. It
had probably been there for years, forgotten until now. They
used to rely on Jackie's pills for the most part, but that was a
long time ago. The wastebasket by the toilet was empty; the
shower was clean, and so was the floor. Discouraged, Tayson sat
on his bed and sighed, almost wanting someone to hear, then

leaned onto one arm and felt something small and rigid under his palm. It was the tip of one of Jackie's nails, no wider than his wedding band and less than a quarter of an inch long. It must have broken off during the night. As he held it up to the light, he noticed something strange. It had been polished a deep brownish red on one side, but on the underside. He held it up again to be sure. The portion of nail had just a hint of curvature, and on the convex side was the polish. It rubbed off easily when he scraped it with his own nail, and turned into a sticky substance between his fingertips.

He glanced again at his watch—time to leave and begin his day of work at Stratton Publishing. Tayson had worked there twelve years, publishing many works and rejecting many times more, and had even helped to found the company's successful monthly magazine. As managing editor, he had most of the company eating out of his hands. If he ever left, the business would fall apart.

During the short drive to work, just a few blocks from home, he grappled with the ideas filling his mind all at once: Jackie being with another man ... her being with so many men ... why he had never seen the same one twice ... the unusual stains she had worn home but which were gone in the morning ... the mysterious nail fragment in the sheets ... The thoughts stayed, circling and repeating in his mind even as he pulled up to the old, rundown building.

Just as on any other day at the firm, Tayson walked in, grabbed a cup of black coffee, nodded to William at the front desk, and stepped into the elevator. He could close himself up in his office, secluded from everyone else in his division, or any other division for that matter.

The building was narrow and squeezed in between two

others, all three looking ready to fall. Stratton had the first two floors of the ten-story building. Each floor consisted of three to four small offices, each with its own half-bathroom that people dared to use and which made the rusty pipes throughout the building scream with agony each time a toilet flushed. The unsteady elevator jerked to a stop on the third floor, where Tayson got out.

Each of Stratton's floors housed a different division. Tayson's division included editing, but also handled delivery and filtering of prospective manuscripts. Unlike larger publishing companies, his worked primarily with local and unknown writers, and because they were small, most divisions handled multiple responsibilities.

Tayson's three peers in his division were few but productive, mostly handling simple editing and revisions. He had the power of saying yea or nay and loved it. He was in charge of doling out any editing projects; the ones he thought boring or too time-consuming he passed to coworkers further down the totem pole—people who actually enjoyed the work. For himself he set aside the most promising poetry, short stories, and occasional novels. Everyone else tended to get stuck with advertisements, flyers, pamphlets, essays, documentaries, and the odd textbook or study guide.

As he sat at his old wooden desk, with the mini-blinds shut and the outside world a safe distance away, Tayson looked over various projects piled there, to the blank wall in front of him, remembering the picture that had once been there. The portrait was of Jackie on their honeymoon in San Diego—one of those sexy-body cardboard caricatures with cutouts for heads. It was taken down long ago, seven men ago. They had spent the first week of vacation on beaches, catching sun, and taking wacky photos. Jackie was the love of his life back then. Now he could kill her.

But first he had to work.

With a sigh, he sat up straight and glanced at the tall pile of poetry submissions on his desk. A few of them would find their way onto the pages of this month's *Brenden Talented*, a once-free city magazine originally created to publish the works of talented Seattle authors, poets, and artists. Tayson had helped found the project years ago to showcase talent that normally went unrecognized. It was now a successful newsstand magazine in high circulation, and he still played a part in its publication. It was his job this month to plow through the different works, playing God by choosing which pieces would achieve fleeting fame and which would be doomed to literary oblivion.

If only he had the same power to decide who should live and who should die.

Tayson worked through the stack of poems. He plucked them from the top of the stack, imagining Jackie on top of a stranger. He held each thin manuscript in his sweating fingers before he ripped them apart and tossed them into the wastebasket—hearts of poets poured onto paper, only to be crumpled and tossed.

He loved the sound.

The callousness would get him fired, he knew. These were just copies, he could argue. The originals would be returned with a rejection slip, dutifully signed by Tayson, of course.

As he picked up the sixth submission, he realized he hadn't read the first five, and laughed.

He focused from the wall to the paper now in his hands.

Throughout the rest of the day he read, winnowing out twenty of the best of what seemed hundreds of poems: some good, some mediocre, a handful of gems, the rest garbage.

At the end of the day he had nineteen poems that would probably make it, three of which he liked. He had plenty of short stories and artwork to fill the rest of the space. Someone knocked on his door as he was about the leave.

"Yes? What is it?"

The door opened.

William held a broad yellow envelope.

"This arrived. Some old guy dropped it off in person."

"Put it on my desk," Tayson said, uninterested.

"He's published with us a few times."

"That sounds very nice, thank you," Tayson said, trying not to sound annoyed but wanting to get rid of the earnest young man so he could get away and see to his wife.

"He was afraid he wouldn't make it in time for the cut. His wife just died, like an hour ago. It's a poem for her."

"Aren't you just a receptionist?"

The "just a receptionist" tossed the envelope like a Frisbee to his desk and stalked out, closing the door hard behind him.

Tayson found the decency to give the poem a chance. Sitting back down, he opened the envelope and pulled out the manuscript. He sighed heavily and leaned back in his chair, holding the paper to the light.

THE MOST BEAUTIFUL PLACE

Shadows eclipse gray suns on white canvas
Escaping light is scarce
Revealed refractions of brightness dance
My heart thunders loudly
Wild flames spark in the darkness around
And in the center of it all I see myself
Surrounded am I by mountains and riverbed
Silken plains, soft pathways
Leading to more beautiful bends
My legs tremble with anxiety
In every direction a new journey awaits
And in the middle of it all I feel I am myself
At day's end a masterpiece is covered
A protection of compassion
With it comes great purpose
My body gains warmth
A comfort of pure completion, blanketed love
And under it all: you and me
You are the most beautiful place

The words were written in calligraphy with an old-style dip pen on cardstock—probably thirty-pound. It looked like something from long ago. It was original. Once in a great while, a work came in that had been typed on an old manual typewriter, but just about everyone worked on a computer.

Never had he seen a handwritten submission.

The script was beautiful.

He tossed it in the wastebasket on his way out.

6

MIDNIGHT STROLL

I made it out of the house by seven after running a small load of laundry and spraying my boots off in the backyard with the garden hose. All evidence erased. The thick, crusted black mud had to be scrapped off with my pocketknife and took longer than expected. I had expected the field to be muddy, since there was a hard rain, but I never thought the sludge would cake on so thick.

One of my fingernail tips was missing completely, probably left in the mud. I would have taken a shower last night, but that would have stirred Tayson. He'd never know what happened with me and my number seven. Like with the six before.

Work wasn't important to me. I gave it up three months prior. Tayson didn't have a clue. He was convinced I was making ninety grand a year selling real estate in Seattle. Really I only made around seventy to seventy-five thousand, not working at all, but from the stocks and bonds I fell into at an early age—a portfolio Tayson knew nothing about. Instead of depositing my commission checks each month, I had an automatic transfer from my overseas account made in the appropriate amount. He had no way of knowing, unless he ever showed up where I used to work.

Real estate was never my profession to begin with. You always had to be nice and kiss ass in order to sell. I hated kissing ass. I would rather *kick* ass, and was never any good at selling overpriced houses to under-waged, young couples ready to buy the first thing shown to them. Selling to old people was worse. Sometimes sixty, even seventy-year-old couples wanted homes they could die within, signing away more years than they had left for a mortgaged money pit. Quitting solved all my conflicts.

I usually waited a few weeks before finding a new man to play with. It took almost a month after the first, but my urges became more and more frequent—a few hours afterward, and the urges were already starting to set in again. I needed an average-size man, hair almost black, dark blue eyes. He had to have a shapely, defined chin and a scruffy face that would tickle my cheeks. He had to be strong, but not too strong; I had to be stronger. Such a blend of a man was hard to find. I was on the prowl for my father.

He wasn't the type of man you would want to meet in a dark alley. For years Mom pretended to love him, as I pretend to love Tayson now. She used to come home from work each day, weak and fatigued, and cook dinner for the family. If dinner wasn't on the table by six, she would feel the bruises later on her face, neck, chest, back. Anything could set him off, and it was different every time. Dad eventually learned to leave the bruises where others couldn't see. It was hard to keep track of the times he had hit her. Mom hid under makeup. She never told anyone.

I was quiet, too.

If Mom knew what he was doing to me, she would have killed him somehow.

It took most of the day to find a man who looked like Dad. I found him at The House of Modern Art—a building that resembled an oversized glasshouse. I observed the beautifully odd art, acting lost. The sky started darkening, as well as my hopes of finding him. And then *he* found *me*.

Our eyes met and connected like the north and south ends of a magnet. Number eight was a few yards away, a perfect likeness. He was standing next to the door with his upper body leaning on the glass, his hands in his pockets like a schoolboy. His eyes followed my swaying hips as I approached. He was nervous and shifted his weight, his feet resting in turn on the wall.

I was about to tell him to take his dirty shoe off the wall when he glanced at my left hand and smiled when he didn't see the metal band of burden. I had stopped wearing it years ago.

His voice held an edgy rasp, like Tayson's, but was deeper and less methodical.

"Looks like rain."

When doesn't it rain in Washington?

"Are you the courtesy weatherman, or did you just now put it together that it never stops raining here?"

This would reveal his character. If he let me pass, it meant he was weak and had a personality the consistency of unsettled chocolate pudding. If he answered sarcastically, it meant he wasn't beaten as a child and had lived a little. If he snapped, he probably lived too much and was a prick like Tayson. I was hoping for sarcasm.

"I'm just filling in; he's on vacation. Stupid icebreaker, huh? I should have said something catchy like 'How's it hanging?' or 'Nice jugs, babe.'"

He wasn't as nervous now.

"Are they?"

"Are they what?"

"Nice," I said. "I think they are. You can call them jugs if you want. I hate the medical terms we use for body parts. Which genius came up with 'vagina' anyway?"

"I believe it was Professor Phil McCrevis."

I think he made it up on the spot.

"No, probably Mike Hunt," I said, not even smiling.

We stared at each other for a few moments. I brushed my hair out of my eyes once. Guys usually liked that. A smile started on his face and then I mirrored it.

The ice wasn't broken between us; it was crushed. He followed me out. We stood outside in the cold, talking and joking about stupid things: strange words, funny sounding body parts and functions, what kind of movies we liked, favorite foods, favorite music, and other things we both would not remember after the night. Typical first date stuff. Not that any of it mattered. I only had to gain his trust long enough to satisfy my craving and then I'd be done with him.

"Want to grab some coffee?" he asked.

"I could use a pick-me-up. Let's go."

Like potatoes in Idaho, coffee wasn't hard to find near Seattle, home of the biggest coffee grinder of them all, Starbucks. They're at just about every corner downtown: next to shoe stores, in malls, next to other coffee shops—everywhere. One was across the street; he pointed at it. Its bright green and white sign illuminated the dark street while the moth-like creatures that roamed the city at night, us included, fluttered toward it.

An overabundance of dark-eyed Gothic louts, longhaired save-the-planet poets and wannabe songwriters filled the tables. They hung off each other like loose clothing. The preppy guys and suited types occupied the center.

I pulled him by his arm, our elbows chain-linked.

We muddled our way through the living cemetery and flower-garden people and entered, not making it past the doorway. A sign on the wall read MAXIMUM OCCUPANCY 23. We were probably numbers sixty-two and sixty-three.

"You sure you want coffee?" I asked above the noise. "Maybe a movie ended, or a football game or something. There's probably another just down the street."

I pulled him out of the horde, without a choice.

No more than ten blocks away was the subtle light of another green and white sign shining in the darkness. Its glow was dulled by the sky as dew began to settle.

"I'm still game," he said.

We decided to walk, and along the way he talked about his job and offered me his jacket more than once. I said not a word as he blabbered on and on and on and on and on. I barely listened. He was another computer geek, so it seemed. I didn't even catch his name yet and here he was explaining his profession.

The scent of espresso beans hit me, making me want caffeine more now than before. As we approached, I noticed that the shop wasn't a suite within a building like the other had been, but a small freestanding building with a steep-pitched roof, reconstructed from some old fish-and-chips restaurant. It had a drive-through window so it wasn't as crowded inside, and all its seating was indoors, which kept the strange ones from loitering about.

I let him order first—a hot white mocha-something—and for myself, an iced caramel macchiato. I never drink hot coffee—can't stand the stuff. I like my coffee the way I like my men: cold and devoid of horrible aftertaste.

"What are you thinking?" I asked.

"Maybe a midnight stroll?"

I wasn't really paying attention.

"Sounds like fun."

His eyes bounced from me to the table, to his drink, and then back again, as if he were afraid to stare at anything for too long. He was insecure, just what I had hoped for.

"But first tell me about yourself. I've been talking *me me me* this entire time and I know nothing about you."

I'm married. I was beaten and raped as a child.

I didn't say those things, of course.

"I'm a serial killer," I said with deadpan calmness. I took a sip of my drink.

He laughed.

I laughed.

"Not what you do in your *spare* time … What do you do for a living?" He was unable hide a yawn.

"You mean when I'm not cutting people?"

I returned the smile.

"Yeah, all blood aside."

"I guess you could say that I'm an insurance broker. And I like Starbucks and meeting strange men in the middle of the night."

We talked for hours and I grew to like the guy. He was different from the others, but I still didn't know his name.

I watched countless barely-awake people filing past the drive-through and thought of Tayson. He was probably wondering about me as I was wondering about him.

My cell phone told me it was just past 11:30.

We never went on our midnight stroll, but he eventually gave me his name and number and walked me to my car like a gentleman. What love used to feel like …

7

SEDUCED

Tayson couldn't get the poem out of his head. The inspirational words touched him deep in his black heart, haunting his coldness with long-lost memories of love. He threw the poem away because he didn't want to have to see or read it again. It was well worth publishing and deserved to be published, but it wasn't worth the risk of seeing it again and reliving its beautiful words.

It wasn't uncommon for Tayson to stay late. Stratton was his surrogate home, a place to do what he liked to do and a secure place to hide when he needed to. The only incentive to going home was the possibility of catching Jackie in the act. He had imagined it many times."

Moaning, naked bodies wrestling in the sheets, a stranger entangled with his wife. He pushes open the door with the barrel of the gun.

He had bought the gun from his neighbor. Karen Steven-something. She had returned early from work one day to find a note on her bed, a hole behind the bathroom mirror, and shards of glass behind the toilet. She had called police to help find her husband, in hopes that he was still alive, and when they found him, they took him away. She had no idea that attempting suicide was illegal.

So Tayson bought it from her. He could still see the desperate look on her face. He imagined the same look on Jackie's face as he pressed the barrel against her forehead.

The luminous moon behind the clouds made the night a dreary, yet romantic painting. It seemed that it could rain, but the moon said otherwise. He unlocked his car and got in, shivering, not ready to go home yet; not ready to face Jackie—if she was even home. Maybe a note would be waiting for him on the pillow.

Instead of going straight home, he drove into the big city for a late-night drive, checking out the bright lights, wasting time. It was an electro-scenic drive.

The lights wore heavy on his eyes, so he stopped down one of the side streets at a Starbucks that, fortunately, had a drive-through. Tayson ordered a double-shot cappuccino. He never liked that iced crap that the young preppies and night freaks were so fond of. His coffee had to be hot. Coffee was supposed to be hot—burning hot. Hot enough to sue McDonald's and make a few million.

Baristas inside had the system of measurements and mixtures down to a science, pumping out gallons of drinks by the minute. He watched the people inside, mostly people dressed in suits—the older types, not the young freaks and tree huggers he had passed by earlier. He was starting to see Jackie everywhere.

The part of Tayson that wanted Jackie to be home when he arrived lost the bet. There wasn't even a note.

She could be anywhere. Doing anything.

It was close to midnight when she pulled in. He waited for her this time with the lights on.

A battle raged the instant she stepped through the door.

"Happy to see me?" she said, glaring across the room.

She had a guilty yet devilish expression.

"Couldn't be happier," he said.

She kicked off her shoes and peeled at her stockings, leaning with one hand on the doorknob. She ignored him and started her routine of undressing. As if he weren't there.

"Where were you?" he asked, smiling stupidly.

She shook her head.

"When did you get home?"she said, redirecting.

"Where the *fuck* were you?"

He sat in his chair, gripping the arms like weapons, appropriate for their duel, ready to draw at any point. He thought of the gun in the little fireproof safe hidden deep in his sock drawer, which only he knew about; only he had the combination.

She undressed at the door. It was part of her way of ending the day. She stopped after a few buttons.

"Does it matter?"

"Yes."

"I could have worked late, for all you know. You seem to do a *lot* of that lately. Or maybe I was out with a friend, or shopping. I could have been stalking someone, for all you care. But you *don't* care. You haven't cared for a long time. And neither have I. You're pathetic, Tayson."

"Who was he?"

She took a while to respond, possibly realizing that he had seen a few of the men. Her face reddened.

"Someone from work."

"Who was he?"

"James. You saw him at the bar last night."

Her responses sounded rehearsed.

"We had a few drinks, he trimmed my grass, that's it."

Tayson knew she was lying, but about what, he didn't know—and that was menacing. So she knew he had seen them at the bar.

Was she fooling with him?

"And the other one?"

"What other one?"

She was calm again, testing his knowledge.

Tayson eased his grip on the chair, stood, and walked slowly toward her. She had resumed unbuttoning her blouse, as if nothing of any importance was going on. He stopped with his hands in his pockets, his face a small distance from hers, close enough to feel her warm breath.

She smirked.

"Oh, you're good, aren't you?"

"I know there have been others."

"So you watch me, huh?" she asked, tranquil as ever.

"Hard not to."

"You ever watch me suck a guy off?"

An evil, leering smile.

She was testing for a reaction, he knew. She let the ends of her silky blouse slip to her sides, like a gate opening.

"You're sick," he said, inches away.

Jackie pushed him back.

"Don't ever get in my face," she whispered.

Tayson stepped back, or had to, after losing his balance from the shove. He seethed inside, and his mind filled with rage. If only he had the gun, he might have pistol-whipped her right there. He imagined knocking her to the ground.

"When I get in your face, you'll know it. You never answered my question, not truthfully. Where were you tonight, last night, and all the other nights, you little whore?"

"Why, you want to be my pimp? We could make good money." Jackie leaned in as she spoke in a softer voice, "Me sleeping around like a bunny"—leaning in even closer, her voice wispier, more seductive—"spreading myself."

She ran her tongue across her lips, put a hand on Tayson, used the other to slide the side of her blouse off the shoulder. The blouse dangled loosely, as if she were its broken hanger.

Tayson clenched his teeth until they hurt. He wanted to head-butt her and shear off that mocking, snake tongue.

"You could watch me …" she said.

Her tongue slid across his lips.

His hand moved down her partially bare chest.

"Beat the living *shit* out of you!"

A knee slammed deep into his groin.

Tayson doubled over, gasping for air.

Jackie stepped back, menacingly, laughing.

He shooed her away and cupped the pain between his legs. His knees buckled. His breath gone, in no hurry of returning.

Her boots, so pointy …

She casually slipped them back on.

And she kicked him senseless.

Beating Tayson to the floor felt pleasant, but there was something missing. It was like going to a burger joint and forgetting the fries, or like sex without the orgasm. Tayson on the ground with his head tilted back at an awkward angle, eyes rolled back and looking into their sockets, it was quite amusing. But something *was* missing.

He wasn't dead. If I had wanted to kill him, I could have, but what I needed then was my number eight to fill my hollow place, but I had let him go earlier.

Then I remembered: he gave me his number. Thomas was it? It was written on a note still in my pants, so I fished it out and gave him a ring, not realizing that it was one-something in the morning. Leaving my number, I told him to call me in the morning—well, later in the morning, when normal people were awake, and that I *needed* to see him again. Guys liked feeling needed.

A few minutes later my cell rang.

"Still up, huh?"

He sounded tired, but not as if he were in bed yet.

"I couldn't stop thinking about you," I said.

A hint of satisfaction filled my void. It was just his voice, but enough to do the trick—enough to calm me.

"I had my cell next to the bed in case you called," he said, and then yawned.

It was loud at first but soon muffled, as if he had moved the phone away so I wouldn't notice.

Tayson was knocked out cold, bleeding through his nose.

His mouth didn't look right. A small pool of blood was forming where the constant drips fell. One of his hands was still grabbing at his groin, and the other was bent funny under his back, which arched up a little. His legs were straight, feet pointing up to the ceiling.

"That's sweet."

I imagined number eight lying on his back and in bed, covered up, pillow-talking with me as if we were back in high school.

"What are you wearing?" he said, laughing. "Just kidding. Are you in bed, though? Come on, tell the truth. I am."

"As a matter of fact, I am."

He was about to come up with something clever to say, I could tell, but laughed instead. Apparently, my raspy voice was a little too over the top. It was a pretty abysmal hooker's voice and sounded more like someone with asthma, or an old lady with lung cancer.

It took a moment before I controlled the conversation.

"Breakfast," I said.

His voice told me he really wanted some sleep.

"I work from six to three. How about an early dinner?"

His work was in my way. It needed to go.

"Breakfast."

"I would love to, but it would need to be around four in the morning, and I don't know about you, but—"

"Four is only a few hours away."

Tayson was a rock on the floor.

"Hold on a sec," I said, and set the phone on the table by the door before he could answer.

The blood on the tile was really starting to bother me. Tayson wasn't going to stop bleeding anytime soon. I grabbed his armpits and propped him up, then dragged him so that he leaned against the wall. He looked like a teddy bear the way his feet stuck out and his head lolled over. Blood smeared across the floor.

I pulled a length of paper towels from the kitchen and shoved them in Tayson's swollen and crooked mouth.

I picked up the phone.

"Still there? Sorry about that."

"I thought I might have lost you there for a minute. What were you doing? It sounded weird."

Before answering, I looked at the now gagged Tayson, with a blood-dripping wad of paper hanging halfway out his mouth. *Poor guy.*

I should have duct-taped his mouth, feet, and ankles.

"I had to move some things around; it was bugging the crap out of me. Sorry it took so long."

"Where were we?" he said, yawning again.

"Breakfast," I said, almost demanding. "Call in sick."

My husband does all the time.

"What?" he said, as if he had never done such a thing.

"Everyone does it. Like peeing in the shower. Come on, do it for me. It'll just be this once, I promise. What—you never peed in the shower before?"

"All the time. I mean, not *all* the time, but I have." He sounded like a kid caught in a lie.

"Are we talking hooky or peeing, here?"

"You're a strange one when it comes to conversation. It seems all we do is talk about bodily functions."

"We'll do more than that."

"I'll call in sick. You owe me. Tomorrow at eight, then. I need *some* sleep."

It was as if a huge burden was lifted from my chest, knowing that tomorrow would be the day. And it would start *at* eight, even more appropriate.

"You pick the place," I said.

"I have the perfect place. Got a pen?"

He sounded excited yet terribly fatigued.

The pen wouldn't write at first, so I ran it around in circles a few times before the ink started to flow.

"Yeah."

It took him a moment.

"Two-three-two Feagleship Road, ten minutes from where we were earlier. You have to look for the street sign, though; it's hard to see. Someone messed with the letters to make it read Seagleshit Road. It's a small place called Ed's Diner. Looks like a dump, but the food's good."

"So, eight, then?"

"Eight," he said, and hung up.

9

THE PUMPKIN CARVER

Blackness covered Tayson like a heavy blanket while he slept on the floor for hours, almost in a coma, or possibly coming out of one. His linoleum bed was wet, not from urine—he was a great bed-wetter as a boy—but with blood that still leaked from the gag in his mouth. His nose was clogged with caked blood.

He dreamed of many things as he lay slumped against the wall. A mixture of old and odd remembrances, thrown into a blender and mixed to a puree: a horrific trip to the hospital, waking without any limbs, and a few other dreams that got more and more obscure as he stirred on the floor.

Along with the red stream that had flowed from his faucet of a nose, blood had also traveled back into his throat, causing him to unconsciously swallow a good amount, gagging him, as evidenced by the spatters on his shirt. His jaw held shards of teeth, and a pain that would hit him like a train when he woke.

Tayson's fingers traced the red-slimy floor, leaving trails like a tempera finger painting. A barely mobile hand made its way to his forearm and drew three red lines down his face, and then fell to his lap again. The darkness filling his head throbbed.

A thin curve of cracked light split under each eyelid as his eyes rolled and peeled away from their lids, like a waking cat's. He could feel the burning now; growing more resolute the more he came to. A popped blood vessel made his left eye seem to look through a cloud. Two of everything crammed the hazy room, every object spinning a little before returning to focus.

The next ache came from between his legs. It started with the right inner thigh, which was numb and prickly, and worked its way up in needles. The throbbing in his scrotum was dull compared to pain that had come with the initial impact; his pelvic bone felt as if it had been split in two.

Tayson squinted and saw a fluffy red image of a bird: his own bloody fingers linked at the thumbs, waving to himself. Those feathery wings traced his cheekbones, but his cheeks couldn't feel them, as if his face had been shot full of Novocain.

A pool of red surrounded him. He was seeing two of everything, so maybe he was seeing twice the blood. It made him feel a little better, thinking that. The back of his head had a bump from when he had hit the floor.

Paper towels were wadded in his mouth. A lump of red slipped from his lips and plopped onto his lap. Feathery wings transformed to fingers that picked up the bloody, ice-cream-scoop-size mess, which dripped and tore as it stretched, releasing two peculiar items from its center. He strained to bring the two images together and realized it was a good-size piece of his tongue.

His eyes rolled as Tayson slipped into unconsciousness.

When he woke the second time, his head throbbed even more, as did the rest of his body. The sun was close to the horizon, and its yellow light filled the entryway. He rubbed his throbbing groin, his sore jaw, and everything else on his body that ached; then, with a mighty effort, he stood on noodle legs.

Tayson glanced at the morsel of tongue on the floor and held back developing gag reflexes deep in his throat.

The faint sound of the radio could be heard down the hall— the alarm clock. It was too early for the alarm, though; it had to be Jackie's. And it wasn't the annoying buzz he was used to.

Maybe Jackie was still in bed.

He went upstairs to check.

No Jackie.

No sign of her anywhere.

He took a long shower and sat at the base of the tub with his legs crossed, too tired to stand. Water beat down hard and swirled counterclockwise at the drain in a whirlpool of cherry Kool-Aid. After the water's color lightened, he rubbed grisly stuff out of his hair with shampoo and felt the burn as sudsy water hit the open wounds on his face.

Tayson stayed there until the water ran cold, which eased the throbbing, except for his tongue, which was on fire. He could not stop moving it around and touching the sides of his mouth. He remembered losing teeth when he was young, how it was impossible not to probe his tongue across the raw, fleshy hole where the tooth had been. It seemed ironic now that the tip of his tongue was raw and fleshy, and he couldn't help but press it against his teeth.

After a quick check with his finger, it seemed that three teeth were missing: an upper canine and the two teeth directly beneath it. His lower lip was split and nearly twice its normal size. Not even daring to touch his tongue, Tayson stopped exploring and spit at the drain. A splatter like that of a red paintball hit the tub and dissolved in chunks as the water rained down. Dark tissues took the longest to meet the drain.

Tayson eventually turned the water off but stayed sitting there until he was completely dry and had the energy to lift himself out.

The mirror above the sink reflected an entirely differ-ent man: a man whose jaw, face and neck had turned a mix of orange and blue with bruised eyes and a mangled lower lip.

Tayson reached for a few squares of toilet paper. The man in the mirror blew his nose. Out came a black clot. He spit once more in the sink, realizing he wasn't going to stop bleeding from his mouth anytime soon unless he did something about it.

He concocted a glassful of saltwater—a first aid remedy he had learned in Boy Scouts—then gurgled and spit the grainy water until it ran clear in the sink. He rinsed with regular water to get rid of the blood taste and then drank at least five glasses more to rehydrate.

Strength gradually came back to his legs, and the pain subsided a modest amount.

He would probably kill Jackie if he ever saw her again, wanted to kill her in fact—badly. So much that he went back upstairs and loaded his gun, nestled it in back of his waistband like they did in the movies. With his luck, he'd blow himself a new ass crack.

Tayson searched everywhere in the house, but could not find any clues as to her whereabouts. And then he saw the notepad on the entryway table. Engravings of a swirling pen—a remnant left by someone squeezing the last drops of ink. He looked even closer to notice fainter markings below it—an address of some kind. From the desk he pulled out a pencil and rested it so that the conical tip and exposed graphite point lay flush against the paper. He rubbed the paper and faint, ghostly lettering formed wherever the graphite did not reach. As easy as rubbing names off a gravestone.

In Jackie's sloppy, boyish cursive: *232 Feagleship Rd.*

Tayson rubbed more to discover the numeral "8."

He looked at his watch: 7:45.

If he hurried, there was enough time to join Jackie and whoever she was meeting at Ed's Diner. He knew the place.

□ □ □

Ed's looked as run down as a crack house, but with fewer boarded windows. The neighborhood was run down as well, probably with crack houses. The first time he ate at Ed's was summer three years ago. The appearance wasn't the greatest, but the food was good.

His watch read 7:06, but it was an hour later because of the time change. He had never taken the time to adjust it.

Jackie's car was parked in front of the restaurant, so he parked in the back lot, around the corner from the bent-up SEAGLESHIT RD. sign. A few older people parked in the back and looked at him funny. He gave them the bird and then looked past a few dusty cases of Budweiser stacked by the window, which also helped hide his snooping figure from the patrons inside.

It took him a moment to spot her. Jackie was facing away from Tayson, wearing a ponytail. Her dark hair, pulled up tight like that, gave her head a shiny black look. She never wore a ponytail unless she planned on playing sports, working out, or sweating sometime soon. She wore the same tight, almost see-through mesh shirt she had worn two nights ago; it stretched over her figure like skin.

Maybe she *was* planning on sweating.

A man was sitting across from her, his face partially covered by the silk flower in its plastic vase. The "floral arrangements" were dusty. Everything inside seemed dusty—even the beer bottles.

Jackie ordered first, then whoever-he-was.

He had an abnormally large head full of thick, curly black hair. It was the same color as Jackie's, only tight and thick like

Velcro. He looked nervous and he was trying not to stare at her chest, but he was failing miserably. It was like trying not to notice a burn victim, or someone in the supermarket picking out cantaloupes with a deformed hand.

Tayson watched them eat. Their hands brushed, which caused a childlike smile to break over Jackie's face.

Interrupting his voyeurism, a side door to the building opened and slammed against his side. It didn't hurt, but startled him. It was Ed emptying trash. The lanky old geezer asked if he was all right, and then offered him some food. Tayson shook his head no.

It felt strange to be thought of as homeless, of not being able to care of himself, unable to hold a job and eat like a normal working human being. It was disturbing to think he looked that terrible in his current state.

Ed went back inside and Tayson returned to the window. His heart jumped when he didn't see his happy couple. He raced to the corner of the building and was relieved to see them in Jackie's car.

He watched as they pulled out, and let a few cars on the road go out behind her so she wouldn't notice him following. Then he pulled out, cutting a car off in the process. It was almost a fender bender, and he was lucky the guy never honked. Tayson looked in the rearview mirror and guessed he was an older guy, maybe some kind of medical doctor, cell phone glued to his head.

The Space Needle glimmered in the sunlight. Jackie was a fast driver, so keeping up wasn't easy. He almost missed the turnoff.

◻ ◻ ◻

Tayson parked a few blocks down and watched as they entered a house on Newman Court. It was a small house in a strange-looking neighborhood. A few of the cars along the street looked broken down, and the beater Honda Civic parked in front of Tayson was on blocks and missing all four wheels.

Jackie entered the house, and her date followed. The front door closed, but not all the way, as if the doorknob was sticking a little. The house was once white, but time and weather had turned it more of a pot-metal gray, with the paint cracking in many areas. It was a single-story on a standard lot. The yard was overgrown and spotted with leaves from the maple trees.

He had a hard time watching through the partially closed mini-blinds. Tayson got out and moved casually to the next house over, which looked like a deserted methamphetamine lab, and acted as if he were the resident. The yard had nothing but dead grass and rosebushes; a faded banner across the fence read HOME DAYCARE and gave a phone number that was probably disconnected. After lighting a cigarette, he leaned against a tree with a foot against the trunk, continuing to watch from this slightly better vantage point. They were still far away, though.

Tayson was able to see the top of their bodies through window frames, like scenes from a comic strip. They weren't doing much, but they would soon enough, and he was ready to watch. It would give him motive to use the gun that now dug into the small of his back. Jackie would sneak back into the house later and he'd put the gun barrel against her face and pull the trigger.

He smiled and took a long drag from his cigarette. He held it like a joint, the way he always did. He knew the cancersticks would kill him someday, but so what? Tayson flicked the butt and let it fizzle out. He moved closer.

Jackie now stood alone, pacing. Her hands moved from side to side, fingers stretching then balling. The man reappeared in what seemed to be the kitchen, maybe pouring them drinks.

Tayson was about to light up again when he caught something odd through the window. Jackie had pulled some kind of baggie from her pocket.

Drugs?

Tayson dropped the unlit cigarette in his shirt pocket like a pen, took a few steps closer as he strained for a better view.

Jackie pulled something white from the bag. She moved slowly toward her new friend, tossed the bag on the ground, still holding the drugs or whatnot, and put it to his face. She grabbed him hard around the waist with her free arm.

Pissed and trembling, Tayson grabbed the cigarette he had put in his pocket, not once looking away, and tried to light it. He let it fall from his lips as his bruised and swollen mouth gaped open.

The man she was with fell to the ground.

Jackie eased the fall with her hand still by his face and her arm around his waist. It happened in what seemed like slow motion—a dancer moving behind strobe lights. She helped him to the floor and closed the mini-blinds.

What the hell?

Tayson ran to the door and stopped, not knowing what to do. He pulled the gun from his 'waste' and thought again of the joke he'd made at the bar, to the girl with the tattoo.

He slipped through the front door, which was still ajar. And he waited, frozen at the doorway, as she dragged the man's body into one of the back rooms.

Holding the revolver in both hands, he nudged the door with the barrel, enough to squeeze through. His heart pounding hard and fast, he tried swallowing but couldn't do so past the invisible lump in his throat. Tayson's legs shook as he gripped the gun even tighter in his damp palms. He felt the urge to urinate, and crouching didn't help any.

Seeing the plastic bag and white washcloth, he put it together. It wasn't drugs; he could smell the chloroform. He slunk toward the back of the house, where Jackie had dragged the body. Tayson froze when he heard what sounded like someone puncturing a milk jug with a ballpoint pen. Odd that he thought of milk, which somehow reminded him of how badly he needed to pee.

What's she doing now?

At the end of a claustrophobically tight hallway, a bar of light escaped from below the last door, along with other exotic noises.

The handle in reach.

The door ajar.

The back of Jackie's head.

All he had to do was kick in the door and blaze away.

Using the gun barrel, he eased the door open, praying it didn't squeak. He waited, taking in the strange sounds.

Just don't squeak, you motherloving crack-house door.

If Jackie turned around, she wouldn't see him before he put a bullet in her head.

She straddled number eight; he sat on the floor with his legs facing Tayson, his feet pointing to the ceiling. She had her back to Tayson and her crotch in the stranger's face, as if he were going down on her ... or being forced to go down on her. Jackie's left hand pushed down hard on the top of his head, her right struggling, as if she were trying to pull out a lock of his hair.

Tayson switched the gun from hand to hand as he wiped his

damp palms on his pant legs. Streaks of sweat stayed behind like claw marks. He took a deep breath and let it out, ready to make his move: kick down the door; bury all six rounds into her skull; save the damsel in distress—or man, in this case.

Jackie stepped away to grab something from across the room, giving Tayson a clear view of what he never imagined or wanted to see. He forced down the rising bile and covered his mouth.

Blood surrounded the man on the floor, towels around him, soaking up his life. Red fingerprints and handprints covered his body like body-art. A ring of red outlined the dome of his skull. Arms limp, shoulders hunched over like Tayson's when he first woke up in such pain this morning—pain he could not even reflect on now.

Out of the center of the man's head stuck an orange-handled object, the handle of a children's pumpkin knife—the dull kind that came in those cheap pumpkin-carving kits.

When Jackie came into view, Tayson wanted to barge in and shoot her dead, but his legs wouldn't budge. He looked over the gun barrel, the hammer to his lips, staring, terrified.

Jackie held pruning shears.

He watched her scissor the man's cheeks apart from ear to ear, giving him a wide and bloody zigzagged grin.

The squelching sounds reminded him of his mother cutting raw chicken. With relief, he felt the warm stream run down his leg and puddle on the floor by his immobile feet.

Swiftly, if it were a hobby she had practiced many times before, Jackie worked the heel of her boot into the dead man's mouth. She forced a gape with her hands, then slid in her heel. Gripping his upper teeth with both hands, she pried him open, and there was a quick, disturbing crack that broke a few front teeth loose before fully dislocating the jaw.

She wiped her hands on her pants.

He wore a melted look on his face, for his jaw gaped open in the biggest evil grin imaginable.

Jackie then stepped away, the artist standing back to check her work. She leaned over and pulled on the orange handle protruding from the elongated head. Along with it came a wedge of skull.

Faint, nauseated, and wet, Tayson pointed the revolver to his piss reflection. Jackie was there, picking up another orange-handled pumpkin knife. She carved out his eyes.

Then came a knock on the front door.

PART THREE

the whiteness

TAHAT

[slavak: *pull*, sometimes found printed
on bi-directional glass doors]

1

GETTING OLD

Old age doesn't hit you as they say it does; it pounces suddenly. You get new things when you're old, though. Not presents or anything like that. Cards and forgotten are what old folks get. I'm talking about new things us oldies can use. Like teeth. Teeth you can take out and wash overnight in a glass. Sometimes you might get a new liver, kidney, an external rectum. My friend once lost his colostomy bag at the market. He thought it might have come off around a display of cantaloupe, because that's where he remembers going last (pun not intended). It probably got stuck on a cart. But who wants to carry around their whiz and feces in a colostomy bag all day anyway?

Not me.

I'm glad I have full use of my ass: sitting *and* shitting. A ruler on the knuckles or a paddle on the rear was what we could choose from for saying such a thing … Some memories never seem to go away. Memories like those at the orphanage: lye soap and other such things.

Knees don't bend as they used to either. They crack now, like the Barbie and Ken dolls I used to get for my granddaughter, Julie, when she was just a little thing.

Don't really get to see her much anymore.

She lives a rough life. Not as rough as we used to have it back then, but rough by today's standards. Her baby's getting older every day—starting to sit upright. Too bad she hasn't got a father to raise her properly. But who does nowadays? He was one of those one-night flings, or so she told me. Wham, bam, thank you ma'am, and nine months later, out pops little Hannah.

Palindrome Hannah, she calls her. She had her young, during high school last year. Sixteen, seventeen, maybe eighteen at the time—a while ago, can't seem to remember her age. Anyway, Julie's young, a baby herself even.

Julie isn't really my granddaughter as I may be leading you to believe, not blood related. She's kind of an adopted grand-daughter of ours, yet I think of her as my own sometimes. See, she was abandoned as a child like I was, and grew up raising herself. A ways back, the wife and I took her into our residence, made sure she was clothed, fed, and looked after. We gave her a place to call home—something she lacked but deserved, same as everyone does. We brought her in off the streets. She was a beautiful child and seemed to grow up fast—pretty much had to, given her situation. In her teen years she was rebellious, as most are, staying out late at night, rock'n'roll music blast-ing, piercing her body with metal—three on one ear and one through the navel.

Julie went to school till just recently. I can't reckon now how we managed getting her enrolled in the first place without being her birthright parents or legal guardians, but it really doesn't matter now. It was the right thing to do at the time. Now she's stopped going and stays out more than in. We can't make her go back to school. We can't make her do anything. She's living her life; we can only do so much to direct her in the right path.

She comes and goes when she wants and stays out nights— some nights at friends, which is probably how she got pregnant in the first place, if you ask me.

She began working not too long ago. Night jobs mostly. That was about the time she started not staying out as much, earning a pretty penny working the night shift, the day shift, and the morning shift. She did it all … to support her Hannah. If

I made money when I was her age, I don't know what I would have done.

I have no idea why I'm speaking of her in past tense—it's not like she's passed on like most of my peers, just away longer, is all. She still comes and goes, has dinner with us now and then, comes by for Thanksgiving and Christmas dinners. Sometimes she just pops in to tell us the important things in her life, like the baby.

Just last week she was talking about getting another tattoo as we ate a fine dish she had helped my wife prepare. I don't think they'd let her get one, though, being young as she is. Or maybe she's old enough, I don't know. She said dragons symbolize both strength and protection, and that she was getting it for Hannah, to help look after her, I think.

My mind forgets now and then.

It's a tricky thing, the mind.

Hearing is one thing that has never given me trouble, if I may stray from the topic and go back to being old. My ears have always treated me right. Sometimes hearing things they shouldn't, sometimes hearing things they should, but always listening.

Eyes are the worst because you have no idea that they're slowly dying with you. You go around believing everything in the world is as blurry as it seems, until you put on a pair of spectacles from a drugstore and—holy Moses, smell the roses—the miracle of sight is upon you. Well, okay, sort of. Let there be light, but let it be less blurry than normal.

Then you check your blood pressure, pick up your pills, and get on with the day. For most folks, this is their day, the day they went to the drugstore. Or the day my [*fill in younger living relative here*] took me to the drugstore.

Drugs? Well, yes, I've done those, but what old-timer like me hasn't? I'm not talking drugs like marijuana or acid or anything like that. Those have always stayed their distance. I hope they've stayed from Julie, too. I'm talking about prescription. The little orange-brown bottles with the white childproof, old-folk-proof caps that are damn near impossible to open. Horse pills, once-a-week pills, daily pills, pills to keep you from coughing, pills to keep you from soiling your pants, pills to keep your equipment saluting, pills to counteract all the other pills you're taking, and others to counteract those. I could die tomorrow and still have enough juice in me to not let me know I'm dead and to keep me horny for three weeks.

Not everything about being old is bad, though, like dining at Denny's or IHOP on seniors' night, bowling, bingo (okay, maybe it still is pretty bad), falling asleep on the recliner with a good book in your lap, like my Barbara. She's never going to finish that book.

My point is that you need some kind of positive to keep the old ticker going. Once you add in the negative, life rolls downhill.

With me, it's my lovely wife who keeps me running. She's my Energizer. She's my Duracell. I love her dearly and have for the last sixty-two years. She's quiet now, but you should hear her voice, like an angel when she speaks.

It may seem like a long time, sixty-two years and all, but every year that's passed is a year cherished with Barbara. She's my complement. And I'm hers. And Julie is sort of both of ours.

Barb hides her age better. She's still as beautiful as the day we met. She sleeps a lot, like a cat, day in and day out, basking in the sun. I swear the book on her lap hasn't turned a page in a week. She rests so peacefully, though. Never makes a peep. Never snores. Sometimes I just lay a blanket over us and sleep next to her on the couch. I think about her a lot when I'm out in the yard pruning the roses, or when I'm in our den writing. She usually checks in on me late at night to make sure I'm not sleeping with the typewriter, but the last week she seems to like staying on the couch.

She hasn't moved since Julie came over last to help her make dinner, as I mentioned before. I hope she's not sick. But like I said, she's getting old and so am I.

Writer, did I say? Yes, that too. Retired from the profession of counseling children for thirty-something years, but still a writer.

Ideas and thoughts just flow, or have you not noticed already? I write poetry mostly—for Barbara. She loves poetry. Sometimes short stories, but I never publish those—they're just for the fun of it. No one will ever read them but me. Sometimes Barb. I will share one of my more disturbing stories later, or at least a poem or two.

I publish my poetry every once in a great while, something like once a year or so, but over the course of my life, it still adds up to quite a few. I've been in the *Post*, the *New Yorker*, countless newspapers—mostly letters to the editor complaining about articles—and one magazine, admirable since its first issue: Stratton's *Brenden Talented*. It's Barbara's favorite magazine.

One of my poems, which we'll just call "Sixty-one" (because I wrote it to commemorate our sixty-first anniversary) will hopefully be published there for Barb to read on our special day. That is if I ever finish the damn thing. It's had me in a vise for the longest time—one of those writer's block deals where you can never seem to find the words.

Inspiration comes like a eunuch, though, I have always said—from a single source. (This is where you'd normally hear two beats of a snare drum and one from a cymbal, signaling my death for saying such a horrid thing).

Now, I must apologize for my crude joke, and also for not mentioning my name up until this point, but it should probably be mentioned so you don't refer to me as that funny old-timer who babbles on too much and gets off topic and forgets so often what started up the whole single-sided conversation in the first place.

It's a name no one ever uses any more, like Harold, Irving, or Ruth, but someday I hope it becomes used more regularly. Names go through cycles, don't they? Nowadays people choose between the regulars or just make up names entirely. Sometimes they go as far as picking regular, modern names and spelling them with like-sounding characters, as in one that made the headlines in the paper recently: Aeron.

But I do have to agree that names sound better these days. Who in their right mind would name their child Ernest or Howard anymore? Names like those are dull, like something you'd name a donkey. If I've offended you, I'm sorry. I blabber.

Where was I again?

My name.

Earl.

Yes, is a donkey-like name, but back then it was as common as a last name like Smith or Jones, of which my last name is neither. I won't tell you my age, for you may laugh or perhaps lay out a rather extended sigh. Nevertheless, you probably have calculated some age in your head that will indeed be close, since I earlier told you about my marriage of sixty-two years to Barbara.

Sixty-one?

Another thing that goes is the memory.

The memory goes …

Anyway, below the dreadfully primitive date, on the barely legible document that is my birth certificate, is the full birth name: Earl J. Heimlich. Don't ponder the J. too much, for it has been a running mystery. My sister, who was the only family I ever had and is now deceased, used to tell me it stood for Jay. That always got a laugh out of me. I sometimes blame her for my crude humor.

My mother died delivering me into this world, minutes after my sister. We grew up in an orphanage away from our abusive father. They took him away from us when we were both too young to understand what he did—probably all for the better, as he was later shot while attempting armed robbery—and as for the rest of the Heimlichs, that is one of the mysteries of my life, for all the genealogy work in the world hasn't been able to link my sister and me to a family.

My sister and I were born into this world with fake documents—and likewise fake parents, for all I know. We stood together and held together, though. We were strong, the two of us; there was some kind of secret bond keeping us alive through it all.

It was tough growing up with all the other homeless children. Looking for hope, support and whatnot. Bundled up and shoved into a churchlike building, all scared and lonely, pissing their pants. Too scared to ask permission to use to the restroom. Way too small of a place for accommodating us all.

The orphanage, I can't quite remember the name—something like Petersburg Family Orphanage, or Vestabury … something-bury anyhow. I couldn't even tell you what state it was in now. Some far-off place that can stay as far away as it wants.

It was more of a child prison, now that I think of it. The nights were worst of all. All the boys would be lined up on one side of building in a clump, the girls on the other—lots of random crying and sobbing. The floor was cold to sleep on and would ache your neck and joints by sunrise. The air was musky and smelled of urine and wet dog. They would stack us in like cargo, tight pack and side-by-side, as they used to ship slaves back when we didn't know any better. The only differences were the color of our skin and the fact that we got blankets.

Yes, it was awful—until the change anyway, which I'll get to—and packed tighter than a can of sardines. If the boy behind you pissed the bed at night, it looked as though you pissed the back of your seat by morning. You'd both get the paddle, the one with the holes drilled through—Berta, we called her—on the behind when the caretakers found out. They were brutal, those caretakers.

The meals were disgusting. White, clumpy, gooey mush called breakfast. Hope to Hades it wasn't oatmeal; no oatmeal should be so transparent. We all started calling it grop after a while. That's the sound it made when it slapped on your plate. Lunch was something similar, but brownish. You don't want to know what we called that, but let's just say it looked better coming out than going in. Supper was different, you could say. Lunch-grop over toasted bread is the best way to describe it.

One of the caretakers—Brutus, as we called him—was fond of boys. We steered clear of him for the most part, but every once in a while a kid would turn up missing at night and wouldn't return for some time. If he came back at all, it would usually be late the next afternoon, with bruises forming, and a new, guilt-stricken, violated look on his face. You could tell what happened, but no one ever spoke a word, almost as if it were considered part of the stay.

I was never approached, from what I can remember, but many of my friends were. Well, they weren't really friends (except for Eddie, of course) in Westbury—that's the name of the place, Westbury—for friendship wasn't allowed.

We stuck together as best we could, said not a word around caretakers, and steered clear of the girls. Girls were trouble, or so they put it in our minds. Girls would bring Berta, and Berta stung like hell. Berta would make you not want to sit for a while.

That's why I can't remember much about my sister. We were separated by gender. I rarely saw her at the orphanage, and when I did, we would pass and give each other a look of acknowledgment, fearing a beating if we talked, and a killing if we touched.

Brutus punished her with cleaning the latrine. This was, of course, after she was nearly beaten to death.

Her screams were muffled, but not by much, through the steel door leading to the master keeper's office—or whoever he was. We just always had called him that. Some thought he was the devil. All I know is that sometimes when I close my eyes I can still hear my sister's crying voice the way I did back then.

I could feel her.

Please …

The repeated sounds of Berta hitting her arm, her legs, her wrists perhaps. A few laughs from the room. Bad laughs.

I could feel her. She wanted to die so the pain would stop, and if I had even breathed I would have joined in her pain. Everyone felt the same. It was one thing we all shared that night.

A few softer screams and gasps, then the sound a baseball bat would make hitting a sack of potatoes, then silence.

The sound of a wind-stricken lung trying to refill.

Breathe ...

Then a cough or two as air came to her.

I swore I could feel her mind through my mind.

In my head: a cloud headache, and a whine of steel on steel like an approaching train, faster and faster and faster and faster, the headache a spreading wildfire as the railcars approached.

Silence on the lips of all those who heard, a silence we all learned to ignore over time, as well as silence behind the door. Then her body falling to the floor, the way *any* body would sound hitting the floor from a kneeling position.

Everyone was breathless except for the smaller children who were sobbing and sniffling, eyes full of water.

This was the whiteness.

Now I've done it. I've gone and opened a whole can of worms now, mentioning the whiteness and all. It shouldn't have happened this way, but if it hadn't, my story would be done with and you wouldn't be here. The whiteness is something you can't just tell someone about; you have to experience it. You must be ready to listen not only with your ears, but also with your heart and mind. So, if you're ready, relax and travel back with me to the year 1924, ten years after I first entered the Westbury Children's Orphanage.

Though published as fiction in a two-part series in the *Brenden Monthly*, what follows is my story. Sorry if parts seem present tense and others past, or if my present self jumps into the story every once in a while, but hey, can you blame a man who has never had a proper education?

Eddie was a good friend. We weren't supposed to have friends at Westbury, but who was gonna stop us? Berta? Not likely. She may have bled us or broken a few of our bones, but our friendship was much stronger than that. It was the only thing we had.

I'll always remember Eddie, like one remembers a pet—I know that for a fact. I'm not saying he *was* my pet; just that he was loyal. The scrawniest guy I've ever known, but by far the toughest. If he ever got in trouble with you doing something stupid, he'd take the blame, and the pain. Eddie and I were pals for about three years up to this point—my longest friendship besides that of my sister. I had other friends, but something, or someone, always changed that. The caretakers would separate us or beat any form of developing friendship out of us. Sometimes kids simply disappeared.

Rarely, extremely rarely, one was adopted, but that hardly ever happened at Westbury. Folks every Sunday, after services, came to check us out, always picking the best puppy from the lot. It was quite sad, really, to see the faces of the children overlooked simply because they weren't cute enough. Some even dressed up, combed their hair with forks, or slicked back their dos.

Me? I quickly gave up on that. Too many Sundays had passed where I tried my darnedest to look my best, only to be frowned at as a pointed finger passed me over to another boy or girl who was much younger and much, much cuter than yours truly.

My sister and I were twelve and had lived at Westbury long enough for our adoption hopes to expire. It was a well-known fact that you had to be under three years of age to catch the eyes of lonely couples wanting children. We had missed our chance long ago. We were past our prime, overripe for cuteness.

The rest of us, well, we were lifers. Until we turned eighteen and could sign ourselves out. Until then, we had to trudge along and pretend not to have friends—the only thing that keeps us alive.

As I mentioned, my twin sister and I were twelve. We had been there for ten whole years. What went on in our lives the two years between the time we were born and the time we entered Westbury? I can't tell you. My sister and I never had a mother and father. I heard that my mother passed away giving birth to us, but that's about it. One of the caretakers told me once, *You killed your mother.* I had heard tales of my father as well, but those were stories told by the older kids to harass me. Maybe my father was a good guy, maybe not. Who knows? Maybe an aunt I never heard of took care of us until we were two, until she realized she couldn't love us and threw us into the orphanage. I've wasted many nights trying to figure these things out, but I've finally learned I don't really care.

Eddie cared. He was always telling me how we were all gonna get out of there, one way or another. If we had to stay long enough to sign ourselves out, we'd get out. Maybe someone lost a twelve-year-old son, he'd say, and wanted another to replace him. And a sister, too, he'd throw in to make me smile. He never gave up. And we all got out of there eventually.

As children were adopted, few as that may have seemed, more took their places. Lots more. The ratio seems to be around three to one in the last of the years.

One day a kid named Johnny was picked from the lot. No one really knew him much because he'd only been there a few months. He was a lucky son of a gun, four years old and all. His parents died in a car accident, and the authorities had taken him to Westbury. We hated him for leaving, but we hated everyone that made it out of Westbury, unless they had died. We never wanted anybody to leave that way.

Some of the older kids wanted to smack him around a bit, but they never got the chance. Once someone got a new set of parents, the caretakers took him or her away for a cleanup job. Those left behind never got to see what this consisted of, but I had always imagined a fire hose shower and a fresh change of standard Westbury clothes: dark blue pants, light gray, prison-style shirt, and a pair of socks and briefs.

The clothes we wore as we stared daggers at him, you see, were the same ones we were given at the start of the year. You were considered lucky if you got a pair of shoes that weren't holey and fit within a range of one or two sizes. Some kids even got two lefts or two rights. And if you wore out your clothes before the New Year, then tough luck, live with it. If you wore out your socks or lost support in the underwear, well, sometimes they gave you replacements. If you wet yourself at night, or the person next to you was so unfortunate (which happened quite often), then you lived with that stickiness for a while.

They made us wash our clothes in the same oversize buckets in which we took our weekly baths. We used beat-up old washboards, so we had to be careful not to further rip or ruin our clothing. And the water in those buckets ... don't ask. Just imagine what it would be like to use the same cold bathwater that every other boy in there had used. Everyone's socks were brown and falling apart all the time, and the pants were so flimsy that even new ones ripped. We were an army of scabby knees. The girls had the same outfits (and probably the same problems). Sometimes it was difficult to tell the boys apart from the girls.

"Hey, Eddie," I asked one day, "who's the new kid?"

You could tell he was new because it was late November and his clothes were still starchy and dark with color. He could have arrived earlier in the day, maybe during Johnny's departure. I asked Eddie if we should beat him up and take his clothes, and he just laughed, knowing it was a joke.

"I don't know," he said. "Look at his hair, though."

He was referring to the kid's long Beatle-style hair. It was dark brown and covering his ears. He also wore round glasses that made him look a little like John Lennon. They sheared us once a month or so, usually a buzz, to make sure we all looked the same, I guess.

We stopped talking as a caretaker (or prison guard, you could say), walked by, giving us the eye. He strode with a dignified look: chin up; hat straight; shoulders tight, Berta behind his back with the handle held loosely with one hand and tapping its edge into the other. He was one of the smaller caretakers, but every bit as mean as the others. I glimpsed a name badge that read ANDY and quickly turned my eyes down to my lunch. Eddie did the same. We stared at our food, as all the other kids were doing, forcing the ill-tasting stuff down our throats. Swallowing was the worst part. Sometimes it didn't want to go down, and you'd have to force it.

Eddie whispered something and snickered as Andy passed my side of the bench. I ignored him for my safety.

Berta came full swing onto the backs of Eddie's hands, knocking the fork loose. He buckled with pain. All ten plates of food on the table jumped. Utensils rattled.

It rattled us all, really.

Some kids looked over; most continued to grovel at their food, not saying a word.

"What did you say, boy?" Andy said.

He leaned over Eddie, with his hands on the table forming a triangle, and Berta waiting patiently for her turn again.

"Nothing, sir," Eddie said matter-of-factly. "I'm sorry, sir. It won't happen again."

Andy backhanded Eddie.

"You got that right."

He walked away in the same manner he had approached us in the first place: eyeing each prisoner for signs of trouble. The backhand was hard enough to land Eddie's head in the shallow dish of brownish lunch-grop.

It wasn't until supper that same day that I asked Eddie about the joke he had been trying to make. I made sure there were no caretakers anywhere near before I asked him.

"Just that it must hurt to have a Berta up his bum all the time," he told me.

I laughed but wasn't sure why. It just sounded odd.

"You know, 'cause he was walkin' around like he had a stick shoved up there."

We just smiled at each other. It was hard to have a good time in Westbury, but without Eddie it would have been impossible. We would usually talk and joke around during supper. It seemed that fewer caretakers were around then. Breakfast and lunch were different—then Berta was everywhere, it seemed.

I was about to say something smart when another table took a pounding and another row of kids jumped in their seats. We dared not look, just listened.

"What did you say?" spoke a louder voice than Andy's.

Silence.

Another thump at the table, louder and more terrifying.

"I asked you a question. What. Did. You. Say."

Silence again.

We all knew who the voice belonged to; it was the silence that had us curious. The voice belonged to the caretaker we all feared most: Brutus. His name really wasn't Brutus; we all just called him that because of his gargantuan size. His real name was Chadsworth,

Bruce Chadsworth. He made me piss myself one day and I cringed each time after that whenever I heard his voice. He had made a lot of us piss ourselves during our stay there.

Then he'd beat us silly for doing so.

The silences scared us most during supper. We could handle the yelling and the crying, but the quiet was uncanny.

Just about everyone had turned to look by this point, including myself. I felt the whiteness returning but wasn't sure why. It came slowly, presenting me with a headache and dizziness beforehand.

The whiteness was coming … and it was coming from the boy, the new boy, little John Lennon.

Something bad was going to happen.

As I turned to look, the feeling proved right. He was different. Not just that his hair was buzzed and his glasses gone. Tears had worked their way down his cheeks. Sweat had formed as small droplets on his forehead. He was crying and scared. A small puddle appeared near his shoes as Brutus spoke again.

"What did you say, you little faggot?"

Berta rose above his head, ready to strike. And after a few long seconds, she did.

Blood flew from the boy's nose, splattering the horrified faces next to him. Everyone but the beaten boy rose in a panic, and the other caretakers approached the table to sit them back down. They sat, but not at that same table.

The boy was alone, blood flowing out his nose, down his face, neck, shirtfront. He was shaking, probably trying to catch his breath as he cried to those who had left him.

Everything turned brighter in my head as a hairline of white light streaked my mind. I forced my eyes shut to dull the pain but failed at shoving that line of white away. After reopening my eyes, I could still see that line, and it obscured my vision as if a single white hair lay across my eyes.

The headache worsened.

"Answer me, boy," Brutus continued.

Everyone saw the bulge in his pants. He was enjoying this in a very wrong way. He raised Berta above his head in preparation of swinging her a second time.

The boy muttered something indecipherable.

"Speak up," the caretaker edged, raising Berta higher.

The boy spoke up.

"I want my mommy," he said.

Not until he said this did I realize how young the boy actually was—probably no older than seven. A few of the boys around me had tears in their eyes.

A mommy was something we had all wanted.

Ruth and I, she was my sister, we exchanged glances across the room. She was holding her temples like me.

Could she see the whiteness as well?

I had heard twins often shared things like that, a connection between souls. I never thought of asking her about it before then, and decided right then that I never would.

The whiteness was penetrating, the bars of brightness growing in number and in hue. Downright blinding, actually, like a flashlight shone in through venetian blinds, but from afar. And the headache was still there; I could always count on that. Through these blinds came faint, ghostly images. I was capable of seeing what was going on in front of me, but I also saw other things. A glimpse of this, a smidgen of that—puzzle pieces, really.

The boy took another beating, but on the side of his head—a horrible sound. Everyone looked down just before it happened. Everyone but me. I heard it as everyone else had: the hard wood of the edge of the paddle breaking cheekbone and splitting his cheek open in a bloody V-shape. I saw it through the blinds of whiteness.

The kid slumped and slid off his seat.

The glimpses and smidgens of puzzle pieces flew in front of my eyes, filling the seat where he had been.

I saw a boy, a beaten boy, but not the boy on the floor.

Piercing, this headache.

My eyes straining to watch.

The boy in his place: taller, plumper.

Brighter now.

So bright.

Everything.

The reason I named it the whiteness.

A young boy—

(Matthew)

holding a gun in a blurry painting splashed with white, fading to nothing as the boy on the floor replaced him on the seat.

Other images flashing, but out of focus.

Remaining *in* focus was a beaten boy, barely conscious, looking up at Brutus who had helped him from the floor. Tears had stopped and so had the sobbing, but you could still see that he hurt. Blood soaked his shirt.

I looked around in my line-striped vision.

Brightened peers all staring at me, empty, faceless.

Brightened peers all looking down.

Brightened peers all crying inside.

I had sensed earlier something bad would happen, but it hadn't happened yet, and that scared me more than anything.

I again spotted my sister, and she looked up at me long enough for me to see her tears before looking back down like the rest.

Brutus shook the boy and snapped fingers in front of his face.

"What have you learned from this?"

Blood oozed out of the boy's lips and off his tongue. The right side of his head was swollen and steadily pumping blood from the gash and broken bone

(something bad)

as he was asked once again, "What have you learned?"

The boy stared at me from across the room, faceless, just a flat stretch of skin staring at me

(something bad)

as red leaked from the hole in his head and he waved to me, but only I could see him through the light, I knew, waving to me like I were floating adrift. Fading away

(white)

and hidden, all I could see was white, only white, white everything, whiteness all around, *the* whiteness.

The kid tried to say something out of a mouth no longer there.

He tried to say

(something bad)

with his scared-angry voice, "I want my mommy, *you kid-fucker!*"

White.

My head hurt, and I felt the pain of the little boy. I swore for a moment that I *was* the boy and had taken the broken cheek-bone and nose, that it was my own blood collecting on the floor.

But it was the boy on the floor again. I don't want to explain in detail what happened, but it was bad.

They assured us the next day that the boy was released because his parents wanted him back. We all knew that wasn't true. The boy was dead. Brutus had killed him.

No, Westbury killed him.

February 1925

Thanksgiving passed, Christmas passed, and so did the New Year. Holidays were just days of the week. No celebrations. No gifts. Not even birthdays. No paper calendars posted on the walls. We only knew what day it was when Sunday came around. It was always the most favored day of the week because the chapel was a lot cleaner than where we ate and slept. And we could sit wherever we wanted.

Eddie and I always sat in the back so we could talk. In other words, where we pretended to listen to church services My sister never sat with us. She could be found in the front row. I don't know why. Maybe church gave her hope.

We really never talked much, my sister and I. Ever since we got into that stupid place, it changed us in a way. I was always the more rebellious type and tried making friends; she was the quiet, good-girl type, following the rules and playing the game.

Survival.

That's her thing.

Just after the death of the little boy, my sister spoke to me. It was the first time in a long time. She told me to be careful, to be safe and to survive. That was all she said. I remember I was going to say something back, but by that time she was gone.

Maybe it was a dream. Maybe she sent the message through a dream or in a thought. Some sort of telepathy. Maybe she sensed something bad would happen to me.

Who knows?

The death of the boy—I have to keep referring to him as the boy because I never once learned his name—lasted in our minds for the next few weeks following the event, but soon faded as they drilled it in our minds that he had been adopted. Not beaten to death by Berta ... adopted.

I knew the truth and felt what had happened; the whiteness showed it to me. I also believe it showed my sister, either first-hand or through me.

The master keeper, also a self-proclaimed priest, didn't speak at church service as he normally had. He was on vacation for the next few days. Sometimes that evil man could talk and talk for hours at a time, mostly about how the fire of the earth would cleanse us all. Instead, Brutus spoke—Father Brutus. He read from a page or two (most likely written by the master keeper himself) on the wrath of God. It was scary, actually, and kept the attention of us all, all but Eddie and me.

We weren't really listening, just catching a few key points here and there in case we were tested later or picked from the crowd for a quick amen.

Since the lecture was shortened, we stayed in the chapel

until supper. Not one of us complained. It was four hours less that we would have to spend elsewhere.

Plus, we had visitors.

Westbury rarely had visitors.

These were strange men: black suits, shiny shoes, white shirts, ties—clothing unfamiliar to us. We were used to the standard-issue clothing for us, and the uniforms the caretakers wore.

They spoke with Brutus and the others took notes. They looked at us, took notes. Always, they were writing.

I must say I was tempted more than once to run up to one of them, revealing everything: how we ate, how we slept, how some of us were beaten, how they had killed. But Brutus was always there, or one of the other caretakers, as if they knew my intentions.

Another strange thing happened as well. We were allowed to talk after the service. Now, I don't mean talk as if we were asked a question by one of the caretakers and were required to respond in a prompt and orderly fashion. *Talk*, talk—chatting with our peers, and such. I'm not sure if it was coincidence or a planned detail, but it was strange that our visitors arrived the same moment the master keeper was out, the same day we were allowed to socialize.

As if the caretakers were trying to hide something.

That night, when we returned for supper for our normal white and brown grop over toast, the place had changed. The dining hall was spotless, and the food wasn't that bad. They had cleaned the place while we were at service and cleaned the cement floors and the old, falling-apart wooden tables and benches as best they could. They were indeed trying to impress somebody.

The strangers, they ate with us. Well, not *with* us; they had their own table, covered with a tablecloth, in fact. They must have been some kind of inspection crew or something.

And we ate some *real* food. Toast, *real* toast, covered in something that wasn't grop, but probably what grop was intended to be: steak, potatoes, carrots, celery, gravy. Distinguishable foods. It was good, and we ate like kings. Seconds and even third helpings were served if we could hold it.

And milk. Lord, we had milk.

That night we were princes and princesses.

The strangers left just after supper with their filled notepads in hand and their jackets flung over their shoulders. They shook a few of the caretakers' hands before leaving and bade them farewell.

They'd eventually come back, but not for three years.

We later returned to our sleeping areas to discover not everything had improved—same old tight pack, holey blankets and all were waiting for us. Nearly everyone whispered stories in secrecy that night, exchanging their wonderful experiences from earlier. It wasn't really wonderful if you think about it—just not as horrible, I guess. The chatter lasted until almost early morning.

Eddie and I talked about the strangers. He thought they were special agents, coming in to take down the place, to give us new homes. I told him he was crazy and that they were future caretakers looking for work.

He didn't like my idea that well.

The next morning, everything returned to normal.

It was my birthday, or so my sister reminded me. It felt like I had aged ten years since the last. She gave me a flower she picked while working outside, I suppose. It was crumpled and wilting, but it meant the world to me. A dandelion. Dandy indeed.

Around my birthday, she always found time for gifts. It would come, not gift-wrapped, as is the common custom, but in a quick handoff. She might cut me off in line for food, or something of that sort, with her hand held open behind her back.

It was amazing the things she'd find in this bleak place: an interesting-looking rock, a folded piece of paper. Once she gave me coal. Sounds great, huh? Well, it was the best gift I ever got, and one of the few gifts I didn't lose to the caretakers during my stay.

One night I found a loose piece of cement around where I slept, about the size of a tile, and was able to pry it loose after a few attempts. There was a small hole, half-filled with small stones.

I hid the few folds of paper in there, the flower, and my coal—the primary tool of my creativity: writing.

They taught us to write like any school would, taught us our math, science, history, reading, writing—the normal subjects. Westbury wasn't a school by any means, but we had classes. Twice a day: three hours in between breakfast and lunch, and three hours between lunchtime and supper. They started us in our schooling at around age six.

I hated it from the start, especially the hours and hours of lecture. But I took a liking to writing. I learned quickly to read and write, and Eddie took a liking to mathematics right off the bat—a subject I couldn't grasp at the time.

After basic comprehension of drawing letters, forming words, and composing sentences, I grew to love writing.

And wrote poetry.

I created lines, stanzas, used rhymes, the whole lot, all in my head. During my studies, I learned by heart the entire poem called "The Raven," by someone named Poe, along with a few others that were signed "Anonymous," and three others that I made up in my head. Unnamed poems by an unknown poet, Earl Heimlich. It was something I enjoyed, but most of all it was something they couldn't take from me. They couldn't take my thoughts.

Now, this is where the coal comes in to play.

The pens we used during classes were immediately returned. If we were caught with one outside of class, it probably would have gone through our hand, or worse. All books and paper had to stay in the schoolroom as well.

My sister knew what she was doing all those years in giving me those strange little gifts. Somehow she knew I wanted to write.

It was that connection we had. And it took her three years to find me the coal, and another to get the paper. I'm sure she must have stolen a half sheet from class somehow.

My sister, the kleptomaniac.

So, after nearly four years' time, this is what I wrote late one cold night just before bed:

A LIFE UNLIKE THIS

The wind is haste, and quite cold,
Like the floors beneath.
Foul air, dank sheets, wet with mold,
Bound tight like a wreath.
Our mad caretakers don't smile,
Not once in a day.
Berta striking, vile,
So in bed we pray:
We may live for a life unlike this.
The food is sick, like mucus,
And hard to swallow.
Steak, carrots, and potatoes
Maybe tomorrow.
We sleep with dreadful crying
Each and every night.
Hope living twice, then dying.
Trading God, we'll fight:
We would give for a life unlike this.

I never signed the poem or signed my name at the beginning or end of it. Instead, I kept it in my secret space, buried in the cement bed where I slept. I told it to Eddie, for by that time it was memorized, and he thought it sounded kind of queer.

"Why'd you write a poem?" he asked late after supper.

We were lying down for the night, staring up with hands bracing our heads. He had a confused look on his face.

"They're just words … to keep the memory of this place alive, I guess, Eddie."

Saying that out loud sounded stupid. We all hated this place. Why would anyone want to preserve it the way I had?

"To keep the memory of this place alive, huh?"

I could see his lips mouthing, *Hope living twice, then dying?*

Everyone else was asleep.

"Maybe it's a part of me I don't want to forget. We'll have to reflect on all this one day, no matter how bad it is."

"Yeah, I guess," he said.

He was still going over the last few lines in his head. *Trading God* … possibly beginning to understand, seeing past the humor and into the sadness.

"You should write one about me. I could get you some paper. Just don't put my name on it … or yours."

"How about—" I started, and then thought for a few seconds while squinting at the dark ceiling cracks above us.

"Eddie, Eddie, Wets the Beddie." Poem number two, "by Earl J. Heimlich," I added at the end.

It was quiet for the few seconds following, and then he gave me a charley horse on the arm. We both snickered as I rubbed my arm. We made snorting sounds from deep within our nasal cavities, the kind of noises your body makes while trying to laugh and be soundless at the same time. Both of our voices were just starting to change with our age, so our snorts were in between high and low pitches, almost like giggling.

The caretaker asleep in the chair not too far from us stirred, so we feigned sleep.

After a while it got quiet again, so I added, "Want me to write that one down for you?"

He was asleep. Moments later, so was I.

December 1926

We were toward the back of the line at supper, twenty kids away from the nearest adult, and I cut in front of my sister. I held my hands behind me in a secretive fashion. It took her a while to recognize the plan, but eventually she grabbed the folded parchment nestled between my waving fingers and the food tray, and shoved it deep in one of her pockets. We finished the food parade with our fellow child inmates, held out our trays to the hair-netted servers, received plops of ladled grop as we would any other day. Then it was off to sit on opposite sides of the room, the boy side and the girl side.

See, it was Christmas Day (I had counted down the days since my birthday and was sure of it) and was time for presents. At least, that was customary in the real world: families giving presents back and forth under a tree, some fat guy in a red suit and white beard handing out gifts to kids from his big black bag. What any of us would give to sit on his lap. We could sit on one of the bigger caretakers here, but that wouldn't come close. Some of us had, in fact, but not for gift ideas. In the older books there's a story of a certain St. Nicholas, who gave all he had to children in need. He went around the world giving everything, including his life. Somehow, I think they're the same person in spirit: *St. Nicholas, Saint Niclaus, Saintni Claus, Santa Claus* ... Either way, reindeer can't fly, but the names merge well and it only makes sense.

My silent and personal saint, Ruth, risked her neck every year for a present for me on my birthday. Have I mentioned her name was Ruth? Well, it's Ruth, and anyway, I had not returned the favor until this day.

Now it was her turn for a gift and my turn to play the role of the saint. Saint Heimlich.

It was the poem. Not the "Eddie Wettie" one, but the other, "A Life Unlike This." I had it memorized, yet had never written it down until this point. It was hard giving the paper back, for it was once a gift itself, but she wasn't the type of person who would take it wrong. Ruth would understand its love and meaning, and also the pain behind the words. She would probably cry.

I chatted with Eddie while we ate, with my eyes glued to Ruth across the room. She was trying to find a time to unfold her gift. She tried not to appear too conspicuous and kept the poem under the table. It traveled between her fingers, dancing like a fairy from an Aesop's fable. Her eyes moved across the room, playing lookout.

"Hear what happened to Saul?" Eddie asked out of the blue.

Venetian blinds again, faint.

"From the Bible?" I asked, not really listening.

"No, you twit. Saul Parker, the fat kid."

Saul was the largest boy at Westbury, weighing well over two hundred pounds, possibly more, quite spherical for a nine-year-old.

Ruth focused on her gift, beginning to unfold it.

"That tubby was eating—" Eddie started.

The words faded as the hairline blinds turned less transparent and my attention drifted to the caretaker drawing closer to

(white)

my sister, her legs shaking as she unfolded the gift.

She didn't see him.

Ruth …

"—and he starts this gurking sound," Eddie said, and stopped to shovel food down his throat.

And then I knew why.

Brutus approached, so I started eating as well. The entire table hushed. The monstrosity held his paddle behind his back—Berta waiting to come out and play.

All heads pointed down in a weird kind of shame—shame that really had no basis but that we all seemed to share. We dared not look up. He passed, for what seemed an eternity, and I could only think of my sister getting caught.

Needles of pain poked behind my eyes, which had drifted upward, showing me the edge of the table, then further up to reveal some abnormally bright cement floor. They moved back down to my tray of food. Brutus had paused behind me. I could feel his evil presence and fiery eyes glaring down at me as if I were a nonentity. After another eternity passed and he took his first step forward, my eyes ventured back, painfully this time, to the edge of Ruth's table across the room, and eventually to the caretaker a few paces away from her.

Ruth!

The blinds twisted shut.

The forming headache unformed.

Ruth stuffed the poem under her legs and resumed eating as if nothing were astir.

Had she heard my thoughts, or his footsteps?

"So he was making this gurking sound," Eddie continued with his story, waving his hand in my face. "Are you even listening?"

"What? Oh … So what happened?"

"He was in the middle of eating his fifth or sixth bowl of … something, and then he just set his spoon down with his eyes all wide. He grabbed his stomach and groaned like you do after Brutus hits you or something."

My eyes returned to my sister.

"And then Warden came by," he said excitedly.

Warden, one of the caretakers, was as skinny as any of us. He would usually follow in the footsteps of Brutus, walking around in his oversize uniform, looking to start trouble. We all knew he was a wimp, but we still feared him—and well we should. Anyway, my attention at the moment was not on Warden, or Eddie's story for that matter. I was listening, but not really.

The caretaker passing Ruth had caused the white imbalance of emotion and eruption in my mind. He had looked down at her once, I knew, because I had felt it in my mind; I had seen his eyes as they bore down on her, at the both of us, really—same hungry glare they all carried—but nothing had happened.

"—was smacking Berta on his palm," Eddie said.

Under the table, Ruth folded the poem back into the small, thick square it had started as, and then she put it in her pocket ever so smoothly. I could tell she had no intentions of reading my poem until after supper, so I moved my focus back to Eddie and his story about Saul Parker.

"Warden slammed Berta hard on the table, making all of us jump, as loud as a gun going off. Well, I've never really heard a gun go off, but it's probably pretty loud."

I interrupted at that point, wondering where I was in all this.

I would have remembered a Tubby event.

"Wait, where was—"

"I think you were in the bathroom or something."

"When?"

It wasn't really a question.

"A while ago. I don't know. So we all jumped 'cause it scared the bejesus out of us, and then it all came out."

Eddie set both hands on the table and smiled.

He sounded finished with his story.

"What did?" I asked.

Anything could have come out.

"You know, he puked."

"Gross."

"What's even grosser? He didn't puke on his tray; he puked on his clothes, back in his food, and, best of all, all over *Warden*. It was neat. Grop-puke everywhere."

He never spoke louder than a whisper.

"You get any on you?"

"No, but guess what happened next. Warden started gurking too, and then *he* puked."

The last part sounded less believable.

We looked around, but there wasn't a caretaker in sight.

I gave Eddie a doubtful look.

"Okay, not really, Warden that is, but Tubby—I mean Saul— he did. Warden pulled out Berta and chopped her right over his fingers. Didn't you notice Saul's hand?"

"I was wondering about that."

We both sat there for a few minutes on our cold, damp seats, staring into a great nothingness, after which we both finished our meal. Each bite (or slurp) became harder to swallow after Eddie's story. But I wasn't thinking about the story much, my mind being busy on other things. Like Ruth, and how she must have sensed my warning to her.

The whiteness was mixed in with it all as well. Somehow it was always there, waiting, ready to blind me from that which I needed not see or, sometimes it seemed, to bring forewarning.

I never really understood what it was until later that day. Well, I'm still not sure I fully understand, but it was during our writing class that afternoon that the whiteness returned in full.

Class just begun, and Mrs. Kumberson, or Kamberson, or whatever her name may have been, she was at the chalkboard. Back then we had chalkboards, not those dry-erase things that are common today. Black slate boards with the chalk dust scratches of previous assignments not fully wiped away. You'd pick up the erasers and your hands would turn white, as if you were playing with coke.

We were all familiar with coke / cocaine / nose candy / whatever-you-want-to-call-it. Almost everyone at Westbury sniffed lines. Not any of us prisoner orphans, but the bad guys—caretakers. *Them.* Sniffling like they were sick with the cold; that's how you could tell they had snorted the evil pixie dust. Nose candy to those bastards.

Mrs. Kumwhatever was clean, though, yet as evil as the rest. A few thought she was a witch, though, like those they had hanged in Salem. She had an old, wrinkled, question-mark shaped body. Her legs were skinny, like all the malnourished kids, me included. Loose skin melted off her dried-out, tree-branch feet; like a burning witch's legs. A wart with three long, dark hairs poked out from the tip of her pointy nose. The rest of her was pretty much the way you probably imagine: black-

and-gray-speckled cobweb hair, hunched-over shoulders, lips squeezed into a kiss-waiting, fart-suppressing pucker. You could almost use those off-kilter, stained teeth of hers to sharpen a pencil. Sometimes it appeared that she might be trying to whistle as her eyes bore down on you. She kept a yardstick at hand. We all knew that stick. It cracked over fingers now and then.

We sat quietly with our heads at our desks, practice-writing our cursive *K*s. They had to match the *K* at the top of the chalkboard, where the rest of the alphabet lay in near-perfect calligraphy script. The day before, we were practicing our *J*s. You can guess what was on the next day's schedule. Each day we learned just one thing, it seemed. Slow learning.

My hands were sore, cramped. The paper in front of me read *K, k, K, k, K, k, K, k*, over and over again, barely legible, some characters running together and others overlapping.

I remember the piercing in my mind as I recursively wrote the letters on the page. The pain was small, but it was there. What was coming with it I couldn't say, but it was coming fast.

Eddie sat in a desk directly in front of mine because we were almost late and it was the only one remaining, right at the head of the room, closest to the knuckle-smacking witch. Being late was something you didn't want to do in her class.

Our near-lateness was a result of something Eddie spotted and just had to snag: the shiny bottom of a glass bottle, which had been rubbed smooth like a polished stone. It made a perfect round lens, flat on one side and slightly curved inward on the other, with worn etched letters of some sort. Eddie's eyes were glossed and wide like that glass when he saw it on the cold cement floor in the open, as out of place as a Big Mac might have been.

"Keep it down," I had told Eddie.

Bashed and bruised from previous encounters, my finger had pointed in Brutus' direction. I could have sworn he had heard us chatting, and for some reason pretended to ignore it.

Eddie had said something about fetching the glass, and disappeared, then quickly returned with his hand clenched in an obvious fist. A half-smile barely showed on his thin lips. He had shown the glass to me briefly, and before class we had entombed it with the rest of my stash (Eddie was the only one ever to know about the loosened concrete slab that hid my things) and had quickly scurried to our first class of the day, where we sat writing the stupid letter *K* again and again, as if we were Klan member wannabes.

I couldn't stop thinking about the glass and why Brutus had stayed his distance with a look that said *I know and I'll kill you soon enough* as more letters crept along the paper. That trying headache poked through the layer of pain covering my eyes, finally punching through like a spade. Intense pain.

The devil has pierced my eyes from the inside, I thought, pressing my palms frantically against them.

The rest of the class continued the tedious writing practice, a scene that blurred through my vision as if I were looking through Eddie's treasured piece of glass.

I hope Ruth can't feel this, I remember thinking.

"That's not right," a voice said, fading to

(that looks like a damned r)

whispers as more pain shot right through my pupils.

A joke flashed by then; for a second, I may have laughed out loud because the room hushed a second or two as

(it is a k, mrs. k)

lowercase letters floated around me in cursive.

A ruler hitting a desk.

The door.

Heavy footsteps.

You know why cross-eyed folks can't teach?

Can't keep their pupils straight.

Eddie told me that one a few years prior. It wasn't funny then, and I had no idea why it ran across my mind. His glass lens filled the unoccupied space in my head; the rest of my head was full of

(red splattering against white)

something resembling a Rorschach drawing and

(something cold, heavy)

the mini-blinds twisting open, allowing me a peek through as more pain seeped in and the devil worked wildly behind my eyes—always my eyes seeing

(a seagull perched on a windowsill)

the room brightening, light seeping in at impossible angles through the slits of the blinds, pain growing, growing, growing in repetition like our cursive writing practice.

A voice: *I'm here for* him, *Mrs. Kumsf*—muddled.

It was Brutus and he hadn't come for me. Somehow I knew he wanted Eddie. A setup; he had planted it for the dummy to find.

The glass, I thought, and pressed my thumbs to my forehead to ease the pain. It helped little.

A chair in front of me moaned like water passing in an old pipe. I'm sure I looked awful as I bent over the desk, rubbing my eyes and temples while Eddie went to the door like a dead man walking, only to be beaten for the umpteenth time. Bad, this time, too. I could see what was going to happen. I could feel it and see it through the whiteness, along with other things, other people.

Blood, a lot, but not from Berta.

Brighter now.

Eddie was there, faintly, but so were a great many other things, more than anyone could count—maybe everything.

Through the whiteness came flashes of present / future / past, one overlaid onto the other onto the other:

Eddie, beaten / a stranger in some faraway place / a dead field / a rose growing out of a skull / a horse kicking a boy / Ruth / me / my sad reflection / a woman / a crying face / a carved face / the face of a clock with the hour hand stuck between the eleven and twelve / a park / a tree / a man holding a gun to his head …

BANG!

The noise, like a door slamming shut.

A single drop of blood dripped from my nose to my paper, a silent splat I could only sense because my mind was elsewhere, my sight gone. Then red, instantly, lots of red, splotching the canvas. Another bright beam of white flashed, and the blinds were back, only far away this time. *Maybe that's why they're called blinds*, a softer thought mused. I may have even smiled as droplets of red paint fell softly from my face to the constant beat of a metronome.

Then everything went away.

No blinds.

A white—

I thought I was dead, and may as well have been, for everything was a great nothingness. The day the world went away. There was no sound, no sight, no senses of any sort. Only my mind existed, which held nothing at the time, except for the whiteness.

This, I knew, was the whiteness in its truest form, whatever it was. Death, maybe? A white backdrop's all it appeared to be.

I held up my hand where it would certainly cross my face; still only white. I tried to touch my face, but that didn't happen, either, as if I weren't there and this was all a sick dream. Maybe I was dead and in some kind of purgatory. Who knows?

And then a faint but high-pitched sound, like a teakettle miles away, rose from the nothingness. The sound a tuning fork makes when struck against a table; resonating, it grew stronger, reverberating that sick echo, louder and louder. Siren-like, it blared—a siren played in fast forward. The pitch rose, higher and higher, growing, piercing, stabbing, mind-cracking ...

Quiet.

In an instant, and at that exact moment when the sound was at its highest and loudest and when it seemed that everything would break apart, that awful noise vanished, leaving behind the smallest pinpoint of black (where it had to have come from): a hole in the whiteness. I could see it, by God. The smallest, tiniest pin-prick of whatever it was I had seen.

Whether I was dead or unconscious, it didn't matter anymore. Nothing mattered but that spot. I concentrated to make it move, to make it bigger, to make it do anything. I even tried closing my eyes to make it go away, but that didn't work, either. Then something stranger happened. Either it was getting bigger, or I was moving toward it, for the pinprick of black slowly grew into a dot.

It grew a bit more, until I could see that it wasn't even round, but a small rectangular something no bigger than a speck of glitter. Seconds later, it was twice that size, growing exponentially, as if I were being dragged to it at a dizzying rate, with nothing but the white canvas all around.

Thoughts overlapping thoughts overlapping thoughts:

A break in the whiteness / an escape / a way out / a cave / a hole / a door / a window

A mirror.

It scared the living bejesus out of me.

First it was a black dot; seconds later it was a wood-framed mirror floating in thin air.

A shadow swayed beneath it, the only movement in the great whiteness. The mirror didn't scare me. In any other circumstance (not that there are many circumstances where I find my soul caught in a white nothingness of space with a mirror), I would not have been startled. What shook me, however, was that I was looking at my reflection: a small child with mussed hair, pale skin, bad teeth, slight freckles ... and the most unholy set of black eyes—glossed eyes, black as coal.

Not *my* eyes.

The mirror floated with my reflection and someone else's eyes.

After my heart caught up with the rest of me, I suspected it wasn't me at all with those devil eyes. Yet, when I moved left (at least in my mind, for the only presence in this whiteness was the mirror) and the morbid, reflected creature moved to his right. I had a strange feeling conversely that when I moved my eyes, those in the reflection would stay, like in the paintings where the eyes follow you around as you move.

The faint teakettle whine returned, its volume and pitch

came much quicker, passing like a railcar.

And when the sound passed, a new reflection appeared in the mirror, disturbing me once again. I'm sure that if my heart were there, it would have stopped. Before me was the mirror, bearing the reflection of an adult male, probably in his mid-thirties, with tears drying below his fire-red, sunken eyes—looking as though he had simply run out of tears. His hair was straggly.

Help me, please.

The whine amplified to its same ear-splitting racket. And as it did so, the stranger's reflection slowly changed.

Railcars passed, one by one, the sound growing in magnitude.

Likewise, the sad stranger's face transformed into a maddening expression of abhorrence. His cheeks burned red with hatred: hatred of the world, hatred of himself. Tears fell from his eyes.

The sound of the railcars, feeding the stranger rage.

And then the noise ceased, just like that.

My reflection in this floating mirror revealed the smallest of smiles on the stranger's face, my altered face, as a gun raised to his temple and blew the side of his head open.

He crumpled, his body disappearing within the framework of the mirror. A mess of matter sprayed into the whiteness. It fanned in a spatter some fifteen feet to the side of the mirror, from where the man would have been had he been standing before the mirror instead of me. The mirror face remained blank after that, reflecting only whiteness while it floated alone with its shadow below it. The mammoth frame bobbed gingerly over the crimson mess.

And then everything disappeared, leaving empty white.

❑ ❑ ❑

"… Earl? Earl?" said a voice in the distance, as solid white became transparent white and a headache lingered wherever my head lay.

Snap! Snap, snap!

"Earl!" It was Mrs. K, but she was far away.

Voices mumbled to other voices while water-blurred people gathered indistinguishably around in a semicircle. They were cloudy and far away. A ringing also lingered—my ears, perhaps.

Snap!

"Is he dead?"

Snap! Snap, snap! Snap!

"No, I think he may have fainted," said Mrs. K, snapping her bony, brittle fingers two inches from my face. She slapped my face with one of her hands, and then backhanded me, not too hard.

"It's no seizure; he's not flapping around like a fish."

She snapped her fingers a few more times.

"Remember that 'tarded boy?" someone asked. "And how he'd just all a sudden fall to the floor with his fingers curled up, drooling over himself and shaking like a wet dog with his back all bent outta shape? That was seizures."

"Yeah," someone else said.

It sounded like Andy; he had that same educated speech.

"See how his eyes are rolled back, staring into his brain? I think he may have started going into a seizure, but just before he did, he fainted instead."

Did I mention they weren't medically literate?

Andy continued his prognosis, "And the blood running out of his nose, that's from when he fell back'ards and bumped his head. That's all normal. Was he acting strange or anything?"

My vision started to return, and the silhouettes above gradually formed faces. The ringing continued.

"No. Not that I recall. Mr. Chadsworth, Brutus, he'd just taken Eddie from class for something he did—that no-good kid is always up to something he's not s'posed to be doing—and when the door shut, that must have been when Earl hit the floor, 'cause I didn't hear him falling over, and I just kept on teaching."

She was a bit shaky.

"Then that girl"—Mrs. K then pointed to a small, dark haired girl who must have been unimportant and largely forgotten in Mrs. K's world, who also had been sitting behind me during the incident—"she started screaming like a banshee: 'Aaahhh!!! Aaaaaaanhh!!!'" she mocked in a higher timbre, startling Andy so that he nearly fell on his butt. "I went to shut her up for good and saw Earl lying out on the floor with those white, empty eyes."

Hysterical.

More people came into focus, staring down at my body on the floor, some gaping, others whispering back and forth.

An ache jabbed the back of my head over and over, throbbing with my pulse as my head rocked uncomfortably on a large bump, centered strangely on the back of my skull, right above the neck—the result of my head cracking against the cement floor.

"I thought he might've been fooling around—you know how these kids act sometimes, like monkeys—so I poked him a few times with this."

She held up her ruler.

"I poked him in the stomach, not hard, mind you that blood

was there when I first showed up," she said, and poked me in the thigh once again like a piece of meat.

"And that's when you came and got me?"

"That's when I came and got you," she reiterated.

My eyes were almost back to normal when I choked on the blood from my nosebleed. Blood shot from my face.

"Oh, dear Jesus!" she cried.

A few spots of blood hung from the tassels of her shoes, and one from the lace on her dress.

"Oh, dear Jesus, that boy has the plague! Get that thing out of here before we all catch it and die like he's gonna!"

She was more frenzied and said another "dear Jesus" for every drop of blood that dripped from my nose.

A few of the kids cried, and Andy told them to shut up or he would shut them up as he attempted to control the eerie situation.

I remember the rest of the class being told by someone to sit back in their seats and to fold their arms, something about putting away the ruler and to stop poking me, and a lot more hysteria.

My eyes rolled back as things clouded and the ringing quieted. Pain still, lots of pain, especially in the back of my head, circling the knot that felt like Devil's Tower growing from my skull.

I remember Andy chuckling to himself, yet pissed at Mrs. K, explaining, as he would to a child, that I was choking on blood.

Quieter:

"Nothing dangerous by any means."

Fading:

"Get him to the infirmary to be checked by the nurse."

Silence.

Whatever else was said, I would never come to remember, for I blacked out. I was in a dark, timeless world where memories fail to exist and dreams have no place.

A few days later, I was released from the infirmary with a less prominent bump on the head.

While I was in La-La Land, Eddie had nearly gotten the life beaten out of him. I almost didn't recognize him. His face was bruised and his left eye socket filled with a solid red, blood-filled marble. Those were the only abnormalities in his appearance, other than his walk (as if he had been whacked in the bum a few too many times). He looked like a complete stranger with an entirely different face and acted as if nothing had happened.

I'm not sure he knew how badly he looked.

There weren't many mirrors in Westbury.

We talked about my episode. He said he had missed it entirely because he was hauled out of the room by Brutus, but he got some good gory details from a few of the other kids the next day. I was the subject talked about for the following six months.

"He cracked his head open."

"He died and came back."

"He bled from his nose with his eyes all rolled back."

I was pointed at secretly from then on and avoided by most of the younger kids. They would be walking in my direction and then take a wide turn, eyes glued to the floor.

"That's the dead guy."

"That's the coma kid."

These things were said beneath breaths.

I was the hot topic. Well, me and a girl named June, who

died of who-knows-what later that week. She was three. Her name was the only other thing I could recall besides the fact she had died.

Eddie asked what it was like to be dead, if I had seen the white light (quite ironic), what heaven was like, if there was only black, or stars, or if it was like a dream, how long it had felt like.

I didn't tell him about the whiteness. He wouldn't have understood. I remembered him leaving class and then me waking up in the infirmary, that's what I told him.

I asked Eddie if *he* was all right.

"Sticks and stones."

He didn't want to talk about it much, so I dropped the subject, we ate our lunch, and never spoke about either matter again.

October 1928

Almost two years later, and things only got stranger. Andy received a higher-paying job at the county jail. It wasn't much of a career change, just an orphanage for older kids. He left in September, and soon after, a new caretaker named Walt joined the crew. He was a larger man than Brutus, by at least three inches in height, and fifty pounds heavier. His beard was husky and joined to the sideburns of a head of curly brownish-gray. He looked as if they had picked him out of the wilderness— him and maybe his pet bear. He was burly and intimidating, yet gentle. That was what set him off from the others and made him not quite fit in. But enough about Walt—his role in this story will come later.

Eddie's eye never got much better. The swelling and blood-shot look went away, as it should have, but what remained was a light-gray cloudiness over part of the white in his eye. It was in the shape of the state of Washington, and hard not to stare at.

I didn't tell him about it. He had plenty of scars.

Ruth was still distant, and my connection to her grew further each day. Sometimes I thought there was something wrong with her. She ambled around, barely, tended school, went to *The Church of Father Brutus*, as we called it, slept, and that's it. She moved like a machine. She moped around with her shoulders slumped, her arms dangling. I thought she was depressed.

November 1928

Ruth got sick. She began losing weight noticeably. Her eyes were sunken as deep as they could go and were as black as two hematites lined together. The cheekbones stood out the most, giving her a ghastly, drugged image. Twig arms and legs made her elbows and knees seem geometric. Not much held her together. Caretakers passed by Ruth unnoticed, looking past her full plates after meals, blind to her skeletal contours.

"Sticks and stones," I mumbled at dinnertime, looking at Ruth as she dumped her untouched plate into the garbage. Eddie asked what I had said. I told him it was a poem, which it later became:

PAPER DOLL

Brittle sticks of bone
Paper tissue, a gentle skin
Hold together my doll
Brace from within
Stand tall
(tear not, paper)
Strings of vein pump the blood warmer
Carry from the heart; feed the pain
(bleed through, paper)
To the soul
And for the demon
Cast yourself away, depart
Go to another, one without the love
One of hatred, voracity, greed, without heart
(soak love, paper)
Don't fold
Don't blow away

It did fold, though, not just Ruth, but also my poem. I folded it gently, right at the doll-shape of the poem's waistline, and tucked it away with the rest of the stash.

There's only so much one can fit under a loose stone. All the original stuff was there, along with a dozen or so poems. There was the glass Eddie had found a long time ago. Only, just lately, it held the shape of a half-moon, no longer full, and sharp as glass should be on its broken edges.

I asked Eddie what had happened to it. We were supposed to be sleeping. It was one of those nights where we were, fortunately, put close enough together that we could whisper.

"It must have broke."

"Pretty obvious *it must have broke.*' You drop it or something?"

No response.

And then, "You ever notice that Randall kid is always pickin' his nose?"

He didn't want to talk about it, I guess. Eddie didn't want to talk about a lot of things, either, these past few years. Like the day Eddie was taken out of class by Brutus and I had my little episode with the whiteness.

Normally one of us would return from a beating, bludgeoning, whatever you want to call it, and after a few hours we'd be joking around trying to forget it. We'd make up stories of how Brutus, or Andy, or Stan, or any of the other caretakers were abused as children, dropped on their heads, or hit by a truck— fun stuff like that, which would take our minds from the rain and into the sunshine.

Eddie was horrible at cheering me up. It was something stupid he didn't mean to say that would eventually make me laugh and get me talking. Maybe he acted stupid on purpose, perhaps not. It was always an easy task to bring Eddie back to good spirits, until Brutus got to him that last time. Come to think of it, Brutus came around to Eddie quite often. He would appear from nowhere, take Eddie by the arm, and drag him to his office with the doors shut. Eddie would return later in the day, not beaten (at least not physically, most times), but with a defiled and violated demeanor, something he carried with him in the way he walked and talked.

You could tell he hurt inside, and that he wanted to scream, he wanted to tell the world what had happened. You could see in his eyes that he wanted vengeance. He said to me one time that he'd somehow get out of Westbury, once and for all. He'd bring the glass edge to his wrists if need be.

"You'd never cut yourself, would you? We're best friends."

Silence.

"I'd have to stoop to their level to do anything *that* stupid, and that will never happen. Never."

He had a hint of a scary-looking smile, both sad and malicious, a look you'd expect to see carved into a pumpkin.

For the next few months, my sister's health, and the shard of glass, slowly diminished to nothing.

They didn't tell me she died until three days after she had passed.

She had died slowly. Whatever kind of cancer or whatever it was that lived inside her, it ate her away until her body gave up. I know her spirit would never have given up. She had probably held on for longer than she should have. Ruth's body gave up and took the spirit of Ruth with it.

They buried her deep in a field, near the other graves of those who died at Westbury, a few yards from a knee-high wall made of stone. It was a sad burial ground covered in high grass, a grim little overgrowth of death. Everything there was dead: grass, bushes, the bodies underneath, even the oak roots sprouting from the earth like a large, undead hand trying to free itself: dry, rotted and ready to crumble back into the soil. An old hornets' nest hung from one of the taller, sturdier branches of the tree, empty and lifeless. Rock piles in body-sized clumps marked each site. I imagine now, like in that movie *Carrie*, a hand bursting through the soil and through one of those piles of rocks, grabbing me to settle unfinished business.

You could tell which were the older graves; there were fewer rocks, as if some had been pilfered to make less work finding other rocks to cover newer graves.

So many dead children.

It was rumored that the grave closest to the oak tree belonged to some janitor from long ago. There were ghost stories about the cemetery.

Maybe my sister became one of those.

I visited the site a few days after the burial. I was to go

alone and return in an hour, the only time I was ever permitted to see her again, but not the last. It was in the early morning, before breakfast and before the sun had risen. The headmaster of Westbury felt it necessary for me to grieve for her since she *was* my sister.

Imagine a barely-teenage boy, walking through blackness with a crescent moon climbing through the sky, the wind howling an evil tune as it snaps sharply against his face (freezing the skin, drying the lips), walking alone on a deer path within a transparent circle of flickering yellow candlelight to see his dead sister's grave in a far-off cemetery where countless other buried souls lived.

I was scared out of my mind. Who wouldn't be at that age? But that didn't stop me from seeing her. I walked that path, ignoring the ghostly shadows from the lantern and the eerie sounds of birds or crickets or whatnot as the darkness swallowed me in.

Ruth's grave was easy to find because it was fresh. The rocks on the mound were newly unearthed and slimy with earthworms—lost and wriggling. I imagined a hand poking through the mound, *her* hand, but the lantern revealed it was only a stick poking out of the rocks—her makeshift headstone. I cried for Ruth. I wanted to show her how much I had loved her and would continue to love her, but all I could do for her was cry. At that moment, it hurt to live. It hurt to love. It hurt to know that I would never talk to her again, or see her. It hurt to know that each time I wrote, I would be reminded of the special gift she gave me, that first piece of scrap paper that sparked my creativity. It hurt to know that I was alone. I would never have a sister again.

So there I sat in the dead grass, my legs crossed. The dark

sky faded to a hint pale blue of morning. Dried tears caked my face with dirty trails. Before returning to my new life, I watched the sun rise to heaven with my sister.

April 1929

Brutus had backhanded a little girl for talking during breakfast. Her name may have been Ann or Maryanne. She was no more than a tenth his size and fell to the ground like a stepped-on flower. She never cried out loud—never dared to. She was on the floor with tears in her eyes, hands to her face, body heaving.

That's when Walt stepped in and started the fight.

I think Jim, who we all called Jungle Jim—because of his long arms and skinny torso—was there and maybe Francis. Francis was a wimp when it came to muscles, also one of the few who stayed away from the coke so commonly shared among the caretakers. Jim was the tallest but the least intimidating. He stood between Brutus and Francis during the argument, with his arms folded in front and his chest sticking out. The three of them faced Walt.

The entire room silently watched the four men, hundreds of eyes bouncing back and forth between the two fighting sides: Walt versus Brutus's gang.

Spoons of breakfast-grop froze before mouths.

Walt picked up the girl by her waist and helped her back to her seat, where she sobbed, but more softly. Walt had explained to her how she had done nothing wrong and that it was not her fault and everything was going to be all right.

This was what ticked Brutus off. He hated to be corrected or embarrassed before fellow workers and, worse, before his students. You could tell he was plenty mad. His face was beet red. A thick vein poked through his neck like a mountain range, twisting and bending, bulging even. It was a cartoon of a madman if I ever saw one. I waited for steam to start whistling from his ears.

Ann, or Maryanne, whatever her name was, sat upright in her seat, scared and confused.

Walt was unexplainably calm.

"Better think twice before doing that again," he said softly, his finger an inch from Brutus's face.

Jim and Francis did nothing.

Brutus snarled as he swatted the beefy finger out of his face.

"Stay outta my business," Brutus said. "Next time—"

Walt stepped forward so Brutus was forced to lean back.

"There won't be a next time," said Walt. "Because if there is, I'm going to stick my *foot*, so far up your *business*, you'll be begging your posse here," he took a small breath between phrases and wagged his finger to each of the men, making sure Brutus looked at each of them as he did so, "to help you pry it out."

He said all this in his typically soothing, mellow voice. It may as well had been a disgruntled Santa speaking, or a science teacher giving a lesson to one of his pupils—a lesson you'd better not miss.

Jim and Francis still did nothing.

Brutus took a half step back to avoid leaning—either way, he looked unconfident. He fondled the paddle behind his back, patting it against his palms, possibly thinking of snapping that chubby finger floating before him.

No one breathed.

Brutus moved Berta to his side, just enough for Walt to

notice, even though Walt's eyes never left his. He then grabbed a handful of grop from the nearest plate with his other hand and brought it to rest on Walt's shoulder.

"I can't wait till next time, buddy."

Then he turned around, and Jim and Francis followed his lead as they walked away together.

When they were about ten feet away, Walt made his way to the table where I was sitting. He winked at me and smiled, grabbed a handful of my grop and pitched it to the back Brutus's head.

It made a *thwopp!* sound as it hit. Flying gooey shrapnel landed on both Jim and Francis. It was quite remarkable, really, how that stuff could hold together while flying through the air. Most of it clung to Brutus's hair as he stopped for a moment, took a deep breath, and then continued on his way.

Things got steadily worse between Walt and Brutus. The other two guards, Jim and Francis, wisely stopped playing a part in Brutus's power games after the cafeteria incident.

The games stopped one Sunday in the middle of the month, the day the white-collared, tie-wearing strangers returned for their second visit. Same crew, it seemed, clipboards in hand, taking notes upon notes. They had freshly polished, glossy shoes you could see your face in, and pressed pants with a crease sharp enough to cut. Some wore suits, others buttoned vests, but all wore a mixture of black and white and gray, like the moving pictures we occasionally watched in class.

Whoever they were, and for whatever reasons there, most of the caretakers feared them the way a fox fears hounds.

Just about everyone but Walt acted strangely around them.

In fact, Walt was with them every step of their tour.

They must have walked around Westbury for hours.

I heard Ruth's name mentioned during dinnertime as Walt and the group of ten or so strangers sat at a table close to the one where Eddie and I were eating. And the other girl who recently died got mentioned once.

We didn't hear much of what they discussed, just snippets here and there about church, education, adoption rates, death rates—puzzle pieces we couldn't quite match together. We were too busy devouring a meal of beef, carrots, and potatoes for the second time in our lives.

May 1929

The piece of bottle was gone completely. Eddie didn't want to talk about it, either. He didn't want to talk about much by this point. Something was on his mind.

June 1929

I got it out of him. Eddie broke down and told me everything: how Brutus touched him, how he hurt him, how he forced him to do things I dare not mention. And that if he ever did, he'd die and be buried with the rest of the invalids. It wasn't only that one time Brutus had taken him out of class, either, but frequently since then. If Eddie ever told anyone, he and all his friends would never get out of Westbury. As long as Eddie kept the secret.

It took everything Eddie had to tell me this, as well as a mess of tears. I remember holding his hand until morning.

He hurt. A deep headache started as I listened, and I hoped for the whiteness to come and take me away, to take *us* away, to show another mirror, a door, or a gateway to another world—anywhere would do. It never came.

I had nothing to say to Eddie, only listened as he talked, cried, talked some more. I had no words for him. I didn't know where or how to begin, or even if it would be okay. I had nothing to give but my shoulder. I felt about as much sorrow and misery as when they told me Ruth had died.

I didn't want Eddie to die. *I* didn't want to die.

Never odd or even. Never odd or even. Never odd or even.

Eddie must have read it somewhere. He said this over and over as he rocked on the balls of his feet, hugging his knees with one arm, grasping my hand with the other.

"Brutus will get what he deserves," I told Eddie.

"I know."

The sun was about to rise.

Birds sang in the trees to let us know.

Neither of us slept that night.

The next day was strange to the end. There was a mood hanging in the thick morning air that told me something would happen. It was almost as if something (perhaps the whiteness, which stayed away) wanted me to pay no attention to the strangeness of the day and to take whatever happened in stride.

Eddie didn't strike up a conversation during breakfast,

either, which was remarkable; he only gave a little conspiratorial smile and looked down at his meal, leaving the icebreaking and the guessing game to me.

"So what's the smile about?"

He shrugged.

I spooned a big dollop of what we were supposed to believe was food into my mouth and mumbled around it.

"Well"—swallowing—"you know something I don't?"

He looked away, twirling his spoon in a circular motion.

"A secret?"

I filled my mouth again.

"A few hours ago we were in tears, now everything's dandy?"

His eyes were red and puffy from the crying, but he somehow seemed to be glowing spiritually inside.

"You know," I said matter-of-factly, pointing my spoon at his face, "if it's a secret, you *have* to tell me; that's the rules."

It was like talking to a brick.

At this point, I realized the only way to get it out of him was to pretend to drop the subject.

"Who's preaching at church services today?" I asked out of the blue. "I heard it might be Walt. At least that's what the lunch ladies were talking about when I passed by."

A blank look came over his face, and he stared down with a stupid expression.

"You think he'll be any better than the others? Preaching, that is? We all know he's the nicest bloke here. I hope so. We could use a good preacher. Maybe we'll even learn something besides the fact that church is even more boring than school."

The boy was a zombie.

"Walt's a pretty neat guy."

I looked around to make sure no one was around.

"Not like the other *jerks*. He's a big palooka too—probably can lift a horse. Would *not* want him on my bad side, either—not that I have one. Well, okay, I do have one, but Brutus and his goons are the only ones on it. Walt's different. Maybe he'll beat the crap out of them someday. Yeah, maybe they'll get in a fight and they'll try to fire him and he'll get mad and pound them into the ground like waffles. Are you listening?"

A grop-drooling zombie.

"Hey, maybe Walt's an alien from the moon and he's wearing some kind of human carcass as a skin so he can hide at Westbury as a caretaker and sew patches on our pants so we can wear them over and over again while we sing songs about wild, gun-slinging cowboys from Texas who like to burn witches and dance around pentagrams drawn in the dirt."

Nothing.

"After that, we'll sit with Brutus and snort the white stuff."

Anything to get him out of his stupefied daze.

"Huh?" he said. "Oh, sorry. Yeah, Walt's preaching."

The bemused smile was gone.

During church services, there was a low murmur of talking among the children of Westbury. Everyone was anxious to hear what good Walt had to say.

A burly man named Hank was at the pulpit.

"And the youth will be cast down to Hell for their sins, sayeth the Lord of Hosts," he intoned, holding a Bible high in the air. He either had the words memorized or was making them up. "And the wrath of God will be harsh and unforgiving, and he will smite thee down with the mighty hands of his servants."

His hand pounded the podium and everyone jumped.

"The weak shall perish into the sands of the earth, and the strong shall live as kings among men. High and powerful, they will rule with the hands of God as thy swords."

A few of us straightened in our seats; benches creaked.

"With this new power they shall guide the children of men to salvation or cleanse them with the fire they deserve. And *fire*," he added, "is meant symbolically."

He held up the Bible and pounded it on the stand. The boom reverberated through the small chapel, and more people jumped this time—even Walt.

"*Fire* is meant to be *anything* necessary, *anything* required to teach the stupid and strengthen the weak. Sometimes it may be by word of mouth, sometimes it might be by ignorance or avoidance, sometimes it will be our hands alone that teach you and lead you to redemption."

He added more lines from his personal gospel:

"So it was that the high priests and the leaders of men smote them with their hands—by 'them' he means *you*—and some fell and died; others, who were strong, also perished. The strongest of the weak also fell, but learned by discipline and by hardship, and joined as leaders of men. This chance of survival is slim," he said to the crowd.

A few of the caretakers nodded in agreement.

None of the children stirred or even made a peep.

"None of you will make it without our guidance. If we smite you with our strength, it is for the good of men. And you shall get up, and take it again, and fall down again. But you will be stronger as men, as we are."

He spread his arms, encompassing all the caretakers.

Eddie gave me an "oh, please" expression.

I looked over to where my sister would normally sit.

She was the weakest of men, as Hank would have us to believe. But she got up and took it, and fell, and got up and fell, and fell and fell until she couldn't get up anymore, and then she died.

I listened as evangelistically-challenged Hank wrapped up his hypocritical lecture.

"Most of you will find yourselves on the ground many a time, seeking forgiveness, and desiring God's help and His salvation as you take the punishments and teachings He gave us—our swords. A few of you may succeed, but if you seek not our guidance, and stay on the ground when you are put there, then you will not find salvation, and you shall perish, as some of you already have."

A mellow "amen" by the caretakers, and an even softer one by the congregation.

He then left with his Bible in hand and sat back down, just as the next speaker stood up, but it wasn't Walt.

"Children of the congregation."

It was Redmond, a short bulb of a man. He had stubby fingers and hairy arms that waived around as he spoke.

"This cross behind me—"

He turned and pointed to the enormous crucifix, then turned back and grasped the silver crucifix around his neck.

"This cross," he repeated, "it means nothing to you. It means nothing to you if *you* do nothing."

Redmond was known for repeating himself.

"The good Lord gave you His life, and you must do the same for Him."

He thumbed through his bible, running a sausage finger down the pages as he read about Jesus carrying the cross. It didn't have much to do with Redmond's lesson, but dragged out painfully in his melancholy voice.

When he was done with the verses, he added in his own words, "And one individual from the gathering crowd stood up and came to the cross, took it upon his own back, and was smitten down. But he was smitten down for a purpose. A higher purpose. A purpose that means more than just helping out a man in need. The man in need was the good Lord. And though the good Lord had to die for a much higher cause, this man who stood up and helped bear the cross, he gave up everything."

He paused so we could all grasp the importance of his words, an extended pause that made me feel unimportant.

"He gave up his strength. He gave up his will."

Redmond counted them on his short, fat fingers.

"He gave up his family, and he gave up his own life. And for what?" he asked, looking around with four fingers poking the air. It looked as if he were holding an inflated surgeon's glove.

"For what?" he repeated, but no one answered. "For nothing, really. He ended up dying and losing everything. But God knew the plan. God knew His son would die on the cross," he said as he pointed to the cross behind him.

"God knew His son would die on the cross," he repeated with sympathy. "So why would God let this man, this man who gave up everything to help the Lord carry the burden of the cross, waste his life for nothing?"

Redmond looked at the children for a response.

None wanted to answer.

There was a long, awkward silence.

"Paradigm," Walt answered from behind him.

"I'm not sure what a pair o' dimes is, but if it means anything like 'example,' then yes, a pair o' dimes." Walt smiled.

□ □ □

Redmond held the stand for almost an hour of boring repetition. But then, finally, Walt stood up to speak, and what came out was a monologue that turned the heads of every caretaker and raised the eyebrows of every child. Like nothing we had ever heard.

He talked about life and our paths in life, and what we had to do in order to overcome misfortune. He told us to confront everything wrong and damaging, so that it may be remedied. He told us about the light that could be found in all darkness. He reminded us that sometimes we fall, but we can rise, even from our ashes. His words filled us with hope. I composed a poem about it:

SAD PARADIGM

The door closes, creaking sadness
The lights dissipate and fade to nothingness
Darkness everywhere
Feelings of despair
Life is unfair
Sad paradigm
The tunnel's clear, but one stranger
Who stares alone, promising lies of redemption
Shouts twice, silently
Panic sets swiftly
Life says maybe
Sad paradigm
Salt-water pools make up the floor
A reflection is missing,
The white light's brighter
Killing a fighter
Life is higher
Sad paradigm
Dry creeks end and form red half-moons
The sleek, silver heaviness waits for its mess
It shouts loudly
Earth listens proudly
Life smiles wryly
Sad paradigm

July 1929

Eddie returned to a state of semi-normality. Or maybe I chose to ignore normality altogether and trust that everything in this world is eventual … to live is to die and to die is to live all over again, that we are stuck in a never-ending cycle of life.

That's what went through my head.

Was my life worth living?

Sometimes I thought of the man in the mirror, gun pointing to his head, wondering if he found the solution to that conundrum. According to the lesson Walt had shared, we either had to find our path in life, or make it.

I decided to make mine. So did Eddie.

His limping gradually lessened to the point where it was barely noticeable. His body had grown conditioned to the abuse, in other words, and he moved somewhat mechanically, keeping to himself whenever possible. Then, out of nowhere, Eddie surprised me.

Out of the blue one day he was back to normal, cracking jokes, making fun of the caretakers, laughing at times. It was as though he had found his answer to life, as though a veil had lifted and he had passed through, learning his path.

But I was wrong in thinking that.

Eddie had created a path for his life, from none other than the piece of glass bottle, which I thought had broken.

Actually, it had turned to dust. White dust.

Eddie had kept his plan secret the entire time, which is a good thing. I would never have let him do it had I known.

Slowly, over time, Eddie had been grinding away at the glass, using the rough concrete floor when no one was around, saving the sharp, powdery shavings in a little swatch of cloth.

"Check this out, Earl," Eddie said, nudging my arm with that same wicked smile I had seen before. It was one of the few times he had called me by name. It made me feel important.

We ate our lunch-grop as we would any other day, talking only when no one was around.

"Check *what* out?"

"Brutus."

Brutus was about to sniff coke.

"What?"

Sometimes Brutus could be seen walking the halls and dipping a finger in the stuff and would sniff from that finger nudged up his nostril. It was nothing new.

I watched him sniff from his fingernail a few times.

He shook his head, sniffling, wiping at his red nose.

Brutus and his white courage.

Eddie and his stupid smile.

I watched Brutus and his beady eyes.

He sniffed again.

The whiteness was nowhere to be found; with it normally came tragedy, which is why, whatever was coming from Brutus, I knew it had to be something beautiful.

And what he produced from out of that supreme ugliness was a rose, dark crimson in color with blackened edges softly rimming the petals—a moving bloom, alive, a canvas with its paints running downward in curvy streams, gathering at its stem in a splendid pool of red. The most beautiful thing I'd ever seen.

And at once it was gone, replaced by a face smeared in blood that flowed freely from each nostril, dripping onto the table below. Brutus was oblivious. Still high and getting higher, he dipped a finger into his pouch, never looking from my eyes, and sniffed another sniff of the white powder. He shook his head back and forth, rubbed his nose noisily in his hand, spreading the red.

Choking on blood, he at last noticed his condition. He rubbed at his nose and stared unbelievingly into bloody palms. Determined not to waste any of the precious powder, he snorted again, deeply, which sent him into a greater paroxysm of choking.

Blood ran copiously from his faucet of a nose.

None of the caretakers noticed what was going on.

Once the convulsions started, he finally drew the attention of a few caretakers. They circled around Brutus, unsure what to do as he shook violently on the floor, coughing up blood, foaming at the mouth. Andy and Francis held him down by his shoulders, leaving his legs and hips to flop like a fish on dry land. By holding him on his back, they forced him to aspirate more blood, watching dumbly as he coughed, snorted, and hyperventilated all at once. His eyes rolled up in their orbits before the medics arrived, and his shaking calmed, but not in a good way.

Medics rolled him out on a shaky metal gurney with squeaking wheels and padding that looked hard and uncomfortable. They tied leather straps around his arms and legs, another around his head. A long, plastic tube was pushed down his throat, which connected to what looked like a ballcock of a toilet. A medic squeezed it slowly, coating its interior with a milky red.

Eddie was no longer smiling; he was utterly horrified.

In the following months, Brutus made a return. We weren't dismayed by his return to Westbury, only curious in the way kids can be curious about death. We all had seen Brutus die—or thought or hoped or dreamed he had died—and we were all a little curious how he had come back, and why.

Where else, I remember thinking, *would the devil go when he died?*

We were in a hell of sorts—the devil's home.

He had died and returned to us.

Brutus never returned to normal during the remainder of our stay at Westbury. He no longer taught at Sunday school, never again so much as touched another child, and no longer intimidated anyone. He only sat in his seat, drooling and looking stupidly to the ground and sometimes at the lights.

I remember picturing Brutus as Lenny in the novel *Of Mice and Men*, staring into nothingness as he stroked his mice and crushed them under his massive hands, and then wondering why they no longer desired to play thereafter.

I never once felt sorry for Brutus, though, and the challenged life he had acquired. No one did, not even Eddie, who had changed Westbury forever.

Change brings change, and that also happened..

Without the aid of their fearless leader, Brutus's goons became nothing more than schoolyard bullies with no one to tell them who to pick on, and so they were soon tolerable.

Walt took over for Brutus, without, of course, indulging in any of Brutus's demented behaviors. He also took on Brutus's role as the main preacher on Sundays, so church services were enjoyable.

We spent more time getting educated.

We read.

We wrote.

We solved many equations that needed solving.

Smiles budded and then blossomed from child to child, like wildflowers in springtime. The tomblike absence of speech during mealtimes turned to a convivial din of conversations that rose and set with the sun each day, filling our lives with a warmness we had never felt before. We slept each night with dreams of promise and woke to hopes of finding the homes from which we were missing.

February 18, 1930

It was the day that changed our lives forever. Children laughed and played and skipped and rejoiced. Some of us wrote poetry (okay, only me), while others stayed alone, unsure how to act, afraid to act as their hearts had desired to do for so long. It was the day the strangers returned for their third and final visit.

The momentous occasion started at breakfast. We knew something was afoot when we were served what we would come to learn were pancakes: fluffy discs of sweet joy that warmed our bellies, gooped with the sugary pleasures of molasses and melted butter.

A few of the well-dressed fellows sat with us for breakfast and lunch and supper, conversing with every child at least once. They asked us our ages, our views of Westbury, what we wanted to be when we grew up. They were counselors for the day and offered us shoulders to cry on, although most tears had been shed long ago, back when hope was merely an illusion.

It wasn't a Sunday this time, so they followed us to our

classes and observed eagerly, taking down page after page of observations on their notepads.

After our classes and a lunch as splendid as breakfast, and even after our steak-and-potato supper, the day continued in its glory, a glory I wished would never end.

The day took its time to end, though, as we were let outside to run and play. No one knew quite *what* to play, so we just ran and laughed, chased each other, invented games and rules, and held our hands high in the air, screaming and laughing and being silly kids. Eddie and I took turns racing from one tree to the next to see who could run the fastest.

Walt accompanied the most important-looking of the visitors. They met near the main gate, which opened on the dirt road to the next town over. A caravan of cars lined the fence.

Curious children pointed in amazement at the shiny black-and-chrome automobiles. Amazing machines to look at, but most of us were too busy being our crazy selves to pause from our horseplay for even a moment.

I made a visit to Ruth's grave before going in. I wanted to tell her about the day and to say goodbye one last time. I brought her a poem and read it to her, placed it near the headstone and weighted it with what was left of the chunk of charcoal I had kept and used for so long in my late-night writing endeavors.

As the sun made its way down the slope of the mountains, and through the thick clouds that filled a reddening sky, it took with it the suited visitors. When the sun fell and the sky grew too dark for outside play, we were rounded up and led back inside. That night, we all slept deeply and soundly, and with dreams no longer of *if* but of *when*. We would wake the next morning to new beginnings and new endings. The end of Westbury and the beginning of our lives.

2

FEELING OLDER

So that is where my story of Westbury ends. I leave you with Walt, the savior, joining the faculty and inspiring the lives of us pathetic gentiles; Eddie overcoming the evil giant, Brutus, with his magical glass stone; the suited knights riding their mechanical four-wheeled chargers to our castle and banishing the nasty dragons; and me ... well, I leave you with me losing everything I entered Westbury with and leaving with only the rumpled pages I poured my heart into, and with memories both good and bad.

You probably want to know what you could find in part three if there were one. Now, I must tell you that at first there *was* a part three planned, and the editors at Stratton did all but beg.

I must keep it short and to the point, or else I could have you flipping through these pages for ages, for there are many years and stories to tell between the end of Westbury and now, but that is for another place and another time.

The orphanage / prison / whatever-you-wish-to-call-it was taken over by what I can only guess was the United States government or some such organization. They took the / *prison / whatever-you-wish-to-call-it* and cut it off, making Westbury truly an orphanage. Its name changed to the Elder Creek Children's Home soon thereafter.

Walt became head honcho for his continuing efforts to help improve our lives and find homes. For some of us, anyway. Food and education improved, with the help of federal funding, and the Sunday services became no longer mandatory, although most of us still went for a spiritual lift. Some of the original caretakers stayed, but not many. Most were forced out in one way or another. Brutus died and was missed by no one.

Eddie and I, we stayed best friends throughout the rest of our stay. I continued writing poetry and moved on to short stories, but I didn't write as much as before. It's funny, now that I think of it, how I was able to write more when I wasn't able to write at all, and how, when I was able, I chose to live a life outside of pages.

But as age catches up to you, and you start realizing you are getting older, the poetry and stories buzz around in your head; they want to get out before the body dies, before their chance to escape passes. And so you click your pen on and off and on and off and on and off and then the beautiful characters and settings and colors and plotlines jump from your pen and dance to the pages. Syllables form stanzas that reflect on your life. Words form sentences form paragraphs form pages form beautiful novels that reflect your life. Everything, every drop of ink or scratch of graphite comes from the memories stored in the wrinkles of your brain, reflecting your life and everything you've lived.

And again I find myself getting carried away.

I ended up across the country to find myself in the wet end of Washington after living my childhood in the East. Not all my childhood was spent east.

Once we reached eighteen years of age, all of us at West-bury, or Elder Creek Children's-something-or-other as it became, were free to move on. Those entering adulthood were given two choices, really. One: stay at the orphanage to help find homes for others and, eventually, if it was in our hearts, become caretakers ourselves; or two: leave.

It was tempting to stay at the orphanage, which had been

our only home, if you think about it, and it was tempting to help others do what we could not (for remember, only the youngest and cutest of the puppies make it out of the kennel), but most of us had captured enough memories of the place for one lifetime.

There could be many positive memories to gain by staying, but they could never outweigh the negative.

So we left.

I waited around for Eddie to turn eighteen, a few months after I did, and then we both split. Of course, we had no idea where to go, what to do, what to expect out in the world. Heck, we had no idea how big the world was in the first place. We ventured from town to town, stayed up late, kept out of trouble for the most part. We slept behind storage sheds and such. Sometimes we stayed in the sheds if no one saw us piddling around. Most nights, though, were spent sleeping outdoors with blankets we had salvaged—from one of the storage sheds, if I recall.

It was summer when we did this, so the nights were warm and starry. If it were winter, we probably wouldn't have made it.

By that fall, Eddie got the crazy idea to train hop. That's what we called it back then. We stayed in freight car after freight car and ate just about anything we could find in cans. We were kicked off some trains, met up with other hoboes, and somehow found our way to Colorado. Beautiful country it was, but cold. We were a few years older by this time and not the least bit wiser.

One day we had to chase down a train looking to leave without us. It was much too cold in Colorado, and we weren't too sure if this was to be the last train out of town. We ran our little hearts out trying to catch that thing, until our lungs were fiery from panting so hard. See, before we jumped aboard we had thrown up our baggage with all our clothes and food—everything we had, really.

I'm sure you can guess where this is going. So, we're chasing this train down the tracks and its rolling away with our possessions and finally I manage to grab hold of some iron bar and dangle for a bit, being dragged partly, until I pull myself up. I sat there for a bit to catch my breath and forgot for a moment about Eddie, who was right at my heels before I jumped aboard. I looked back to see him trailing farther and farther away, still running but losing ground. He was a stick figure shrinking from view. I watched as he stopped and bent over, holding his sides. I thought about jumping, but the train was moving much too fast by this point, enough to kill me.

A moment later, Eddie was a little dot bending over to pick up a smaller dot on the ground—his baggage. I threw it overboard.

I'm not sure what happened with Eddie, but I hope he found a place in the world. Something spectacular. Who knows? Maybe he made it all the way to the west coast.

I wasn't sad about our parting. I only wish we could've hopped another train and shared one last laugh over a can of beans. That's life, though. You take what you get.

I made it to Washington months later and got a decent job at a refinery shaping steel and pounding metal. It was hard labor. I lived with a friend at the refinery the first two years and saved my hard-earned cash for the down payment on the home I still live in today, with a few additions and improvements over the years.

And in a nutshell, here I am. How's that for summing up sixty plus years of life into a couple pages? I could go on, but then, so could this story.

What of the whiteness?

You may have noticed the whiteness stayed its distance during the second part of my story, and that's because it *did* stay distant. That's because nothing too traumatic happened during those years. Nothing happened for the bad, would explain it better.

I can feel it approaching slowly and steadily like a moving train. This train is on its way to pick me up. I can feel it, and know it as I know my name. I know it as I know my sister's name. It puffs thick white smoke. On the side of each railcar is printed in bold letters, HEIMLICH EXPRESS NO. 78. Maybe 87. Metal wheels scream over metal rails, both rusted with age the way the wrinkles and arthritis rust *me*. There's an evil smile on this train's face, perhaps, with red, fiery eyes as headlights, and sharp, pointy teeth in place of the cow-catcher.

All aboard the Heimlich Express!

I wait for the conductor to proclaim this. Or maybe even the train itself.

All aboard!

There is no conductor.

There is no train.

Only the whiteness.

It's coming: to scare me to show me to blind me to guide me to protect me to take me to—

White hairlines in my vision.

The blinds again.

Barbara rests soundly, peacefully, and there are white lines over her face and torso. The television screen, it's covered in static, the way running a vacuum cleaner used to warble reception.

The whine only adds to the headache growing behind my eyes, poking at them from behind with sharp sewing needles. I wait for them to pierce completely through.

Have I mentioned I hate the whiteness I detest the whiteness I *loathe* the whiteness I am so scared of the whiteness, the blinding, the hurting, the things I am not ready and not wanting to see? I am curious for what it will bring, the way I'm curious when watching horror films with my eyes covered but peeking through to watch—my fingers, metal bars to protect me from anything that jumps out from the screen. The blinds are now my protective bars, I guess, since bringing my fingers up to cover my eyes does nothing.

These blinds are brighter than before, perhaps wider even, and the shriek of the approaching train elevates. The headache behind the eyes has grown to fill most of my head, numbing, pinching, and poking, stabbing everywhere. Screeching like a train laying hard on its brakes, trying to stop itself from crashing.

It grows even brighter, the whiteness, the blinds opening fully, allowing only slits of my normal vision through, as if my true vision and the mini-blinds of white light have swapped roles. The noise, it is deafening. A million rock concerts at once, me standing at the speaker boxes, listening as heavy-metal guitar riffs scream against my ears. My ears, they must be bleeding.

Everything is white. No more lines left from the blinds, and it still grows whiter somehow, brighter and louder and emptier.

And all at once it is gone.

All is white.

All is silent.

All is painless.

The whiteness, whatever it may be, its truest form.

I look left, right, up, down, and there is nothing.

I want to see …

But my mind is a mesh of random: *The day I knelt over Ruth's grave, Barb sleeping next to me, the mirror, strange numbers, children playing in a park, Eddie grinding away at his stone, a little girl dressed as an angel, a field of wheat, a homeless man begging for change, little Hannah—Palindrome Hannah, her mother's black dragon tattoo.*

Random thoughts.

And in the center of this whiteness there is now a black dot; a pinprick of black surrounded by the whiteness.

I wait for it to happen.

A high-pitched whine that starts as a dog whistle and ends with two trains crashing together.

It's here.

The mirror.

My reflection, with the blackest of eyes.

The frame of the mirror is wooden, a light oak, with a dragon carved into the base. The same dragon tattooed on Julie, my sort-of granddaughter. This mirror floats in the whiteness, with its shadow cast on the white floor.

A bright flash, like that from a camera, and the mirror face—my face—disappears, replaced by a reflection of Barbara. She has the same black demon eyes as mine and she smiles. And then there is no face at all as the glass starts to change.

She disappears.

I disappear.

The frame starts to fade, taking with it the dragon and the light oak and the heaviness, and what is left behind is the glass surface of the mirror, which starts to expand. It grows taller and wider until there is no end and there is no beginning. I reach out and see my hand and my arm. I look down, and there are my feet, my legs, my thighs, where they should be.

I am back. But I am without a reflection.

I try to touch the non-reflective glass surface of the mirror, and find it liquid. The surface depresses on contact, causing ripples to flow outward in round waves with depth but no color. They move upward and outward, and as I watch this, I realize I am surrounded in a mirrored box. My reflection is not present, but those of each wave are in this liquid glass chamber, and it is a beautiful thing to watch as they warble in all directions, joining and then separating in their diverse ways, moving in fractal patterns.

And then it shows me what I need to see.

never odd or even

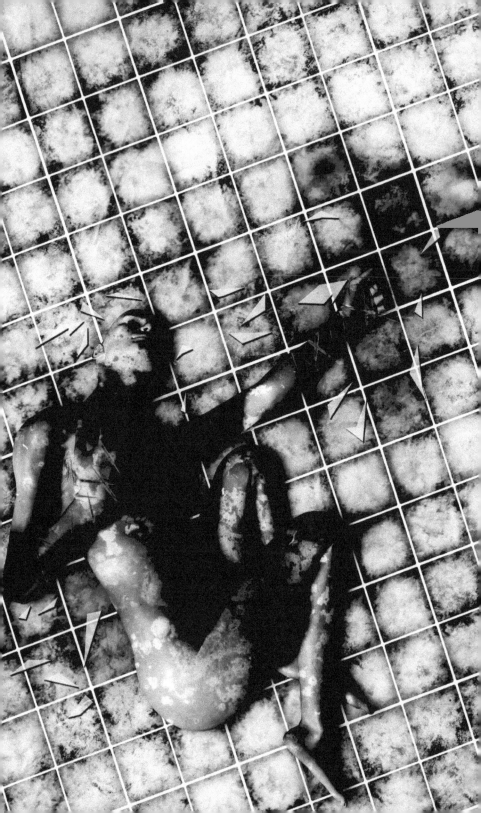

PART FOUR

finding god

se es o no se es

[rough translation: *to be or not to be*]

1

INITIAL INTERVIEW

Deified, he jotted on his notepad.

"You say that you were born with this power?" Doctor Milton asked his patient. He was sick of the runaround. He wasn't getting anywhere with this one and had to hide his frustration. His patients typically showed signs of progress, seldom of regression.

"I never said I was born with anything."

"What do you mean *'anything'*?" he said. "You weren't born with …" He left it hanging.

"Simply, that I at no time said I was born with this power that you insist on uncovering today. I am what I am."

Dr. Milton pondered, searching for the key that would unlock this patient's secret. They all had secrets.

It was revealing those secrets that sparked his love for the profession, like finally completing a puzzle. His ballpoint clicked as sweat beaded at the wrinkled valleys his concentration made on his forehead. His wife had told him once that he wasn't getting old, just wiser, and that the wrinkles were from concentrating so hard.

"I wish you to stop that," the patient said in a flat tone.

Dr. Milton leaned forward, stopped clicking the pen.

"I'm sorry?"

"I meant to say please," he said, "and thank you for stopping."

His patient was referring to the pen clicks.

He clicked a few times out of habit.

"The pen. Right."

He set it on the notebook balancing on his leg and then picked it back up to take more notes. It was all in an instant. He scribbled *annoyed easily* on his notepad.

Calm was also written there.

"What do you think this power is, then? In your own words," the doctor said.

"Who else's words would I use?"

"Hypothetically speaking," said Dr. Milton.

"I wasn't clear we were speaking in hypotheses."

He didn't seem sarcastic, but serious.

"*Hypothetically*, we all have *powers*. Everyone on this earth has power. Some good, some not so good. Some use it in politicking—the president, for example. Some don't know they have it at all—those that are meek and humble, children, Catholics. Others over-amplify. You use your powers for doctoring, healing patients, such as the others in here."

Dr. Milton raised his hand to stop him. Speaking hypothetically had opened a whole new can of worms.

"Let me stop you there."

"Your hand gesture already has."

"So it has. Do you have an issue with religion?"

"I'm not sure I mentioned religion, so to speak."

"You said that Catholics don't have power, that they're meek, humble."

"I could have said Protestants, or Jews, Seventh-Days, Baptists, Muslims, Buddhists." He counted on his fingers. "Members of the Reorganized Church of—"

"They're all powerless?" the doctor interrupted.

"Not powerless. Most just don't realize what they possess, and those that do—"

He interrupted again. "Which religion are *you*, John?"

The hospital had checked the patient in as a John Doe. Since his records hadn't been located and he hadn't stated a preference, this remained his name for the initial interview.

"I am of no religion—I cannot be."

Dr. Milton thought long on this and jotted *problems with religion* on his notepad.

"We'll come back to religion in another of our meetings. That's another day. Now, the president … hypothetical, or could you have mentioned any politician?"

"Yes."

"You say I use my powers for the healing of the others in here. Do you not believe I can heal you?"

"I don't believe there's anything the matter with me, Doc. I am not like the others in here. They need help, especially the window-licker over there."

He pointed to an old man pressed against a window that overlooked the courtyard. The glass was fogged around his mouth with drool sliding down the pane.

"Why are you here, then, John?" the doctor asked, not moving his eyes to the window.

"I was put here."

Dr. Milton decided not to go down that path just yet.

"I have to go back to your power. Why do you believe you have a power at all? And I'm not talking about power in general. Not the pope's power, not the power of an engine on a seven-forty-seven, not kinetic or potential power, but the power you believe you hold. Why do you think you have this power?"

John Doe looked at him profoundly.

"I believe that it is *you* who think I have a power. I have never mentioned before that I have a 'power,' so to speak."

He was still serious, and sounded like a psychologist.

"I might have to start charging *you*, Doctor."

Dr. Milton clicked his pen again. *Differential powers*, he added to his growing list.

"Are you telling me the power you have is not the same power that all others around you share?"

"You don't seem to be paying attention, Doc. It's not a power; I am not some comic-book character … I could continue if you wish, or repeat our entire conversation if you don't believe me."

"John, certain people have photographic memory that pertains to images and objects they remember. In extreme situations, some have described remembrances down to the finest of details. But to recall an entire conversation spanning several minutes is ludicrous. It's not even a visual type of circumstance—"

The patient proceeded to replay their entire conversation, word for word. Dr. Milton sat astonished as John repeated every syllable, every nuance, in which he spoke in a flat, almost emotionless voice. The voice was slightly higher-pitched when miming the doctor.

"'… ludicrous. It's not even a visual type of circumstance,' you said. I never said at any time it was a power. That was your idea."

Dr. Milton was speechless.

Never in his career had he experienced photographic dialogue remembrance, or whatever it was called. There was probably a name for it out there in some obscure diagnostic book. He had heard encounters by other psychologists, but never such an extent as this. This Mr. Doe had a gift.

Extraordinary memory capacity, he jotted on his notepad.

"John, you have quite an unusual gift for remembering."

"Thank you."

He showed no signs of pride or gloating.

Politeness, the doctor added to his list. *No signs of pride.*

"Will you agree on this, then, John, that everyone has a power that we all share?"

"That we share? Telepathy, or thought networking?"

Another subject for another day.

"I was thinking more on the lines of decision making. Thought process, physical power, imagination; everyone has them, these powers. Do you agree that these powers exist?"

"Yes."

"Then, do you also agree that every individual, every being, has access to these powers and has the ability to control them? Can *you* control them?"

"Which question shall I answer first?" John asked.

"Either or," said Dr. Milton.

"Yes."

"Which question are you answering, that every person can control these powers, or that you can control them?"

"You are a very confusing doctor, Dr. Milton." John answered the questions in turn: "Yes. The second question—that I can control them."

Dr. Milton was really starting to get uncomfortable. He got this way whenever he felt he was toyed with. Patients rarely got on his nerves or frustrated him, for it was all part of the job, but this one was getting to him. He took a while to set things in order.

"Let me get this straight. You have access to these powers and can control them. Everyone else has this same access, but cannot?"

John replied calmly, "Yes, and no."

"You are confusing me, John."

"I can access these powers and can control them. So can everyone else. Everyone has them; everyone controls them. All abilities are controllable, except for imagination; that one is a special power, Doc, a gift unlike any other. To be alone and in total darkness and to be able to dance through or fly over a grove as a warm sun sinks into a glorious horizon—a beautiful gift, imagination. Powerful, too. I'm sure you have daydreamed of flying once or twice."

"I have."

The doctor listened, scribbling notes. His pen began to skip, so he scribbled circles on the page until it would write again. It made a nearly perfect circle of ink.

"Picture having the ability to unleash your imaginative powers, to make them alive," John said. "To make imagination reality, you would be the most powerful being in existence. And dangerous, if you go down that path."

"Scary thought," said Dr. Milton.

"Scary indeed. You may cherish your family dearly, but one day you may have a disagreement with your mother and wish her dead. And so she is. Just like that. Dead. Gone."

"Have you ever wished your mother dead, John?"

John took a long time to answer.

"I would never wish *anyone* dead, Doc. That's the problem with controlling imagination. It is too powerful an ability. There would be chaos. That is why only I can bring it alive. No other person can do that, not one other being."

"Why is that, John?"

The hair on his arms and the back of his neck prickled.

"Because no one else is God."

2

C O M P L E X

So he thinks he's God.

Why couldn't all patients have similar ailments? Why couldn't they all need a little Thorazine, a few Valiums? Sarah had said this would be a calm one ... yeah, calm, all right, but cuckoo.

Sarah was a cop who sent various mental cases Milton's way, usually when someone she picked up was too far around the bend for jail. Sarah was also his wife.

He and Sarah had hit it off one night when she delivered a man claiming that insects were the government's army, spying on people as they crawled around all innocent-looking. They had an air force of flying beetles scouting topography, a scurrying horde of cockroach saboteurs, and miles upon miles of ant soldiers lined in battle ranks. Sarah had brought him to the hospital after he had scratched the skin off his arms, muttering about how the arthropod army had gone molecular. When he was patched up and released, Sarah took him to the psych ward for further treatment, to patch up his mind. There Dr. Milton and Sarah met, and their relationship bloomed—nine years now, and running.

He felt like prescribing himself nine years' worth of Valium as he ventured home that night after his first interview with Mr. Doe. He called Sarah from the car.

"I've never seen anything like it. I've had a patient think he was *chosen* by God, or *sent* by God—even one who thought God was out to kill him. But *being* God? This is a personal first."

"I told you he was a weird one. Strange thing, though."

"What's that?"

"Fingerprints. There wasn't a match in the system. You would think a fifty-one fifty like this John Doe would have some kind of criminal background, such as misdemeanors, or indecent exposure. He didn't even have a wallet."

"Fifty-one fifty?"

"Nut-bag," she explained.

"We prefer 'mentally challenged,' but I hear you."

He had his cell set to speakerphone as he drove.

"How long did you have him before you gave up and sent him our way? I mean, it had to have been a while—you wouldn't pick him up, say 'hmmm … nut-bag, let's send him Dr. Milton's way.'"

Rows of headlights battled taillights up the highway.

The sound of running water through the phone.

"We held him at the station after the hospital for disturbing the peace—refusing to get out of the fountain downtown. People had complained, mostly businesses. You know the fountain, the round one with the statue of the children in the middle. And get this: he claimed to be walking on water. He *was*, in a sense."

"How's that?" he asked, turning down the off-ramp.

"The water's only a few inches deep," she said, laughing.

Dr. Milton was tired. He started to say something but stopped himself as he sped through a yellow light.

"When we approached the subject," she said, always in police language, "he didn't resist. He was gentle and didn't mind the cuffs. But anyway, when we approached him and asked for identification, he didn't have any. Said he didn't need ID. So we searched him."

"You find anything?"

He was almost home, but there were a lot of lights to beat,

or miss. He was mostly missing. Each oncoming headlight appeared brighter than normal, as if everyone had on their high beams.

"Not a thing," she said. "Just the clothes on his back and some pocket lint. At least he does his laundry."

The sound of the washer lid closing; muffled water.

"Didn't say a word when we took him to the station. He was humming. Sounded like Metallica, maybe. Still—"

Static.

"Hon?" he said. Still nothing, so he hung up.

A few seconds later, his cell rang.

"Lost you there," he said.

"What's the last thing you heard?" she asked.

"Dead air."

"Funny man."

"Do I have the right to remain silent? Um … you said humming, what was John humming?"

"So you got his name," she said, sounding surprised. "How'd you get it? Did he tell you, or did you find records at the institute?"

"No, Sarah, it's nothing—John *Doe*. He thinks names are just names, nothing more. This guy has a unique outlook on life. Like nothing matters to him."

"He thinks he's God. What kind of outlook *would* God have on life? Anyway, I was saying that he was humming on the ride to the station. It sounded like Metallica."

"God likes Metallica, huh?"

"What else would he listen to?"

3

GONE

Dr. Milton walked through the door humming the only Metallica song he could recall. He couldn't remember the title, or many of the words, but a single verse stuck in his head. It had something to do with never-never land, and exit lights.

"What's the name of that—?"

"'Enter Sandman,'" Sarah said.

"That's it. Thanks for starting dinner."

"Can you set the table? Food's almost ready—just waiting on the bread," she said.

He set the table and pulled a Napa Valley Zinfandel, uncorked the bottle to let it breathe.

"Besides God, did you find other interesting fellows?"

"Nothing out of the ordinary. A call for domestic disturbance; otherwise, nothing else really. Wasn't finding God enough?"

His pager beeped. It was the hospital with a message that read GOD WENT BOATING. CALL ASAP.

He thought of ignoring the page, and shook his head. Boating? What was that supposed to mean?

"The ward?" Sarah asked, almost knowing.

She had a look of disappointment, but understanding. It was not the first time he had been called back to the office. They both had demanding careers.

"Yeah, it's about John. Same time tomorrow?"

The oven timer sounded with a repeating beep-beep. Whatever she had made was ready.

"Maybe they can wait an hour," he said with a smile.

Sarah gave him a look that said, "It won't happen."

His pager sounded, beeping offbeat with the stove timer. The two of them sat there, sighed, exchanged a resigned look.

"Which one do you want?" he asked.

"I'll take the casserole," she said.

She pressed a button and half the beeping stopped.

He checked his pager again: GOD IS GONE. Scrolling down, the message continued: BOATING, and then: ANSWER YOUR PHONE.

His phone wasn't ringing because it was on Vibrate. It buzzed among notepads and notebooks in his briefcase.

"Milton here," he answered.

He watched as Sarah put the wine in the refrigerator. She then dished out a single serving of casserole onto her plate and plastic-wrapped the rest, put it in the fridge, and sat down to eat alone.

He snapped his cell closed, shaking his head in disbelief.

"You'll never believe this. John somehow left the ward, and he left me a note. No one there can find him."

He sat down at the table and watched Sarah eat.

She took a bite and said with a mouthful, "Let me guess, they want you to come in to help locate him?"

"Not exactly. They want *you* to help."

4

THE SEARCH

When they got to the psychiatric ward, a security guard screened them through the door. He was one of the two security personnel who patrolled the grounds afterhours. Police weren't usually called in situations such as this unless the ward was a hundred percent sure that the patient had escaped and hadn't been checked out by a relative—which was rare—and were sure that he or she wasn't just hiding on the grounds. Police tended to draw media attention.

The first year Dr. Milton worked for the ward, three patients found a way to bypass the alarms by crawling through windows in the recreation room. Dr. Milton had panicked and called the police. The headline the next morning read THREE MENTAL PATIENTS ON THE LOOSE. It was blown completely out of proportion, of course. They were found hours later at a Starbucks down the road, waiting for a pizza they claimed to have ordered from the barista.

Media badgered every doctor, therapist and counselor working the ward that night. The article exploded and led to a story on the evening news, a clip with Dr. Milton and colleagues brushing away cameras and pushing reporters. Dr. Anderson, a veteran doctor and friend of Dr. Milton, was taped swearing and knocking a reporter to the ground after some harassment on the reporter's part. With a little biased editing, the video made him appear violently enraged. He was eventually fired to protect future funding.

Ever since, the policy of the ward was directed to avoid calling police whenever possible. Sarah offered her help on future cases of missing patients, and the hospital gladly accepted, knowing that she had no intentions of grandstanding for the media. Missing patients were a rarity, happening maybe once every two years.

Sarah showed her badge. She was in police mode, questioning the admissions nurse who had first noticed the patient missing, and also the security guard who had been sleeping on the second floor nearby to John's room. They had apparently searched all floors and found nothing out of the ordinary.

"How did you determine the patient missing?" Sarah asked.

Heidi was an intern, using the front desk job on the night shift as a means of getting her foot in the door.

"The note on my screen," she said, searching the piles of textbooks and paperwork on the desk. "Here it is."

She held out the yellow Post-it note to Sarah:

GONE BOATING - GOD

"I thought it was a joke," Heidi said.

"When did you last leave your post?"

"When did I leave my desk?" Heidi had a look on her face that implied she had been glued to her desk for the duration.

"Did you use the restroom or go for a cigarette break?"

The light bulb flicked on in Heidi's head.

"I was gone for only a minute," she stammered.

She hesitated and looked around at the faces of Dr. Milton and everyone else standing around, and then said, embarrassed, "I had to check on some feminine things. It was right after Dr. Milton left for the night. I went to the ladies' room. When I returned, the note was on my screen."

"You were only gone for a few minutes?" Sarah asked.

"No one was on this floor but Howard and me. All the patients were in their rooms. The alarms would have sounded if any of the main doors opened."

She pointed to the doors behind the reception desk.

Wired-glass windows on both doors showed a reverse etching of *Personnel Access Only—Alarm Will Sound* in bold lettering.

Dr. Milton explained the security. Every employee had a name badge with a magnetic strip, which granted access to any security door when passed through the reader on either side. He pointed to a device mounted on the wall with its red LED, and explained how it turned green and blinked steadily when access was granted, then turned back to red when the door closed. If the door didn't close in ten seconds, the light blinked red and the door would close automatically. If that failed, the alarm sounded.

"You were here when he disappeared?"

Howard straightened up. "That is correct."

"Did you see Heidi leave the front desk?"

"Heidi checks in with me every time. She's very good at that. She informed me she was going to the little girls' room to freshen up." His tone was matter-of-fact but gentle.

"And you?" she asked a second security guard.

He was a tall, older man, lanky and balding, with glasses thick enough to start a fire.

"I was outside patrolling the perimeter," he said.

"You didn't see anyone go through those doors?"

"Dr. Milton was the last to go through those doors, as I recall. I was watching the monitors and sipping coffee when Heidi let me know she was off to the ladies' room. She returned a moment later. Like I said, Heidi's good at following our policies."

"Nothing unusual on your monitors?"

"Only white tile floors, white walls, white doors. Same boring white everywhere," he said.

The monitors showed empty hallways, doors to patient and counseling rooms, exits, security doors, and the parking lot, where a few cars remained. Surrounding the security desk were pictures of Howard's family. His logbook lay open and listed all the visitors he had checked in and out during his shift.

Howard was correct in that everything was white: the floor tiles, walls, doors, ceilings—everything. At first glance, without moving bodies for perspective, the monitors appeared blank.

"Is this all recorded?" Sarah asked.

"Seven days' worth before it's overwritten. We can see footage from any of the cameras. I've been through it all and didn't catch anything."

"Are there any other angles—patient rooms, perhaps? We have anything on John Doe's room or close to it?"

"Hallway B has the best view," he said.

Howard pointed to the monitor: *Second floor, Hallway B.*

"John's room is the third." He tapped the glass. "Regulations keep us from having cameras in patient rooms."

"Find anything inside his room?"

"Nothing. His bed was made, but that's normal, being his first night here. He wouldn't have had a chance to mess it up."

"Let me see the note," Sarah said to Heidi, extending her hand. Puzzled, she flipped it to the sticky side. "Don't regulations also prohibit allowing your patients access to potentially dangerous items, such as pens?"

"That's correct, Officer," said the second security guard.

"How did he write the note?" Sarah asked, looking at each of the employees in turn. "It's in ballpoint."

They looked around at each other quizzically.

Dr. Milton patted his shirt pocket, which was empty.

"He seems to have acquired *my* pen," he said.

"I use red when interviewing patients for the first time, and use black for other consultations. That way I can ascertain preliminary notes from regulated consultations."

"Is this it?" Heidi asked from the front desk. She was holding a red ballpoint. She clicked it twice.

"Yes, that's mine," he said, and returned it to his shirt pocket. "It must have fallen from my pocket."

"We should look at footage," Sarah said. "It might lead us to when he left his room so we can then piece together the other segments: when he made it downstairs, whether by the stairwell or the elevator, if and how he passed through those impassable doors"—she pointed to the double doors leading to the room they were all standing in—"and figure out how he made it to the reception desk the exact moment Heidi was in the restroom, and without Howie seeing him."

Everyone was in agreement.

Dr. Milton added his thoughts: "Why don't you and Howard go through the footage, Sarah. Robert and I"—he nudged the security guard twiddling his thumbs—"will turn this place inside-out. We'll check every floor and room. Again. He's here somewhere. There's no way he made it out of this place. Most likely, he's hiding."

"That's good," Sarah said. "Heidi, if you could stay at the front desk; maybe he left more than this note behind."

Heidi sat at her desk, searching through stacks of paper.

Dr. Milton took his security key card to the doors leading out of the room. Robert followed, holding his own key. Policy required all staff members to swipe their cards individually. The system kept a log of each entry by employee name and number. A staff member could follow another through the door without a security key card, but everyone followed policy, even though it was bothersome.

He wondered whether his patient could have followed him through the doors as he had left to go home, but dismissed the thought as absurd. He had said goodnight to Heidi; she would have looked in his direction and seen John.

Sarah reviewed the footage. The screen showed Dr. Milton sliding his card. The light turned from red to green and then to green again as the guard passed his card through.

One of the parking lot cameras revealed a stray cat scrounging for scraps; otherwise, all screens were motionless.

"Can you go back four hours? We'll start there, fast-forward through," Sarah said.

"Yeah, all we got to do is turn this knob; reverse or forward. We can go as fast or as slow as you want," Howard said.

Sarah noticed each monitor had its own control panel with identical knobs and buttons. She let Howard have the controls and watched the second monitor again while the first was rewinding. On it, her husband and the other guard were searching the floor around the doors. This could take them all night, but she didn't care. This was the kind of stuff she lived for.

She watched her husband head north to the elevator while the guard took the stairs.

Sarah yawned, and then did a double-take when she got to the fifth screen, the second-floor, hallway B monitor. John Doe's door, third on the right, was cracked open to a dark wedge of black.

5

ROOM 202

Sarah met Dr. Milton before the elevator doors closed, informed him of their discovery, and waited at the stairwell for Robert. When he caught up, he was out of breath—the cigarettes taking their toll. Dr. Milton told him to watch the hall while he and Sarah checked room 202.

Sarah unclipped her Maglite and clicked it on. She nudged the door open and slid into the room. Sarah moved the beam of light along the floor.

Dr. Milton reached past her and flipped the switch on the wall, inches from her shoulder.

At first glance, the room appeared empty.

In 203, the room across from John's, a young patient moaned incoherently, making Sarah jump. It sounded like something from *Night of the Living Dead*. Dr. Milton, more accustomed to the moans, didn't stir. He regularly met with the patient in 203, who suffered from night terrors.

Sarah was the first to notice John. He lay behind the couch in a fetal position, knees drawn to his chest.

Dr. Milton thought the worst, but his patient was only sleeping heavily, his ribcage rising and falling in the slow, restful rhythm of someone who had been asleep for hours.

They decided to leave the patient on the floor without waking him. It wasn't good practice to wake a patient in deep sleep, especially one who had not been fully diagnosed. He lay awkwardly on his side, his long, straggly hair pasted to his forehead and cheeks. He appeared as though he had fallen, but there were no visible bruises or scrapes on his body, or displaced furniture. John had put himself there, as children sometimes do in their sleep.

"God sleeps on the floor, huh?" Sarah said to Howard.

You've got to be kidding, his expression read.

"Did you check his room before you paged?" Dr. Milton asked him. "We came all the way out here—"

"We checked," Howard said, fidgeting. "We checked every inch of this place. That was the *first* place we looked."

"Check behind the couch?" Dr. Milton asked dryly.

"He wasn't behind the couch."

6

THE OTHER PATIENT

The following morning, Dr. Milton was back in his office, going through notes and recordings of patient interviews from the week. He drank his coffee and thumbed through papers, note-pads and microcassettes stuffed within oversized folders.

He cleared a spot under the *Ds* for his deity of a patient, wrote *Doe, John* on a fresh folder, put in yesterday's tape and notepad, and squeezed it into the filing cabinet.

He kept the cherry-wood desk clear except for a notepad, pens of various colors, his tape recorder, and *Terminal Man*, a book about a man with a microchip planted in his neck, which he was currently reading. It was fiction, but barely. Dr. Milton rarely read fiction.

He opened the drawer and flipped through tabs until he came to a folder marked *Stevenson*, another of his patients.

Aeron Stevenson was brought in for court-mandated ther-apy after wrestling with suicide. Dr. Milton wanted to recap the last few sessions before his next session.

The sounds of rewinding, and then his own voice:

"What, exactly, was green?"

Aeron: "Everything … everything was green. Hands, arms, legs, gun. But only me, and the other toys. They were green."

Dr. Milton: "I see."

A long pause of white noise.

Dr. Milton: "Army men. I remember playing with those when I was your son's age. Were you ever in the Army?"

Aeron: "I went right after high school. Barely made it through boot camp because of my size. They beefed me up and shipped me off to Desert Storm."

Dr. Milton: "So you must have worn sand fatigues: browns and beige. Anything you experienced that caused you stress?"

Aeron: "Boot camp and training, we wore green camo."

The patient's mind seemed to fade from the subject.

Dr. Milton: "Was there anything from your military experience in these dreams? Were you injured? You said earlier that your hand was always bleeding in the dreams."

Aeron: "Red flowing down my arm. Man, I could feel it—hurt like a bitch!"

Dr. Milton: "You mentioned you cut your palm with a razor a couple of days before you tried killing yourself. Not too many folks use razors like that anymore."

Aeron: "Call me old-fashioned."

The tape skittered as the doctor fast-forwarded. It clicked to a stop and he took some notes before playing it again. He wrote, *more information on dreams.*

Dr. Milton: "… reaching into his closet?"

Aeron: "For a pellet gun, the one we were getting for his birthday. Well, the one *I* was getting for his birthday. Karen was against it—hates guns. It was just like the one—"

Dr. Milton: "When you first had this dream, your son did not have the gun yet? The dream came before the gun?"

Aeron: "Never bought it. Just thought of buying it."

Dr. Milton: "I see."

Aeron: "Bought a mirror, though. That's what got me here."

Dr. Milton: "A mirror. Go on."

Aeron: "After I, well … missed, I went out to buy a new one, like the old one but better, because I shattered the old one."

Dr. Milton: "From the blast?"

Aeron: "Yes."

Dr. Milton: "Aeron, did you try to kill your reflection?"

Aeron: "I wish I could have. He was starting to piss me off."

Dr. Milton: "Since that didn't work, you turned the weapon on yourself. And somehow you missed."

Aeron: "The mirror shattered from the noise, I guess. I'm not sure how it really played out. I remember being tired. My eyes dry and red. You ever try killing yourself, Doctor?"

Dr. Milton: "No."

Aeron: "Well, it's aggravating and depressing. I had one bullet in the gun, and every time it clicked, I was both angry and relieved. I wanted to see my reflection's head burst open, yet also wanted to save him, but I couldn't. I got dizzy. My body heavy. It was difficult to stand, and to even stay awake. And then I heard the blast and blacked out. I thought I'd done it at first, but then I woke up and realized I had missed myself, and my reflection, and instead put a hole in the wall. I was tired, as if hypnotized. You ever been hypnotized? A few minutes under feels like sleeping half a day."

Dr. Milton: "I *have* hypnotized, but I never been under myself. Back to the mirror."

Aeron: "The infamous mirror."

Dr. Milton: "You said you missed yourself and your reflection. Whom were you trying to kill? You or your reflection?"

Aeron: *"Pull up if I pull up."*

Dr. Milton: "What does that mean?"

Another long recorded pause.

Aeron: "It's a palindrome."

He remembered writing it down during the interview, and reading it from left to right and then from right to left.

Dr. Milton: "Yes it is. What does it mean to you, Aeron?"

A longer pause.

7

TERMINAL MAN

Dr. Milton's session with Aeron was a waste of time.

He discovered nothing new, made no progress whatsoever. He pressed the patient about the mirror, and he broke down into tears. After two or three attempts to calm Aeron, he eventually gave up and put a stop to the session, bumped the patient's medication to 250mg, double what it had been.

During the break between sessions, he gave Sarah a call.

"Found God?" she said.

"Not yet. We meet in about an hour. Is this a secure line? I'm not being recorded, am I?"

"Of course not, dear. It's illegal to record phone conversations without first seeking permission. So, can I have your permission? You know, I already have this line traced."

"Let me guess," he said, "I'm calling from the hospital."

"And you're not at your desk; you're in the break room," she said with confidence.

"You can determine that?"

"We can determine a lot of things. But really, it was mostly just logical reasoning."

"Some kind of call monitoring system, a program that can trace calls by extension numbers? Sounds illegal."

"No, it's logic, as in: one, the time is twelve fifteen; two, eighty-five percent of working adults take their lunch breaks between the hours of twelve and one p.m.; and three, you must be taking yours. It's quite a simple system, Doctor."

"Did you know that eighty-seven percent of all statistics are made up on the spot?" Dr. Milton said.

She didn't laugh.

"It's been a slow day," she said and sighed. "A cop's life is not what it's cracked up to be on TV. There are plenty of criminals, but they don't all show up in half-hour time blocks. And plenty more commercials in the real world."

"I see," he said, smiling.

"Don't 'I see' *me*, Doctor. I'm not one or your patients. Ask me how my day was, like a normal husband."

"You already told me about your day."

"Then ask me something different."

"Okay, then, what's the most exciting adventure you have been on today? If it's too boring, make something up."

"That would have been half an hour ago. I was called to the armpit of Washington, Crack Town central. A neighborhood watch group called it in. Suspicious character moping around, looking in windows, sucking down cigarettes."

"Is that a crime, moping around?" Dr. Milton asked.

"No."

"What do you do for that type of call?"

"We'd confront the individual, ask questions, make sure he just wasn't some locked-out roommate or sub-lessee," Sarah explained. "Check for identification, look for drugs, weapons, the usual. Then we'd have to wait for a second complaint. If he returned, we'd put him in the black-and-white for disturbing the peace or trespassing."

"Was that the case with Mr. Suspicious?"

"No. That was the first time a unit was sent to that residence. I sound like a robot, referring to myself as a *unit*. When I got there, I circled a few times, didn't see anything."

"Besides the overabundance of crack houses."

"Well, yes, besides that. I see more crack houses in a day

than most people see in a lifetime."

"Would you like to talk about it sometime?" Dr. Milton asked. "I could arrange a session."

"Funny. Anyway, where was I? Oh, yes. So I circled the block, still nothing, waited for a few minutes, nothing. It didn't seem like *anyone* was there. Neighboring houses were empty, and so were the streets; not even spectators peeking through mini-blinds at the cop car parked out front. I report my status, S.O.P. and all that jazz. I go to the door, ring the doorbell, and guess what?"

"Ding-dong?" he said, checking his watch.

"The button pushes through, like it had been decomposing the last twenty-some years. It was a ghost town."

"I see," Dr. Milton said flatly.

"So I used the butt of my nightstick on the door."

"Standard operating procedure, I'm guessing," he said. "That's how they do it on *Cops*."

"It just looks cooler—more authority behind the stick. It's the same as wearing shades while patrolling."

"It does."

"And I say, 'Police, anyone home?' and I knock harder. After a few moments, the door opens to the length of a chain lock."

"Was it the killer?"

He checked his watch again, out of habit.

Sarah ignored him.

"A woman stood at the door, drying her hair with a towel. She had another wrapped around her torso. Wet feet making a mess of the floor. You know how I hate that."

"Slow down. This is starting to get good."

"She apologized for taking so long to get to the door. Her left cheek looked red, like she had been slapped hard. She kept drying her hair as she answered my questions. I asked if everything was all right and notified her of the complaints. She told me it was her ex-husband trying to get in. I didn't believe her, though. Instincts told me something else was going on."

"Spousal abuse, or ex-spousal abuse?" Dr. Milton asked.

"I asked about her face and she said she had slipped and fell in the bathroom, smacking her face on the doorknob."

"I hate when that happens," he said, laughing at the absurdity of such a thing happening.

"I asked if I could take a look around, and she instantly found an excuse—grabbed it out of the air. Said her house was a bloody mess. She had excuses for everything."

"How's that?"

"I asked if her ex was still there, to ask him similar questions, but she said he was gone. Go figure."

"Interesting," Dr. Milton said.

He didn't mean to sound like a psychiatrist.

"Sounds like the ex came home, roughed her up a bit."

"I'm not sure," she said. "I have a strange feeling she beat the piss out of *him*. I hope she did—if he was abusive."

"Maybe she might be the abuser and he the abused—a sort of dominance issue. It could be a sexual thing they have together."

"Sexual?" Her voice lowered, the way it would when discussing adult topics around children.

"A dominant-submissive, sexual relationship," he said. "They could be into asphyxiation, S & M ..."

"I get the picture," she said. "That's the extent of my day. You probably need to get ready for your next session."

"John Doe again. I need to review my notes. Quite confusing, really. Scribbles, words here and there. More like a shopping list than consultation notes."

"What kind of notes can you take? After all, this is God you're dealing with."

"Difficult notes indeed. John is extremely difficult. If I had one word to describe John, it would be *difficult*. I feel like I'm trying to consult a computer terminal. Computers only do the things you tell them to do. They have the potential to be infinitely useful, but they cannot function on their own. They need to be told how and when to function. They need someone to push their buttons *for* them—a person with potential to make mistakes. That's how I feel when talking to John: as if I'm only pushing buttons."

"Maybe *you* are the terminal."

8

PLACEBO

As he prepped for his next session, Dr. Milton pondered Sarah's comment and whether it applied to his relationship with John Doe. He hadn't recorded their first session together and had only taken a few notes—a page or two of scribbles.

He decided to delve into religion for the next session—fishing, really, in hopes of unveiling something, anything. Maybe see if the patient had a religious background, or get him to discuss parents, siblings, or children of his own—people to account for his not being a deity by heritage and birthright.

Hypnotizing was also an option, but Dr. Milton would have to learn more of the patient's background first. He left hypnotherapy as a last resort, preferring the path of self-healing first.

He believed that everyone had the power to cure themselves of anything—from common colds to cancer, even mental illnesses. Of course, this theory cut both ways: we could heal, and we could also damage. Dr. Milton went as far as publishing a monograph on his theories, "Art of Self-Mutilation," and a follow-up article called "The Powers of Self-Healing."

In these articles, using case studies to back his hypotheses, Dr.Milton explored how the mind could cause as well as cure disease. The self-mutilation article discussed dynamics of the human mind creating sicknesses, whether physically or mentally, and the reasons behind body piercings, tattooing, even self-cutting. It discussed suicide attempts, which were usually cries for attention rather than serious attempts on one's life. Mainly, he was trying to prove that most sicknesses, physical or not, were caused by the workings of the human mind.

In one such test, Dr. Milton held a meeting with college students he was mentoring at the time. All were completely healthy when they had first met. He held a lecture class in a small room, pretending all the while to have a serious cold. He went as far as applying makeup to feign a sick appearance, blowing his nose, and speaking nasally throughout the lecture. Several times he apologized for being sick and for possibly infecting his students with his bad cold. Later that week, during a second class, a third of the students came in with colds, stuffed noses, coughing. Two students, who were absent for the second class, explained the next day that they had been too sick to attend. During his next few lectures, a constant coughing and clearing of throats could be heard among the students.

Milton, however, was perfectly well.

In his other piece, he theorized that the mind could not only develop sicknesses, but could also un-develop them. To help support his theory, Dr. Milton used his wife, who at the time was suffering stress-related headaches. Being a gentleman, he offered to get her a couple of Tylenol, bringing her two capsules and a small glass of water. A few hours later, according to the article, her headache had all but disappeared, despite the fact that the pills he had given her were nothing more than vitamin supplements.

Dr. Milton checked his watch.

He was late for his second session with John Doe in room 202. On his way, he mulled over the questions he would ask, knowing that once he stepped in the room and started talking with John, the direction of the conversation would shift dramatically. They always did. You never knew what would come up in a therapy session. No matter how much you prepared, it wouldn't matter when the clock started ticking.

9

A LITTLE FAITH

When Dr. Milton first walked into the room, he noticed a cryptic smile on his patient's face. Before pressing the record button on his tape recorder, he again pondered the angle he should take. *Where to go first? Where is the key to this one? Why is he smiling?* He took a pen and notepad from his briefcase and studied the patient before him, the mocking smile.

John spoke first.

In a sincere voice, he said, "I'm sorry if I caused the facility and its staff any hardships last night."

The smile was still there, a well-rested smile.

Dr. Milton realized he had not even thought about last night's happenings until this very moment. He double-clicked his pen with his forefinger, as he might a computer mouse.

"John," he said, and waited. "Tell me about last night."

Dr. Milton assumed he had little if any involvement.

"Were you not here, Doc?"

"I was."

"The most reasonable time for my departure would be after everyone left for the day. You didn't worry, did you, Doc?"

Dr. Milton was startled, but made an effort not to react.

"We found you in your room, sleeping."

"I guess you didn't worry much," John said.

"Honestly, John, I don't believe you went anywhere. You may have wandered the halls a bit, but you never left the ward. Someone would have seen you leave."

"But no one *did* see me leave; they wouldn't have. That's why I left the note."

The doctor had forgotten about the note, too, until now.

"Gone boating, did it read?"

He studied John's face, looking for expression changes.

"That is correct, Gerald."

Dr. Milton wanted to ask about the note, but—

"Did you just call me Gerald?"

"That is your name," the patient said.

"I go by Gerry, and only my wife calls me that when she's not happy about something. *Gerald* ... not even my parents called me that when I was young. Always Gerry."

"I will not tell anyone," John said.

"Not even my paycheck has that name. And it is not on record at this hospital. What I am most concerned about is how you came across it. My name tag,"—he pointed to the golden tag on his lapel, which read DR. G. MILTON—"this is how people refer to me."

He tried to compose himself.

"As *G?*"

"Doctor Milton," he said, a little too snappish.

He was doing his level best to keep John from digging under his skin, which is where problems nested. And getting angry with a patient only slowed the self-healing process, immensely. He took a deep breath.

John's expression: innocent, childlike.

"You could have gotten that from any of a dozen places," he said to change the subject. "Possibly my wife even let it slip. She's the officer who brought you here."

"Nice woman you have there, Doc. Sarah was very nice to me on the ride in. I'm sorry if I caused her any trouble."

The fact that the patient knew Sarah's name troubled him, too, for her badge simply read, OFFICER MILTON, or something like that, and it wasn't very likely she had shared her name with a mentally disturbed individual.

But never mind Sarah; never mind the fact that he knew both their names; it was not relevant to the task at hand, and regardless, he needed to remain composed, or at least appear composed.

John gave another of his concerned looks.

"You still do not believe I am God."

Dr. Milton made it a point to answer promptly.

"No, John, I do not believe you are God. I believe you are like me, like Sarah, and like the billions of people on this earth. But *you* believe you are God, and I have to find out why you believe that."

"I agree I *am* like you and the rest, Doc," he said. "It was in my image that I created you, for Christ's sake."

"I believe you took your own name in vain there, John. I don't believe God would do such a thing."

With a sudden look of concern, the patient said, "I am afraid, Doc, that you are mistaken. You seem to have overlooked the part in the Bible about the Godhead. And I in no way took the name of Christ in vain. It *was* for his sake, after all."

"There are many religions out there that would disagree, John," Dr. Milton said, knowing in advance that he couldn't win this argument. "It is widely accepted that the Godhead is one."

"Some religions agree with that statement," he said. "There are some that believe I am a vengeful god, and some that believe there is more than *one* god, some that believe I am an elephant, and some that believe they can become gods if they come to church a seventh of their lives. Redeemed. Saved. Eternalized. Some think that I am a woman, a goat, a cow. I am just God, nothing more."

"A god with powers," Dr. Milton added.

"We have discussed that. You are skeptical. It is a lot to accept, I know. BAM! I am God. Poof! Something like that."

"Let's say you *are* God for the moment," Dr. Milton replied.

"I am God, for all moments, yes."

"Why is God in a mental institution?"

A long pause.

"Where else would God fit into this world?" John asked. "Take Christ, for example. One day, poof! Here is Christ, Jesus, whatever. He tells those around him who he is, why he's here. He gets asked over and over again, 'Prove it. Make this blow up.' I'm improvising for you here, Doc. 'Turn this water into wine. Make it blood, gold, water. Cure my leprosy.' Things like that, over and over again. And he proves it for them, over and over again."

"I see where you're going," Dr. Milton said, clicking his pen a few more times as he leaned in to the patient.

"What do people do?" John said, "If they had institutions two thousand years ago, he would have gone there to be analyzed, or *healed*, as you put it, because he did not fit in. He scared people. So they killed him because they would not come to understand."

"I guess asking you to remove a corn from my toe is out of the question, then?" Dr. Milton asked, and then laughed.

"You do not have any corns, Doc."

"No, I do not."

"What about that kid you almost hit? He rode his bike across the road and you nearly clipped him. How would I know that?"

"I'm sorry, John, I don't recall almost clipping a kid on a bike," he said. It was true; he couldn't recall such a thing ever happening.

"I guess you'll remember soon enough," said John.

In the silence growing between them he added, "So, then ... let's play a little game of faith. Pick a country."

"Is this like a card trick? Pick a country, any country?"

Looking at his notepad, he realized he had not taken any notes up to this point. He decided to play along.

"In a way it is," John said. "Let's just say I will not be turning water to wine or anything of that nature. So, pick a country."

"All right. I've thought of one in particular."

John laughed.

"What is so amusing?"

"It doesn't work like that, Doc. It is not a mind game. That would take all the fun out of it. Feel free to tell me the country."

"China."

"China is not going to work. They are a little on the large side. Think smaller, maybe third-world."

Dr. Milton looked at the ceiling to mask the rolling of his eyes, and thought of a country.

"The Czech Republic."

"The Czech Republic. Are you certain?"

"Is there a problem with that, or shall I pick another?" He had no idea what to expect from the patient in return.

"No problem at all. It is gone."

"Gone?"

"Gone."

"What do you mean, gone? You got rid of the Czech Republic? It no longer exists?"

"Gone," he said. "Gone from existence, from memory, all but yours, of course—and, well, *gone*."

Dr. Milton tried his best not to sound patronizing.

"What about the people? What will become of them?"

"They will not be missed, for they no longer exist. By this time tomorrow, everything will be back to normal. The world will go on for a day without them. You will check it out, Doc, no? I would be crushed to find that I did this all for nothing. It is not as easy as it appears to be. There is a great deal of rearranging, hence China."

"I would guess so. I will definitely look into it."

Dr. Milton then wrote his only note for the session.

Verify existence of the Czech Republic.

For the rest of the session, Dr. Milton inquired more about John's religious leanings. It seemed that John—or God, for that matter—had no religious background or faith whatsoever. He explained that faith was a temporary thing, existing only until you *knew*, or *saw*, at which point you no longer required faith. Faith was a belief in what one could not see; once that happened, faith disappeared, like one's lap when standing, as John put it.

Dr. Milton was never into organized religion, but the ideas presented by his patient were intriguing. He wondered how long it would take for his faith in healing this patient to disappear.

The idea was absurd. But if it was so absurd, why couldn't he get it off his mind? It was all he could think about ... the Czech Republic. It had him so bugged that he stopped to ask Heidi at the front desk for assurance.

She said she had never heard of the country, but she wasn't the sharpest crayon in the box when it came to geography or history, she said. She remembered Czechoslovakia and Yugoslavia, but never heard that the country had divided. She said

Howard might know—he always kept up on stuff like that because all he ever did at home was watch CNN and read *TIME*.

Howard was no help, either, although he knew that the country formerly called Czechoslovakia was no longer Czechoslovakia and had broken into different nations.

Dr. Milton had a scheduled session with Aeron before the day ended, and needed to make his rounds beforehand. He was rarely late making his rounds, but today he was, for he had spent a great chunk of the afternoon in the library, wasting time searching the encyclopedias and atlases for a country that had ceased to exist.

The only up-to-date books in the moderately sized library were fiction; the nonfiction section contained textbooks and educational materials, but they were too old for the Czech Republic.

Aggravated, Dr. Milton went to the globe. He spun it to show the opposite side of the world to find Czechoslovakia. The rest of the globe revealed how quickly maps of the world changed. Russia was imprinted in parentheses on an amoeba-like red sprawl that covered nearly half of Asia, under bold, black letters: *U.S.S.R.* He kicked the globe in frustration, putting a small dent in southern Africa. If the globe hadn't been on rollers, he might have taken out the entire southern hemisphere. The globe coasted to a stop against the far wall.

He needed Internet, but didn't want to wait until the end of the day. It would nag at him otherwise. The computers at work were network terminals, offering no such access.

Just then his cell phone beeped. He guessed it would be a text message from Sarah, but was disappointed to find the battery LED flashing, reminding him that it needed charging.

Of course, he thought, *the cell*. His phone had limited access to the Internet, a feature he'd never used to this day. CONNECT-ING ... across the top of the screen. The phone beeped again.

A few moments later, a Yahoo logo appeared on the miniature screen, along with a box in which to type search criteria. Using the buttons on the side of the phone, he navigated to the search box. It was an old flip phone, and it beeped again.

The difficult and annoying part of the ordeal: scrolling through the number pad to find the letters to compose words. For the letter *C*, he had to press the *2* three times, since three letters occupied the numbered button. Without a keyboard, it was rather cumbersome.

Dr. Milton started pressing numbers in succession as he translated the nine-button keyboard: *[2, 2, 2]*, *[9, 9, 9, 9]*, *[3, 3]*, *[2, 2, 2]*, and *[4, 4]* to get CZECH, and then *[7, 7, 7]*, *[3, 3]*, *[7]*, *[8, 8]*, *[2, 2]*, *[5, 5, 5]*, *[4, 4, 4]*, *[2, 2, 2]* for REPUBLIC.

It was a race against a dying battery on an ancient relic.

He checked the display to verify the spelling, then hit the Send button. The screen read SEARCHING ... and the dots that trailed it blinked in succession.

The phone beeped one final time as the battery ran dry.

He planned to keep the promise he had made with John, but it would have to wait until he got home. The country would be there.

It hadn't disappeared from existence merely on John's decision. He found it strange that he even felt the need to assure himself of such nonsense, and laughed, shaking his head at his own gullibility. No patient had ever gotten this far under his skin.

Why now?

Dr. Milton checked his watch and got to his rounds more than an hour later than scheduled.

DREAMS

Being an hour late for his rounds resulted in being an hour late for his second session of the day with Aeron Stevenson.

Aeron was busy reading a book about dreams when Dr. Milton sat down and apologized for his tardiness. Aeron marked his place and set the book onto the floor: *Dreams and Their Meanings.*

He had given Aeron the book after their last session, and he was nearly finished, according to the bookmark. It dealt with symbolism of colors and objects in dreams.

Green and guns were not the most auspicious pairing.

"You've been doing your homework."

"It's an interesting book and I can't seem to put it down. Sorry I got emotional on you last time."

"That's understandable, Aeron. You have been under much pressure lately, battling demons along the way."

"You could say that."

"Find anything you would care to discuss?"

"I learned I am really fucked up."

"The first step to recovery is acceptance, Aeron," he said in his best psychologist's tone. He realized it sounded phony the moment it left his mouth, repeating basically the first line of every self-help book on the market.

Aeron stared at the floor and said, "And the first step to killing yourself is pulling the trigger."

Dr. Milton realized his own mind was wandering. He was looking at his patient but fading. He also realized he'd forgotten his briefcase with his pens and paper and recorder. They were still at the foot of his desk, one floor down.

"Aeron, regarding the dream involving your son, where you are the toy, bound, bleeding, et cetera … We both understand what each element represents: where the closet and the rifle fit in, why you are bleeding, and the importance of the colors."

Aeron studied the tiles on the floor.

"I want to focus on the other dream, the one with the boat."

A chill moved down Dr. Milton's spine. The hairs on his neck and arms stood on end, his palms clamming.

His mind left Aeron and their conversation, ventured on its own, recalling the patient's vivid recollection of the dream. He put himself there without trying.

Alone on a boat, Aeron drifts from a shore where his son and wife stand, waving goodbye. Their expressions are emotionless. He grabs an oar, paddles with all his might, but he drifts farther away. Back on the shore, behind him, his son is looking to his mother. Crying and floating above them is Aeron's mother. She is looking to Christ, crying. Christ is looking to God, crying. Dr. Milton is in that dream now, playing the part of Aeron in the boat. In his grasp is no longer an oar, but a handgun, and in God's place is John Doe, smiling a malevolent smile.

Dr. Milton was startled into reality by the sound of what he imagined was a gunshot. It was merely the sound of the room's door opening as Heidi poked her head in to check on them. She looked ready to leave for the day, purse at her side. It also seemed a bit darker in the room.

"Sorry to intrude, but we're about ready to start locking things up downstairs," she said.

"Locking things up?"

He checked his watch, surprised to see that it was a quarter to six. Three hours had passed.

"We'll wrap things up here. Thank you, Heidi."

He leaned forward in his chair to find his back drenched with sweat and his shirt stuck to the backing. Windows overlooking the parking lot revealed that the sun had gone down for the day.

He was about to apologize, but Aeron apologized first.

"Sorry for jabbering like that. I never even gave you a chance to get a word in," he said, this time looking at the doctor instead of the floor. "I guess I needed to vent."

"That is perfectly understandable."

He had no memory of the last three hours.

"I'm sorry I kept you so long. Got a little carried away, I know, but I feel like we hit a few breakthroughs."

"I certainly hope so," Dr. Milton said. "I have more homework for you this time around, since you did so well."

He pointed to the book on the floor and smiled.

"Name it," Aeron said eagerly.

"I would like for you each morning to look in the mirror. Look at yourself. Really look at yourself. If you are able, I want you to do the same with the lights off. If it's too much, leave the door open. Let me know how it turns out in our next session."

"I will try."

"There is another book in the library you may also find useful. *Finding Me*. If it's not in the library for whatever reason, I'll be glad to loan you my personal copy."

He held out his hand and Aeron shook it. His grip was firm, a sign of confidence. His condition was improving.

11

THE SEARCH

The computer was in hibernation so he tapped a key and waited for the screen to flick on. He headed for the big blue e on the bottom left of the display.

In the search criteria, he typed Czech Republic. He had expected a message such as '*13,142,397 hits were found*' but instead he received '*Your search* -Czech Republic- *did not find any documents.*' He hit the search button a second time and got the same result.

He tried a different search engine, then another.

Nothing.

He put in just *Czech* and finally got some half-million hits. After checking the first ten or so links, he discovered they all referred to information on Czechoslovakia. Several sites offered maps, but all were outdated.

A chime sounded as an Instant Messenger window popped up. A user by the name of racecar196 was trying to chat—a friend of Sarah's. He closed the window and searched for *atlas*.

The first returned page was an online encyclopedia with a search window on the middle of the page. He searched again, and ended with a message stating that in order to use full functionality of the site, he would be required to pay a monthly subscription fee and become a member.

He returned to the first search engine, which had an ad pop for a spy cam. Closing the new window, he scrolled through the list of initial search results, past the sites advertising hot, live Czech girls, and clicked on a link to another site listed as an online encyclopedic haven. It brought up a mostly white page.

This page has moved. You are now being redirected ...

That was about all Dr. Milton could read before a site appeared with nude women doing strange things with even stranger objects, animated images galore, flashing brightly colored words like *SEX*, *HOT*, and *LIVE*. The entire page was a rainbow of neon and nudity.

He clicked the Back button of the browser but was forced forward to the same page. He hit the Back button a few more times in quick succession. He closed the browser and two other sex-related sites appeared, along with a pop-up window wanting him to change his homepage, and another to download streaming sex software.

Clicking the Close boxes as fast as he could, he managed to get to the results of his original search. He browsed for hours, clicking the button that read "Next page" again and again, scrolling down list after list of search results, which took him to dead ends, dead links, and finally to dead tired.

Before he called it quits, a link caught his eye. In bold lettering: *The Czech Republic—the Forming of a New Country*. There was no site description below it, but the title was promising enough. He clicked the link and waited for the page to load. And then he waited longer. And longer. A long while later, a white page came up that read *This page cannot be found* and gave an error number.

And he gave up.

When Sarah got home, he asked her about the country and she could only remember Czechoslovakia and Yugoslavia. He informed her that both were gone, split into other countries years ago.

She helped him check the set of encyclopedias in their den, but they were fifteen years old and as outdated as everything seemed to be. Sarah offered to look online but was stopped.

"John probably picked the Czech Republic," she said, and shrugged, "because not everyone knows about it."

"*I* picked the country," he said.

12

SEVENTY-EIGHT

A few minutes before he reached the parking lot, Dr. Milton's cell phone rang. He charged it on his drive to work and answered, cord hanging from his ear. He recognized the number on the display.

"Hi, it's Heidi. I have some bad news about Aeron."

The doctor sighed, glad to hear it wasn't about John.

"We would have called earlier, but everything happened fast. We called an ambulance to have him transferred to the hospital downtown so they could stitch him up."

He could tell by Heidi's cracked voice that she was upset, as if she had witnessed some horrifying ordeal. She took a deep breath and exhaled deeply into the phone.

"He cut himself pretty badly. Blood was everywhere: the walls, the floor, the sink. I just finished helping clean up the trail left from the gurney that took him out."

He was speechless, imagining the worst.

"Someone found him. I don't know who, but someone did and told Howard, who was already upstairs. He rushed to the bathroom and found Aeron laying on the floor in the dark. There was blood everywhere, Doctor. I saw him on the floor with his arms all cut up and bleeding. The bathroom mirror was broken, and there were pieces in the sink, on the floor, sticking out of his arms."

"Is everyone else okay?"

"Howard told me to call for an ambulance. I didn't think to use the phone around the corner, so I ran downstairs and used my phone to call it in. They got here ten minutes ago."

"You think he tried to kill himself again?" the doctor asked. "Is that what it seemed like happened?"

Heidi took another deep breath.

"It looked that way, but then I remembered the glass from the mirror. Pieces poking out from his elbows, through the length of his arms ... Howard wants to talk to you."

"Dr. Milton?"

"What happened, Howie?"

"The ambulance left about five minutes ago. Everything is starting to calm down now."

"What happened, Howie?"

"I don't think it was a suicide attempt. He was lying there on the floor when I found him, in a pool of blood. Looked like he bashed the mirror up with his arms. Bashed it over and over until there was nothing left on the wall. Paramedics said he might make it, said he lost a lot of blood and needed transfusions."

"They took him to the hospital downtown, right?"

"Seattle," he said. "He sliced his arms and wrists bad. Palms were cut up, too, and maybe a little on his elbows."

Dr. Milton couldn't help but feel a sense of guilt.

Aeron apparently wasn't ready to face the mirror.

What went wrong?

"Still there, Dr. Milton?"

"Still here, wondering what I should do. How are things there? Are the other patients okay?"

"It took a while to calm some patients, but everything's under control. Heidi's shaken up. She threw up twice."

"Send her home if she wants," Dr. Milton said.

"One other thing. He wrote the number seventy-eight on the floor with some of his blood."

13

EIGHTY-SEVEN

Questions swirled in Dr. Milton's head the remainder of the drive to work: Why seventy-eight? Had he tried killing himself a second time? Where was the Czech Republic in all this? Still gone? The number bugged him most of all.

1978? Not a birthdate; the patient was much older. His child's birthdate, perhaps. Matty was younger than that, or so he had been told. Wedding? Anniversary? Seventy-eight items of some kind?

It was perplexing.

No one recalled seeing the number except for Howard.

"Everything happened so fast," Heidi had said.

Dr. Milton called the hospital in Seattle from his desk phone to check on Aeron's condition. He was now stable and needed whole blood to replace the two pints he'd lost.

An image of a milk carton falling and splitting open came into Dr. Milton's mind. He shivered off the visual, disgusted. The thought of that much milk—or blood—pooling on the floor ... well, it seemed like a lot of liquid. And that much blood, well, there was a reason he hadn't become a surgeon. Blood put him off.

Aeron had sliced large lengths of a few blood vessels, the way a drinking straw splits down the middle. The backs of his hands took most of the damage from pounding against the mirror. His wrists and arms were sliced, or grated, as the surgeon put it.

He checked Aeron's current medication dosage levels with one of the nurses. Nothing was out of the ordinary.

After searching his room, Dr. Milton came up empty—
nothing but signs of improvement. A few drawings were taped
to the walls, mostly sketches of the dreams they had discussed
in their sessions. He recognized a few of them, some in colors,
others black only on white paper: demons trying to escape
Aeron's body, a boat heading downstream while a family stood
on the shore, a vibrantly green soldier with a red hand. One
had black lines running up and down the center of the paper,
separating a dark man on one side from a hollow-looking image
on the other.

And then Dr. Milton noticed the blank page taped to the
wall. At least he thought it was blank until he saw the small black
dot in the very center. He couldn't quite make out the tiniest
pinprick of black against the white.

He returned with a magnifying glass and let out a small
laugh on discovering what the dot really was: A tiny *78*, in the
smallest handwriting imaginable, in black ink.

Dr. Milton pondered a bit and then flipped the page over
in his hand. On the back was a diminutive *87* of the same size,
with the seven written in reverse. The eight may have been
reversed as well.

14

THE GAME

John sat in his chair, arms folded. He had pulled his long hair back in a ponytail, shoeless, fidgeting with his toes, with one leg crossed over the other.

Dr. Milton sat across from him and started the recorder.

"No need to feel guilty, Doc. Some demons you have to battle on your own."

His voice was sympathetic.

"You are referring to the incident this morning with another of my patients. Did you know him?"

"I know everyone."

"Of course."

He must have befriended Aeron during his stay.

"Did you catch any of the excitement?"

"I was sleeping, but I wouldn't call it excitement."

Dr. Milton's pen clicked on and off, on and off.

"But you know what happened?"

"I would only be repeating what you have already discovered. But if it would make you feel—"

"It would clarify things for me. What did you see, John."

John told him what he had already heard from both Heidi and Howard. He was hoping for more, but got only what someone who had overheard would have known. He either witnessed the event, or had heard about it from the other patients.

"You don't believe me, do you?"

"Of course I believe you. I don't believe you would lie about Aeron's condition, or anything else for that matter. I trust in you as I do all my patients. It is through trust that I can help."

"You still don't believe who I am."

"That you're God?"

The question was quite a *faux pas* in his profession. Answering a question with a question showed disbelief. He tapped the end of his pen against the sole of his shoe, which bounced against his knee to form the triangular lap he used as a backing for his notepad.

"The question should be 'why do you believe you are God?' What makes you *God*, John? Why would God be here?" Unconsciously, he began clicking his pen.

"What makes you believe you are a *doctor*, Doctor? I believe I am God because I am. Why is a door a door? What makes art art? What is, is. I am what I am. And we've already gone over why God is in a place like this."

His voice seemed strained, but otherwise serene.

"This is where modern man would have me."

"I am a doctor, John, because that is the profession I chose. I realized in college the great need for mental healing in the world, so I took all the necessary classes to become a doctor. I am a doctor because I made myself a doctor."

John smiled, unfolded his arms, put them to his sides.

"You figured it out," John said, extending his hand.

Dr. Milton thought about the implications of handing over the pen, but did so anyway after clicking it once more. He offered the notepad, but John only wanted the pen.

"I am God, because that is how I made *me*."

He unscrewed the pen apart at its middle.

"A long time ago—I don't know, maybe a few billion years—I decided I wanted to be God."

The pen was in two pieces, and then three.

Dr. Milton listened and watched patiently, wondering what

his patient was up to.

"So I said to myself, 'let's create time-space, dimensions, make some worlds, create species, and see how it all plays out. Let's control *everything*.' And so that is what I did."

He pulled the spring from the tip of the pen and tossed it over his shoulder, began rebuilding the pen from its pieces.

"I made myself God."

John handed over the reassembled, springless thing.

Dr. Milton clicked it one final time, and the thumb clicker fell inside the top part of the pen.

"Sorry," John said. "It was getting irritating."

He threw the pen over his shoulder, like his patient had done with the spring—the heart and soul of the pen, the one thing that made it alive and useful in the world.

"It's a bad habit, but it beats smoking," John said, shaking his head. "I can't believe people concocted such a thing."

"Cigarettes?"

"No, *cancer*. I can't believe people created cancer. Where were we? Oh, yes, you not believing who I am. What's it going to take?"

Dr. Milton pondered for a moment.

"Making a country disappear didn't seem to get your vote. *Rise to vote, sir.* You ever find the Czech Republic, Doc?"

He wanted to spill everything to the patient: how the books in the library were outdated, the Internet servers being down, and his phone dying. He realized they sounded like excuses.

What was it going to take?

"The country never disappeared or vanished from the world, John. There were coincidental occurrences that may have caused it to appear that way, but nothing else. The Czech Republic is still the Czech Republic."

"Are you trying to convince *me*, or yourself? It seems you are losing control of what you believe, Doc. Part of you believes in me; part of you is lost in confusion. By the way, I changed everything back to how it was, in case you were worried."

And then he had it.

"I'm going to think of a number, John," Dr. Milton said. "I am going to think of a number, and I am not even going to give you a range. No 'one through nine,' not even 'one through one million,' just a number. It may be a whole number, a fraction, a decimal, or even binary or hexadecimal. I will pick a number at random and you will tell me what it is, John."

It wasn't a random number Dr. Milton planned to pick, but the number he had found in Aeron's artwork and blood.

John smiled and said, "Just one number?"

"Only one."

"If it is only one number, I would have to say … 165."

He refolded his arms, looking almost proud.

"That's not the number, John."

Dr. Milton would have accepted either eighty-seven or seventy-eight, but was relieved to hear neither. A trickle of sweat slid down his neck. The hour was about over.

"4,884?"

"Sorry, John."

He was making progress.

"Are you sure?"

"I am certain, John. I would have written it down beforehand, but you broke my pen. Now, I believe our time is up for today."

He stopped the recorder.

"I think we made some progress today, Doc," John said. "But sadly, this will have to be our last session."

15

PUZZLE PIECES

He reached Sarah later that afternoon and told her everything that had happened with Aeron and with John.

"Maybe the numbers aren't numbers at all," she said. "It could be code for something. G, H. Seven, eight—G, H. Does that ring a bell? Initials for anything? Or H, G?"

"I'll check it out. Maybe they belong to his parents or siblings. I was thinking a year, or a number of times something occurred. I'll look over my notes."

"Any progress with God?"

On his notepad, Dr. Milton wrote *78, 87, 87, 78, 78, 87,* over and over again. He looked at the paper taken from Aeron's wall. The number *87* was in the middle of the page. Flipping it over, *78*.

"I don't know, maybe. Any progress on your end?"

He looped figure-eights on one of the *8s* on his notepad. *Eternity*, he thought, and scribbled round and round.

"We put him on the missing persons list," she said. "No one's claimed him. He doesn't take the greatest picture, you know. Looks like a street bum."

Sarah started in about her day but was interrupted.

"I'll call you back," he said, and hung up before she could say goodbye. He stared at his doodles. He was getting somewhere but couldn't put his finger on it.

It had something to do with what Aeron had said in one of his earlier sessions. *Was it the last session or the one before?* He tried his hardest to remember as he went through Aeron's folder. He tried one of the tapes in the player. Searched, played …

searched, played. Finding nothing, he switched to a different tape.

As the second tape rewound, Dr. Milton looked at his note-pad, thinking of the numbers but also of John Doe.

There was a connection between the two patients.

As he searched Aeron's second tape in one hand, he readied a tape of John Doe in another player.

"Only one?" the player sounded.

Dr. Milton rewound further and stopped.

He held a player in each hand now, a therapy maestro: John in the left, Aeron in the right.

He started Aeron's third tape and remembered which session it was from, recalling nearly the entire conversation.

Aeron: "Red flowing down my arm. Man, I could feel it—hurt like a bitch!"

The sounds of fast-forwarding, and then a click.

Aeron: "—ver try killing yourself, Doctor?"

Dr. Milton: "No."

The room filled with fast-forwarding noises.

Click.

Dr. Milton: "You said you missed yourself *and* your reflec-tion. Whom were you trying to kill? You or your reflection?"

He was about to search further but let it play out, remem-bering what came next, what he was looking for.

Aeron: *"Pull up if I pull up."*

Dr. Milton: "What does that mean?"

A long pause, scratchy hums from the tape.

Aeron: "It's a palindrome."

Dr. Milton: "Yes it is. What does it mean to you, Aeron?"

He looked back at the numbers on his notepad, realizing that they could be considered a palindrome too if put side by side. That wasn't it, though. There was something deeper; it had something to do with this man who thought he was God.

After fruitless puzzling, he played John Doe's tape in his other hand. He could imagine John's little smirk as his voice sounded.

John: "No need to feel guilty, Doc. Some demons you—"

He fast-forwarded to about halfway through the session.

John: "… believing who I am. What' it going to take?"

A pause. He let it play out.

John: "Making a country disappear didn't get your vote. *Rise to vote, sir.* You ever find the Czech—"

Click.

Why voting? He rewound the tape a few seconds' worth and played it over again.

John: "—ote. *Rise to vote, sir.*"

Where have I heard that before?

He wrote it down next to the numbers.

The phrase, too, was a palindrome.

John had been playing with him.

Dr. Milton cued the tape further along in the session. It clicked and then played on.

John: "If it is only one number, I would have to say … 165."

Dr. Milton wrote the number down with the others, continued listening. He remembered John's smile at this point in the session.

Dr. Milton: "That's not the number, John."

John: "4,884?"

He wrote that number down as well, also a palindrome. He let the tape play to the end.

Dr. Milton: "Sorry, John."

John: "Are you sure?"

Dr. Milton: I am certain, John. I would have written it down beforehand, but you broke—"

At this point he had pieced it together. The puzzle was not yet finished, but key pieces had been placed. He had the corners, most of the borders. Now came the job of filling in the middle mess of scattered pieces that all looked alike.

He called Sarah back.

"What did you find?" she asked.

"Seventy-eight and eighty-seven."

"Okay …"

"One is the flipped version of the other. Add them together: 165, the same number John had guessed earlier."

"That's great, but it doesn't make much sense. Where are you going with this?"

"Do the same again. Add 165 to its reversed version, 561, and you get—" He summed the numbers on his notepad. "726. And do it again: 726 + 627, and you get 1,353."

A long sigh from Sarah.

"This is where it gets *weird*. Add 1,353 to its reverse, 3,531, and you get the second number John guessed: 4,884. It's a number palindrome, Sarah."

"Well, what is all that supposed to mean? I mean, it's cool and everything, interesting, but what do you think it means? Seems like you're finding clues left by a serial killer."

Dr. Milton's excitement plummeted, an empty-stomach feeling. "I have no idea," he said softly, realizing he was now more confused than ever.

16

NUMBERS

He spent his lunch break gnawing fingernails and inner cheek as he struggled with puzzle pieces that wouldn't fit without the aid of a ball-peen hammer. Dr. Milton sat at a desk piled with notepads and microcassettes, while pulling out what little hair he had left.

He was drawn to the numbers.

Drawn onward, another palindrome.

He could take any number it seemed, be it single, double, or even triple-digit, add it to its reverse, and if repeated recursively, he would eventually get a palindromic result. It intrigued him. Feeling a little addled by all the calculations, he gazed down at his notes:

1. $78 + 87 = 165$
    $165 + 561 = 726$
    $726 + 627 = 1353$
    $1353 + 3531 = 4884$

2. $94 + 49 = 143$
    $143 + 341 = 484$

3. $912 + 219 = 1231$
    $1231 + 1321 = 2552$

4. $325 + 523 = 848$

5. $4139 + 9314 = 90708$
$90708 + 80709 = 171417$
$171417 + 714171 = 885588$

Dr. Milton went through each of the tapes at least half a dozen times. Nothing he heard made sense of it all. He went through the written notes as well. Nothing.

Aeron, was he like the numbers, his reflection simply an inverse of himself? What, then, if they should meet?

John Doe knew something.

Aeron was fighting a demon inside.

Could it be Aeron's inverse self, Aeron's palindrome?

The questions flashed through his mind.

What would happen if his patient met the man in the mirror? What if Aeron's problem wasn't psychological at all, but deeper, darker than Dr. Milton could handle? Maybe he had multiple personalities or, worse, multiple souls. Maybe this was a fight Aeron needed to face alone. Perhaps there was nothing he could do.

And what to make of John—a man who truly believed he was God? A man who thought he could make countries vanish from all thought and memory, and then reappear.

Was it a psychological problem with this one?

The absurd thought of John actually being God *had* crossed his mind, but only briefly. John could be convincing, but he was just a man with a mental disorder.

He would not give up on either patient. The entire expanding universe was intelligible, and its every equation ultimately solvable. The equal sign never budged and could always be found, as well as the variables, the X, Y, and Zs of the equation.

Like any mathematician worth his salt, he was determined to

find that variable, break or wound or trauma in life that caused or fed the problems that triggered the mental disorder. He had a feeling John Doe's condition sparked from incidents, or *an* incident from long ago.

The incident could be physical, sexual, or purely psychological. It may not have been a spark at all that started his condition, but years of slow, smoldering abuse.

If he could just find that one special piece hidden in John that made him who he was; the one piece that made him think he was God almighty, then Dr. Milton could press that button—with the patient's help, of course—and find a way to help John heal himself.

He was handed the missing piece at a quarter to six that night as he made his way to the hospital downtown to check on Aeron, in the form of a call from Sarah, which nearly made him smack into the back of a Lincoln Continental as he grabbed for the phone that had slipped to the floorboard. He pulled it up by the charging cord.

A bumper sticker by the left taillight read JESUS LOVES YOU. EVERYONE ELSE THINKS YOU'RE AN ASSHOLE.

After fumbling with the phone, he flipped it open to answer a call from Sarah.

"I've got something you want," she said.

"Excedrin?"

"No, but it's good news. Are you sitting down?"

"I would sure hope so. I'm driving."

"A young woman came in to the station claiming she knows our John Doe."

17

THE MISSING PIECE

Her name was Julie.

And John really was a John—a crazy uncle of hers by the name of John Hinclan, who had disappeared some two years ago and had magically reappeared on a missing persons list posted downtown at the Home Depot where she worked. She had called the station the moment she saw it, and agreed to come down.

Dr. Milton would meet Sarah and this Julie at the station in the next hour, right after he checked in with Aeron at the hospital.

He had to wait in the lobby, and then in the reception area, and again in the waiting room—to see a patient who was *his* in the first place. After all that, Aeron didn't want to see him.

He left the hospital around the time he was supposed to meet Sarah and the young woman. He called Sarah to keep Julie at the station until he got there. She possibly held the key to the riddle.

Sarah told him she had not yet shown, so he offered to make a coffee run—he could use the caffeine. He pulled in to Starbucks and ordered three coffees. Four cars were ahead of him in the drive-through, but he waited it out.

He put two of the drinks in the cup holders and nestled the third between his legs. The cup at his crotch made him nervous, so he moved it out a little, toward his knees.

As he pulled in to the station, a kid on a bike nearly caught his right front fender, forcing him to brake. Hot coffee sloshed on his thighs, making him cry out, and gradually wicked up his trousers to his crotch—no longer hot enough to scald him, but it appeared as if he had wet his pants with black coffee.

He swore through the closed window, shaking a fist as the kid pedaled away. He was a small boy, hat turned backward, and he looked familiar in a way—maybe from church. And then it hit him: this was the kid John told him about—the kid he "almost hit." *How could John have even known? How could I even be seeing—*

The kid was nowhere to be found.

Had he slammed on his brakes for a delusion?

He parked at the station and brought the surviving coffees inside, still shaking at his pants, thankful that they were at least dark. He gave one to Sarah, the other to the young woman who must be Julie, sitting across from her.

They both saw his pants and grinned.

A small girl about three years old sat beside Julie, swinging her feet above the floor.

"And this is my husband, Dr. Milton. He likes his coffee with, well, his pants."

Julie held out a hand.

"Nice to meet you."

Milton shook it after wiping his hand on his shirt.

"Yes—uh, delighted," he said.

She displayed her midriff like a piece of art, with the tattoo of a dragon inked on her waistline. She looked like a troubled teenager who had been through a lot.

Sarah's frown told him he was unconsciously ogling.

"And this is my little Hannah," Julie said.

The younger version of Julie hid behind her mother.

"Say hello to the doctor, Hannah."

Julie must have been in her late teens when she had her,

now facing the responsibilities of motherhood, a single parent, juggling babysitters while she worked one, maybe two jobs to provide for her daughter.

You could tell Hannah meant the world to her.

"Hello, Hannah," Dr. Milton said, offering a smile.

"Dr. Milton's working with John in the ward," Sarah explained.

"Yes," he said. "What can you tell me about him?"

"Well, besides the fact that he's finally in a place he belongs, he is a complete bag of nuts. He's my uncle, a *very* long lost uncle. I've only met him a few times, but once I saw his picture, I knew it was him. Looks like a homeless Jesus. The little moles below his left eye gave him away, though. They make an upside-down triangle."

Dr. Milton hadn't noticed the marks, and wondered if he really had the "bag of nuts" Julie was talking about.

Sarah joined in, saying, "Julie was telling me about her parents. They died when she was young. She doesn't have any relatives that she knows of, besides John."

"A long while back," Julie said, "I spent some time at a church doing genealogy to find out more about my family. The folks I'm staying with now pointed me there. They put up with my hectic life and treat me like I'm family. I only came up with one name on my father's side, and that was his brother, John. The rest of my family tree must be burned down or something, 'cause that was all I could find on my father's side. My mother's side, well, her maiden name's Smith, so you can probably guess how that's going."

"I see," Dr. Milton said, although he didn't.

"I found out where John last lived. And he was evicted, hadn't paid rent for a couple months. The landlord said he was a weird guy. Always preaching about salvation and stuff from the Bible."

Dr. Milton's pager beeped.

"He said I should look in Seattle, in the bad parts of town, to ask around. A few days later I saw him walking the streets. My only known relative and he's homeless, barefoot, crazy, preaching about the end of the world. I introduced myself as Julie. He tells me he's *God*. How weird is that?"

Dr. Milton had experienced *weird* over the last few days.

"You said you met him a *few* times in the past?"

"I gave him money once, first time I met him. Bought him McDonald's. I'm not making much working the few hours they give me at HD." She blushed and said, "Pays most of my bills, though, keeps food on the plate for Hannah. I'm hoping for more hours. And I've been cutting down on other bad habits."

"We all have our habits," Sarah told her.

Dr. Milton checked his pager after it beeped a second time. It was a 911 page from the ward.

"What now?"

"The hospital?" Sarah asked.

"No, the psych ward."

He looked at the message again and scrolled down to the next line of text: GOD MISSING AGAIN. He scrolled further: LEFT ANOTHER NOTE. The last line read ON VACATION.

God.

While Dr. Milton called in, Sarah told Julie about the last time they found a note from John—how they both had gone there, searched, and later found him sleeping peacefully behind his couch, curled in a fetal position.

He closed the phone, told them the news.

John was missing.

"If it ends up being something," Sarah said, "give me a call."

Sarah, Julie, and little Hannah remained at the station, chatting and coloring beautiful pictures of a utopian life, and of dreams not so far from reach.

18

GONE

The security system showed no signs of John going to or from his room. Not one patient had come downstairs to the front reception desk, so who could have placed the note?

John left it on the reception monitor:

ON VACATION – GOD

No one had seen him since Dr. Milton left for the night.

The security camera labeled *Hallway B, Second Floor* had revealed nothing but the dark sliver of cracked doorway of room 202.

Dr. Milton shook off the déjà vu and forced himself upstairs to look behind the couch where they'd found him the first time. That is where he found John Hinclan, curled up, smiling peacefully. He didn't need to bend down to his patient to determine he wasn't breathing.

He was gone.

inside/ outside

draw putrid dirt upward / lived as a devil

[the pact]

1

THE BLACK / THE WHITE

Ray Duschenne grew up in abuse, and often watched his mother take a beating from his father; Ray was not above giving out a little rough treatment to his peers, either. And this wasn't *nouveau* "child abuse" kids got these days, like spankings, insults, or arm tugs. Ray dealt out the real thing—abuse parents lost children over.

They were punks: Steven, Michael, Richard and Allie. Even Billy, the youngest, needed lessons now and then.

Richard, who he often called dickhead, was his worst rival. Ray had nicknamed most of the gang. He called Steven a skinny queer-boy because everyone in the eighth grade knew he was a homosexual and would grow up to be like his queer dad. Michael, in thick-rimmed glasses, carried around books wherever he went and spent recesses with his nose buried in them. One day he might grow up to be the founder of some business and make billions, but not if his fingers were broken enough times beforehand. Allie, she was cute, yet she hung out with the rest of them, so she was a punk by association. And then Billy, the follower of the bunch—a regular Bobby fuckin' Brady. He was years younger and not yet in the sixth grade, making him the easiest to pick on. He threatened to tell his father sometimes and cried. He was nothing like Richard, the group leader, if they had one, the one who decided what they'd do, what they'd eat, for how long. He sometimes stood up for his friends and took the brunt of his punishments. That's what Ray called it: punishments.

Ray Duschenne thought of these kids and the ways he'd

deal with them next the moment he woke up, came to, or whatever it was that happened when his eyes opened. He thought he
was dreaming at first, but feeling his eyelids with the tips of his
fingers, he knew they were open. It was as black as black could
get. The only thing not black was the starry fuzziness behind his
eyes. Waving hands in front of them, he saw nothing.

His first thought was that he had gone blind.

Ray was on his back and fully clothed, as he could feel with
the palms of his hands, and numb in the head. His head hurt
the most, as though he had been whacked hard with a blunt
object. The back of his head throbbed, giving him the notion
his scalp was bleeding profusely. He felt around and licked his
fingertips—no blood, just a killer headache, the type he would
get from incurring his father's wrath—grabbed by the hair,
thumped on the head, or worse.

He had seen his mother take a good number of thwacks to
the head. And then there was the belt. Every so often Ray would
be in a heap of trouble severe enough to merit the belt. Curs-
ing—that would do it—or getting caught bullying his mother
around. Once it was for threatening to call the police to take his
father away. His father hadn't taken the threat too kindly and
brought out the belt. It was brown leather, the kind that didn't
leave marks unless there was contact with the buckle—but then,
there generally was.

His dad might beat him blind someday.

Am I blind?

He could tell by the silence that he was in a place where
sound could not escape. He screamed, hands beating the soft
surface above, until his throat was dry.

A close softness eight inches above. He pushed against as
hard as he could—a silky, plush material slipping around and

through his fingers. Wood behind it.

"Help, someone help me! Help!"

Ray was soaked in sweat.

Panic seeped in as he pushed against the enclosing walls with his knees, elbows, hips—everything he had.

Claustrophobic thoughts assailed him: collapsing mines, caves closing in, rooms shrinking, ceilings falling, elevators crumpling. Ray wasn't a claustrophobe, but quickly became one, given the circumstances. Fatigue moved through his joints; they hurt the way his wrist sometimes did after hours of homework, or after finishing a comprehension essay with those stupid number 2 pencils. *Ticonderoga.*

He remembered the tip breaking one time in class and how he screeched his chair back and had to walk in front of gawking classmates to the sharpener. At times like that, he'd take out frustration on Michael by shoving his books to the ground or even ripping out pages, or maybe he would go after queerboy Steven, who he sometimes called "Step-on." He would pull down Steven's pants so the other kids could laugh and point at his Transformer briefs with the blue Decepticon logo on the crotch. Better yet, he'd pull those down as well so the kids could laugh and point at his little pecker. Billy, he'd just run off, hide, cry like a baby. Richard might stand up to Ray at first—it was possible, but he'd have to eat a mouthful of dirt while his goody-goody girlfriend watched.

But Ray couldn't dwell on these thoughts. His mind was busy with ghosts and skeletons and bloody, oozing corpses, for he had finally realized what contained him.

A coffin.

A skeletal hand under his own.

Sweat dripped from his forehead and hair as he banged

against the lid. He swayed from side to side, hoping to tip it over, maybe break it in two. He felt the bony hand for a moment more before realizing it wasn't decayed skin over bristly bones, but metal support rods under silken material and padding.

Ray sunk into hysteria, thinking of his father.

It was a few weeks ago, the day he had brawled with Richard Nelson over a small incident in Canford Park. Ray thought it was small enough. He had been strolling through the park, not looking for trouble, when he happened upon Richard, alone at their hangout, which was nothing more than a curvy creek bend and an oak tree set deep in the park. Ray visited the hangout sometimes to poke fun and push them around—simple fun.

"What's up, dick?"

Richard had pretended not to hear, the way Ray ignored his mother when she wanted him for chores. Richard was collecting river rocks for a creek dam that he and his friends were planning to build, piling them near the water's edge.

"I'm talking to *you*, littledick, littledick, Richie has a tiny prick."

He started for the pyramidal stack of rocks.

Richard had his back to him, crouched on the ground.

Ray mocked in a whisper as he approached, "Here, dick-dick-dick-dick-dick; here, dick—"

"My name is Richard, and that's what you can call me."

"Fine, Richie-Ditchie."

It didn't quite work as an insult, but it would do. Ray flicked the backs of Richard's ears, hard.

"What are you building, a sanctuary for you and your boyfriend Stephanie to mess around in?"

Richard's face grew redder.

"It's none of your damn business what I'm doing, Ray*mona*. I have a girlfriend. And Steven's not a homo. His dad, maybe, but *he's* not. And what would it matter anyway?"

Ray smiled.

"Little dick and little Allie Hart, holding hands. Isn't that sweet?" He then waxed poetic about them sitting in a tree …

"Leave me *alone*," Richard said.

He and Allie had been 'going together' for three weeks, which meant they held hands when they walked down the halls. Ray had teased him every one of those twenty-one days, it seemed.

"And leave this place alone. This is *our* hangout, not yours. It's none of your business."

"So you wouldn't mind if I knocked over some of your business, then," Ray said, and kicked at the piles of river rock until they were no longer piles.

Ray picked up a round, heavy rock and threw it at the tree house he and his friends had started constructing in the oak tree. Hitting one of the wooden steps, it made a loud crack as the weathered board broke in two. One piece dangled briefly and fell to the ground.

That's when the brawl began.

Ray, older and bigger of the two, had come home with a black eye. Richard left with two black eyes, a swollen lower lip and a bloody nose. Ray left him crying and whimpering in the cold creek as he tossed a few rocks from the demolished piles to splash water into the crybaby's face.

Richard had deserved it, though—he *and* the others.

They deserved it because Ray got a beating when he got home. Later that day, Ray's father, dressed in military garb, took one look at him before the belt came off and the lashings started. He was beaten for getting into a fight, and was beaten more for wasting the cold cut his mother would later use on his eye.

Ray added temper to the flux of fear, fatigue, and the lurking fear of never escaping his current condition. He pushed the coffin's ceiling to no avail, contemplating premature burial.

What if I'm really buried? Not just stuck somewhere in a coffin, but actually buried six feet under the earth, with a mound of fresh dirt and clean, green artificial grass. Would Mom be weeping on the surface for her buried young boy?

"I'm not dead."

He repeated this phrase a dozen times until the crying made it impossible. Tears rolled down his already wet cheeks as he cried in a tantrum, scared and enraged.

Why would they think I'm dead?

A conundrum he wasn't yet ready to solve.

Why would they bury me?

Six feet of fill-dirt above his body.

It explained why he was unable to burst open the coffin's door. There had to be a hundred pounds of earth holding it down.

Was it possible to tunnel through so much dirt, or would his escape route cave into itself? How much air? An hour's worth?

No one could hear his voice. No one would guess there was a ghost of a chance he was alive, because of the burial.

But Ray wouldn't give up; he couldn't afford to. He needed to clear his mind, calm his shakiness, and then he'd try to escape. And he would have to be fast.

Whether he was done crying or simply out of tears, he couldn't be certain, but at least he was starting to calm. He thought of happier things—things, at any rate, his distorted mind could perceive as happy.

Another memory surfaced.

He recalled a confrontation with Allie Hart during the school year, before she and Richard were a pair. Ray had to admit she was cute—which is why he had tried kissing her.

He had been sent from class for back-talking his social science teacher, Mrs. Felder. In his hand was a note to see the principal—a crumpled ball in a tight fist slamming against lockers. He got a kick out of the noise.

He found Allie at the water fountain. One arm held her long brown hair behind her head; the other pressed the button on the fountain. She was three years younger than Ray and two grades lower, but he had a crush. He admired her innocence and liked the way she held her hair back. Maybe it was only developing hormones. They made him do strange and stupid things—perverted for a fourteen-year-old—things that made him feel complicated, such as talking dirty around his friends, playing pocket pool, or ogling over pictures of women in *National Geographic*.

"Cutting class, Allie?"

He leaned an elbow on the cold porcelain surface of the water fountain.

"Buzz off, creep," she said, and turned away.

Ray blocked her path.

"What are you up to?"

Allie's skinny body worked its way to the left and to the

right, at last settling in the middle when it could find no way around him.

He had matched her moves in perfect unison.

"I need to get back to class, Raymond."

She tried moving past, ducking, but failed. She looked to the room she had come from, avoiding eye contact.

"Call me Ray."

"Fine, *Ray*, I need to get back to class. *Really*."

What came next was unplanned; it just happened.

He grabbed her by a lock of soft straight hair and pulled her face to his—the way actors and actresses dramatically kissed in movies, the only way he had imagined kisses to be.

Their lips touched and he felt mostly upper lip and under-nose before Allie stomped on his toes.

"Get off me, you creep!"

Her words crushed his heart.

If the vice principal hadn't walked around the corner just then, he may have held her against the lockers for a while to feel her up.

He wanted to punch her in the gut.

"You two. My office. Right now."

He pointed a finger at the ceiling; he was serious.

"But—" Ray had started to say.

"Both of you. Now."

He waggled that same finger between the two of them.

They both followed him to his office. When he was asked what had happened, Ray lied about Allie splashing water in his face, and so on ... but it hadn't worked. The vice principal saw through his story. Allie told him the truth, which got Ray a three-day suspension, a result he later regretted when his father left marks.

Ray learned a lesson that day: actions speak louder than words; words had got him nothing from sweet little Allie, but actions had gotten him his first kiss.

Ray smiled as he lay on his back, his sweat-soaked shirt and pants stuck to his skin. He breathed more heavily, whether from lack of air or the earlier bout of sobbing. After gathering his strength and mustering the will to perform the task ahead, Ray made ready for his escape.

The execution had to be flawless the first time—his *only* time. He reached deep into his pockets and retrieved his cigarette lighter. At fourteen, Ray was a two-year smoking veteran, up to half a pack a day—sometimes only a pack a week if he couldn't snag a pack at the drugstore when no one was watching. He flicked a flame and the coffin's interior lit up—a morbid sight.

Shadows danced between illuminated satin ripples of the coffin walls. He half expected to see the body he had fantasized lying with him, but there was no such thing.

The lighter moved back and forth to reveal what one would expect to see inside a coffin. What he hadn't expected was his clothing. He had assumed he'd be wearing funeral garb, and couldn't imagine why he would still be in his jeans, pocketed T-shirt, and sneakers. He didn't give it another thought and held the lighter up to the satin material. Bits of charred fabric fell, singing his arms. His thumb burned and blistered.

After creating a hole in the fabric large enough for two fingers, he turned off the lighter and put his scorched fingers in his mouth.

In complete darkness, Ray reached his bony fingers to the

hole and pulled apart the material. It ripped jaggedly and took effort, like when he had ripped Steven's shirt. He pulled until the entire top half of the ceiling was bare.

Flicking on the lighter a second time, Ray inspected the wood until holding the lighter became unbearable.

Breaking through would be impossible.

His only chance was to break the hinges, squeeze out.

Was there a latch? Was it physically possible to open the lid under six feet of dirt?

Ray's body shook uncontrollably. He wished for his father to save him, or beat him first and *then* save him. His lungs hurt from crying, and his breathing slowed as the dank air thickened with carbon dioxide.

The lighter flicked on as Ray attempted the impossible task of burning the thick oak above. The light finish bubbled as polish burned and blackened in small rings of soot. Smoke quickly filled the coffin, making the air even harder to breathe. He coughed and it made him think of his grandmother's emphysema—a smoker's cough, something he may never grow old enough to experience.

With smoke building and the flame feasting on what little oxygen remained, Ray hoped the earth above was still wet, muddy, and easy to swim through.

He tried to keep his mind occupied.

His thoughts moved Michael Farley and Billy Jones, the smallest of the bunch. It was a rainy day, one of what seemed like three hundred or so days it rained in western Washington—the fifth of July, primetime for leftover fireworks from the holiday season.

Most of the explosives were spent the day before, but Ray kept some for the rest of summer, like Pops, the white, sperm-looking things one threw on the ground for a quick bang, spinning flowers that changed from red to orange to greenish-blue, colored smoke bombs and, last but not least, whistlers, which were great for mailboxes or doorsteps late at night.

They weren't really whistlers when he was through with them, not the high-pitched Piccolo Petes they were originally designed to be. Modified slightly, with help from a few pyromaniac sites, his Piccolo Petes, or 'P-bombs,' as he like to call them, were wrapped in layers of duct tape. He'd remove the blue base and pinch the bottom of each cylinder with a pair of pliers, then break the remaining contents until powdery inside. The result: *BOOM!* Throw and run, in other words.

If only he had a P-bomb with him on the day he stumbled on Michael, with his fish-eye glasses and sidekick wonder twin, Billy. They sat in their tree fort nailing shards of two-by-fours and wood scraps to the giant oak. It was amazing the fort had made it so many years without falling to pieces.

A glance toward the creek just beyond the tree—dam not yet complete—verified the boys' vulnerability.

They hadn't seen him approach, and this made it better. While Billy held a board and Michael pounded a nail into it with both hands gripping the hammer, Ray pulled a pink flower from his pocket. He lit the fuse with the tip of the cigarette hanging from his mouth, and cocked an arm back, threw the flower through the cutout window of the fort. His timing couldn't have been more perfect.

Just as it hit the far wall, the flower bloomed to life.

Shhüisszz, üzzz, üzzz.

It hummed as it bounced fiercely against the interior walls.

Ray imagined the flower's cycle as it buzzed: a flash of white before a steady red *shizzz* turning to a yellowish-orange *iizzz* bouncing *iizz* and going from yellowish-orange to a greenish-blue, *iizzzz, zzz, zz, z* and stopping, leaving dark burn marks on the walls. Michael Farley and tattle-tale Billy Jones clung to each other in the corner like scared lovers, holding on for dear life while a war took place at their feet.

"Stop! Stop it!" cried Billy, scrunched into the corner and holding his knees to his chin.

Michael had left their embrace and looked over the side.

"That one came really close to hitting us."

His mother-combed black hair lay neatly parted to one side as he readjusted his glasses.

"Did Mommy's boy almost get burn-ded?"

Ray grabbed for more fireworks in his pocket. He then asked a question neither of the boys had expected:

"Have you and your friend ever been to Yellowstone?"

Michael looked at him questioningly and answered yes.

Billy was still in the corner, crying.

"Why?"

Ray pulled from his pocket a handful of smoke bombs: yellow, blue, and purple.

"Then you know what these smell like."

"They smell like *you* when you fart," Michael said.

Ray turned to the creek and the not-yet-finished dam. He lit the purple smoke bomb with his cigarette and tossed it in the water.

Probably thinking it would explode and destroy their project, Michael said, "Why do you have to break everything? Can't you just—"

Michael's raving was interrupted by the sight of bright

purple smoke billowing from under the water.

"Whoa, cool," he said.

It brought Billy up from his crying.

They both watched as a violet cloud spread along the surface of the water from the little ball nestled at the base of the dam. The smoking ceased, and purple water filtered through and over the top.

"Do it again," Billy said eagerly.

"You got it," Ray said, and lit the others.

Ray smiled and threw them into the fort.

They ducked out of the way, but both smoke bombs landed at their feet. There was a small hiss as yellow and blue smoke filled the fort.

Michael had tried throwing one of them out, but it probably burned his fingers.

The two hunkered down as heavy green smoke filled the cabin. They coughed and eventually hung their heads out the window and away from the sulfurous stench.

Later that night, Ray's parents got a call from both Michael's and Billy's parents. His dad was drunk and that was a good thing—Ray never received punishment. "Boys will be boys," he'd said. And if they didn't understand that, they could bend over.

This got another smile out of Ray, despite the lighter going out. He had managed a charred six-inch burn that resembled a black pie plate. Both thumbs now scorched, Ray gave the lighter a break. He scraped a quarter-inch chunk from the burned portion, where the flame had been hottest, and charcoal powder filled the gaps under his fingernails. Even if he could scrape an inch into the wood, he still had a hell of a long way to go, and there was no way the lighter would last that long.

Fire breathed oxygen, and for every second he used the lighter, another breath of air was sacrificed. His breathing grew heavier in the coffin, smoke filling his lungs.

He was going to die.

There was nothing he could do.

The grim reaper on his way to lop off his head.

Ray let out another banshee cry and then another, the air so thick, so hard to breathe.

Breathing through a trembling hand holding his nose, Ray searched deep in his pockets. He knew he had one somewhere, reaching past the stick of gum, a melted chocolate bar, a quarter ... and finally the object that might get him out of here. It would only work if he hadn't been buried yet and was merely awaiting burial.

From his pocket he pulled an unmodified Piccolo Pete.

Thank God I hadn't pinched it yet.

The firework was wet from sweat, but it would work. His plan was to call attention to the hopefully unburied coffin, to let someone outside know he was still alive.

He imagined himself in a funeral session, pictured the faces of grieving family members. A scene straight from a horror movie: "Our dearly beloved," a priest would say, or the like, "we are gathered here today to mourn for a boy, our friend, our son, and a well-loved member of the Brenden community. Like many, he was taken from our world in a time so—"

Screeeeeee! the sound would echo through the chapel, giving sudden chills to some, heart attacks to others; then, when everyone realized this had all been a mistake, Ray would be rescued.

What if I'm in a mortuary?

A mortician would hear the noise and make the discovery then. It was worth a shot anyway, unless he was buried six feet under.

Before giving it a go, he thought of one last muse.

Stephanie Johnson was one of the many names he gave to Steven. He wore jeans that were one size too small, supplemented by pink shirts, purple shirts, yellow shirts, or those polo shirts with the cat stitching on the pocket. Even his haircut looked gay: a clipped-by-mom bowl-cut. Like a Portobello mushroom. He carried a pocket day planner wherever he went, attempting professionalism in a child's world, wore penny loafers with copper pennies actually stuffed into the flaps above the toes.

"Hey, girlfriend," Ray teased.

Ray had followed him into the boys' restroom, banging the door open as he entered.

Steven back-stepped into a hand dryer mounted on the wall. The back of his head hit the stainless steel tube. Steven's eyes squinted shut, enough to form wrinkles around his eye sockets.

"Please, don't do anything."

It appeared as if he were smiling, the corners of his mouth coming to visit the corners of his eyes in fear.

Ray's smile was real enough.

Homophobia had kept him from doing anything *too* serious to Steven/Stephanie.

Gays were contagious; that's what his father had said.

Steven shrank against the wall like folded paper.

"My parents … they know *your* parents, and they'd get you in a heap of trouble if you do anything to me."

"What, from church or something?" Ray said.

"You guys sit in the back. Me and my mom and my dad always sit in the front, so you probably see us all the time."

Steven's eyes were slivers. He held onto the dryer for dear life while his loafers slid on the floor.

A yellow fold-up sign at his feet read: CAUTION / WET FLOOR and then PISO MOJADO. It showed a stick figure slipping wildly on the floor and cracking his neck, the same stick-figure character seen at pools, diving into the shallow end. Funny more than threatening.

"My dad, he'd talk to your parents. My dad—"

"Your dad is Ned Fuckin' Flanders, Stephanie. The only thing your daddy can do is other people's daddies."

Ray held him by his lavender polo shirt, splitting

(a sound identical to the coffin's silky interior ripping).

at the seams.

"He's a fruitcake. He sits down to pee. A sword swallower like his little protégé," Ray said.

Steven slipped down the tiled wall. His knees buckled into sharp peaks when his butt hit the floor.

Then the bathroom door opened. Whoever it was turned right back around where he came from.

"Must have thought it was the girl's room with *you* in here." Sometimes he could really make himself bust a gut.

Steven whimpered.

Ray pointed to the sign and forced Steven's chin away from his chest so he could see.

"You ever have a *Piss-o Majiado?*" Ray asked.

"It means 'wet floor,' you stupid moron," Steven said. "It says so right above the Spanish part."

There was pride in his eyes, but only for a moment.

Ray kicked the plastic sign; it folded onto itself and slapped the recently polished floor.

"Wrong. 'Piss-o' means *piss*; 'majiado' means *flush*."

Ray lifted Steven to his feet. He had fight in him, but only as much a girl his age would have. He grabbed Steven's wrists in a tight grip and pulled him to the nearest stall.

Steven planted his legs and slid as he was dragged.

The first stall was locked with no one in it, so Ray slid the boy to the next, and then to the next; he paused at each one to glance in the bowl and also to use the stall frames for leverage. He finally maneuvered Steven's dead weight into the last stall. He looked into the bowl after lifting its lid, one hand holding Steven's wrists, and was disappointed not to find floaters—only a mellow yellow.

Ray pulled and pushed, shoving the gaunt little pervert into the stall. With much effort, Ray held Steven's wrists behind his back with one hand, the back of his neck with the other, and forced his head to the rim.

Just when the tips of Steven's hair made contact with the lemon-tinted liquid in the bowl, the bathroom door swung open again. Heavy footsteps worked across the floor, followed by lighter ones.

Ray let go of Steven and was soon alone in the stall. He heard the door flap open as Steven ran out. The door creaked to a stop.

"What are you boys up to in here?"

A familiar voice.

Ray peeked out of the stall and saw Mr. Spiegman, the janitor. Billy's stepfather. Everyone had teased Billy for having a janitor dad, especially Ray.

Mr. Spiegman had a mop and a bucket with him and started

on the bathroom floor. He smelled like urinals and was missing teeth.

Richard Nelson stood behind him.

The janitor fixed the fallen yellow sign and mopped.

"You better not be causing any troubles."

"No, sir," Ray said. "Just doing my business."

Each breath became a giant heave-in, heave-out effort that required concentration. His body no longer perspired, not a good thing. Dry sweat coated his skin. His eyelids weighed two tons each and wanted to close.

Sleep tried its hardest to take over, but Ray knew it would be a forever sleep, the *long* sleep. For a moment he forgot all about his plan to get out of the coffin. Every joint and muscle ached.

No one can hear me anyway, so what's the point?

Maybe I'm dead already.

It was the first time he'd considered it. Maybe everyone went through such a thing after dying. Some sort of purgatory. Maybe a soul stays trapped in its body after dying.

Ray took a heavy breath, exhaled slowly, and flicked the lighter. It sparked, but with it came no flame. He tried again, and then again, and then again and again and again, and just then there appeared a small flame at the lighter's tip. He stared at it, amazed by its yellow essence, mesmerized by the way its light made shadows dance inside the coffin like phantoms—shadowy creatures come to whisk away his soul.

Breaking the enchantment of the flame, Ray lit the wick of his last Piccolo Pete. Sparks hopped as it burned. The strobe effect made his movements and shadows seem slower. A jagged, interrupted view of his hand placing the firework at his side made him think of a scene from one of those *Alien* movies. He remembered lights flickering white/black/white/black, and how it made the same strobe effect as the alien put its face to the woman, reaching out with first a mouth, and then a mouth from within that mouth.

And then he screamed, for contained in one of those strobe flickers, he saw a face. And then it was gone. And then back again, flickering. A dead man's gaping jaw with a mouth cut open from ear to ear in an impossibly wide smile. Blood gushed from the nose and mouth and carved-out eyes.

It was at this point that the high-pitched shriek of the sparking blue cylinder harmonized with his insane cries.

2

THE RED WAGON / ALLIE

Allie Hart came home violated. It was only a kiss, but it had been forced on her, the way her parents forced Sunday school on her every week of every month of every year as far back as she could remember. This time it had been a kiss. What next? One day he might rape or molest or even kill someone.

She'd help out with Richard's idea. It was the only surefire way of stopping Ray Duschenne from becoming a monster. Richard was the idea man; that's why she liked him. He stood up to people like Ray. Allie liked everything about him. Sometimes she'd stay up late and write her name with his last in different ways: *Allie Nelson, Allie A. Nelson, Allie Alain Nelson.* They held hands between classes and at recess and lunch. He carried her books and she would look dreamily into his eyes.

She planned to spend most of her summer break with Richard Nelson and her other friends at the park on weekends and after school. They had planned the ordeal weeks ago. Once summer break came, the five of them devoted their time to finishing the clubhous—*tree fort* to the boys—in the giant oak at the back of the park. Next to this tree was a small creek with barely enough water to keep it running—never more than a foot across after it rained. They would build a small dam from boards and river rock and create a swimming hole.

Replacement steps had been nailed to the trunk of the oak, and two-by-fours nailed to its limbs as a frame for the walls, but both the resources and time to build such a thing were hard to come by.

From time to time, Allie gathered scraps of usable wood

from behind the shed in her backyard and carted them to the park in her red wagon. It was her younger sister's wagon, really, but Molly only used it to stroll around with dolls and stuffed animals. It was one of those Radio Flyer wagons with black rubber wheels and a glossy red shine that never dulled. It had a black handle as long as the wagon, which turned on a pivot.

The day Allie left the little red wagon at the park was the same day she had made two arduous trips with loads that kept toppling over and spilling onto the street. The loads she took reminded her of her dad when he would take loads to the dump in his beat-up truck, piled high with trash and yard clippings.

Allie organized the pieces into neat piles in a clearing behind the oak that would eventually become their playhouse. Some wood was already there—scraps of flat wood and particleboard. They had two sheets of drywall with broken, jagged edges, which Billy and his friend Matty brought. Allie propped the sections against their sides to make a white canopy. She put the coffee can of rusty nails under it as well. Somewhere in the vicinity was a hammer; her dad was probably looking for it.

The fort was mostly out of sight.

Allie looked from the clearing to the squiggly racing branches of the oak and imagined what the playhouse might look like. The boys kept calling it a fort, but to her it was a playhouse. She pictured a dollhouse, high in the tree, with sturdy walls and open windows to let in the sunshine. Maybe they could plant flowers: snapdragons or daffodils, preferably.

The pond will have to come first, she thought, and decided she'd run it by Richard. It was going to be one hot summer.

It wasn't the same sort of hot as on summer trips to California, where temperatures stayed in the dry triple digits, but more like a humid hot that left you feeling sticky. She was looking forward to staying cool with the pond, and kissing Richard in the playhouse, a moment that would now forever *not* be her first kiss.

Allie took a nail from the red Folgers can after brushing away a spider web. She used it to carve AH into the bark, added RN below it, and scratched a heart around them both. Smiling, she threw the nail over her shoulder and kissed the tree and its proclamation.

The wagon stayed behind the oak tree for the next few weeks, untouched, waiting to be rolled out one last time during summer break. It was Richard's idea to keep it there while they constructed their fort/playhouse, and she would later understand why.

As she walked home from the park, she kept replaying the incident with Rayomnd It was her first kiss from a boy. First kisses weren't supposed to be forced onto you by some creep. First kisses were supposed to be magical with hearts pounding, stomachs churning, arms and legs trembling. Little girls lived their entire childhoods waiting for that first kiss, and Ray had taken it away from her. It made her sick.

When she got home, her dad was pulling into the driveway. He smiled and waved, but Allie only held her stomach with her head down as she made her way into the house.

"Allie?" her mother called. "Dinner's about ready."

Sure enough, it was ready and waiting as Allie walked into the dining room. Her two sisters giggled and poked at each other with forks. Each held a paper doll in their opposite hand.

Her mother walked in from the kitchen carrying a hot dish. Like clockwork, her father appeared through the door to the garage and set his briefcase and keys down before joining them at the table.

"How is everyone?" he asked to no one in particular.

No one said a word at first, and then her mother said, "The school called today."

Allie started to cry.

3

THE BED SHEETS / STEVEN

Steven Johnson was too old to be wetting the bed and felt shame the moment he woke in that warm wetness.

He dreamt of playing with one of those octopus-like sprinklers with tentacles flying around and spraying water in all directions. He had danced around the yard in the middle of the fun, with his own hose adding to the spray of water.

It took a while before Steven realized what he was doing. *You're pissing the bed again. Wake up. You're not in the backyard, get up, it's not three in the afternoon, it's morning, wake up, get up and go to the bathroom to finish what you've started*—but it was already too late.

There was no water-spouting octopus in the yard; his dad had thrown it out after killing it with the lawn-mower.

Only a dribble was left in his bladder.

When would he get over it?

When would he ever wake up in dry underwear?

These questions beat relentlessly into his mind most mornings, no solutions in sight. But then he realized it was the first day of summer break, the end of seventh grade.

Steven peeled the sticky briefs from his skin, dropped them onto the middle of the bed. He dried himself with a pair of socks from the floor and threw them onto the bed as well, then grabbed the wrinkled corners of the darkened bed sheets and made a pile with a ball of clothing in the middle. He stuffed it into the hamper, a length of sheet hanging out of it like a dog's tongue.

Steven called his friend Richard Nelson after a shower.

It was a quick call—only a few words exchanged over the

line, mostly in fragments.

Richard: Hello?

Steven: Hi, is Richard—

Richard: Hey, Steven.

Steven: I didn't know it was you at first.

Richard: You coming to the park today?

Steven: I still have to ask.

Richard: Go ask.

Steven: Okay, hold on a second.

"Hey, Mom?" Steven asked, covering the receiver.

She was in the kitchen.

"Yes, Steven?"

"We're going to the park to work on the fort. Can I go?"

Steven chanted *please, please, please, please, please.*

A moment later her ever-joyous voice answered, "Yes, sweetie, just be home before dinnertime."

Steven: She said yes.

Richard: We might be out later than dinnertime.

Steven: Okay, hold on.

He reaffixed his palm to the receiver.

"Allie and Billy are bringing hot dogs. Can I stay late?"

"I don't know."

"*Please.*"

It sounded more like 'police.' He nearly promised to do some chores, but the chanting must have worked.

"I guess so," she said with disappointment. "Don't be out *too* late, and *no* fires. If you guys are having hot dogs, they either need to be cold or already cooked. Got it?"

"Ok."

Steven: Yes.

Richard: Awesome.

Steven: We're having hot dogs if she asks, and I can't be out too late. Before dark, anyway.

Richard: When's she gonna ask?

Steven: Never mind.

Richard: Don't forget to bring some sheets.

Steven's heart bottomed out, realizing his dilemma.

Richard: We all bring something, or we break the pact.

Steven: I'll bring 'em.

Richard: Good. I just have to call Michael. Billy's not coming, because he's got relatives over, but that's all right. We can deal with what we've got. I don't think we'll need tape, and he'd chicken out once we got there. Allie says the wagon's already there.

Steven: This is going to be so cool.

Richard: As long as no one tells anyone.

Steven: See you there in half an hour. Bye.

Richard: Bye.

Steven ran to his bedroom.

He was responsible for bringing only one thing, and had pissed in them not too long ago. He knew they'd still be wet, but checked.

They wouldn't have dried in the last few minutes. They might dry on the way to the park, though. What if they don't?

All his friends, except for Billy, would find out that he was a bed-wetter within the hour.

Even if they dry, they'll still smell like piss.

After finding nothing in his dresser drawers or in the laundry room, Steven settled for plan B. He raced his wet, urine-soaked bed sheets into the dryer and added a stack of fabric softener sheets.

4

THE ROLL OF TAPE / BILLY

He really did have relatives at his house; his brother was on break from the military, had been for a few weeks.

But Billy Jones was chicken, and that was the real situation. He didn't even know why Richard wanted him to bring the tape in the first place, and hadn't been told the plan or let in on the pact. But that was probably because they knew he would chicken out at the end—which he had. And he wasn't known for keeping secrets well. It was maybe better that he stayed home.

Deep down, Billy wanted to help his friends, regardless of what they were doing. He wanted to fit in, to be part of the gang. He had helped construct the fort in Canford Park, occasionally, and helped collect river rocks for later use in building the dam in the creek, yet he never seemed to fit in with the others.

They were a grade above him in school, yet treated him as an equal. What made him feel most welcome was that Ray Duschenne would pick on him when he picked on the others. In a weird way, it helped Billy feel welcome.

When Richard called him, Billy simply told him that his parents said he couldn't go because he had relatives over.

There was no way he'd confess he wasn't going because of the yellow blood running through his veins. Instead, he spent the day with his best friend, Matthew Stevenson. They played in the backyard popping holes in soda cans with Billy's Daisy. Matty wanted one for his birthday so they'd each have one and wouldn't have to take turns shooting.

But before any of his fun times with Matthew, Billy had called back Richard. He let him know there would be a roll of tape on the back porch if he wanted to swing by on the way to the park to pick it up. While Billy and his friend spent the day playing Cowboys and Indians and shooting copper BBs into Pepsi and Dr. Pepper cans, the tape lay undisturbed on the back porch.

Sometime before five o'clock it was gone.

5

THE DRAGON / RICHARD

It was babysitting night, one of those nights when his parents were out on a date—most likely dinner at a fancy restaurant, followed by dancing and maybe ice cream or coffee. Richard looked forward to the babysitter. She was untouchable, he knew—brought a kid with her one time, and it was hers—but Julie was hot.

Before his parents left for the evening, they reiterated the rules for the hundredth time in Richard's life, leaving numbers for every place they would be at, in case of emergencies. They left a twenty-dollar bill behind for him to give the pizza delivery guy.

"Make sure your brother is in bed by nine and you both brush your teeth and go potty," his mom said.

This made him blush a deep red. He couldn't hide it. Julie saw his cheeks. Dimples darkened around her mouth like two symmetrical beauty marks.

"I'll make sure they both go *potty* and brush their teeth before bedtime," Julie said with a cute, knowing smile. "Have a great time, you two."

Richard couldn't help but notice everything about Julie. There was something about her that pulled all eyes and concentration to her stunning form, as if all matter revolved around her and gravity was just a sick game of false love.

It was forever before the door closed, forever before his parents left for the night.

Kyle, his younger brother, required a nudge.

He nudged back, embarrassed, because he was staring.

Inconspicuously, or so he thought, Richard studied Julie as she set her things down and got comfortable.

She wore black running pants, the kind with the white stripes up the sides and buttons running the length of the legs. The two or three buttons at the bottom on each leg were unbuttoned to make room for her clunky black boot-like shoes. They reminded him of military boots, appropriate for the blue-black-gray camouflage tank top—thin straps, he noticed. Richard admired her strawberry blonde hair, which was pulled into a ponytail.

"So what are we doing tonight?" she asked.

It startled him out of the trance.

"Uh … um, what?"

Richard put his hands into his pockets and looked toward the kitchen at his brother, who had dropped a stack of paper plates on the floor and was spilling more as he tried to pick them up.

She pulled a scrunchie from her hair, ran her fingers through waves of strawberry gold as her eyes met his.

"Wanna play some games, or watch a movie? I can teach you how to paint your nails."

As she smiled, Richard smiled.

His cheeks were probably rose blossoms.

Richard wished he were her age.

"The pizza should be here in a few minutes," he said. "We can probably only watch one movie. Kyle can only watch part of it. I might be able to watch all of it, but I have to be in bed by—"

"I won't tell if you won't tell," Julie said.

He liked the way that sounded.

"How about this?" she said. "You both stay up for a movie

before going to bed, but you have to go to bed *right* after. And remember, if you mention any of this to your parents, they might not let me come over again. Deal?"

"Deal."

She started laughing.

"Kyle, you're so cute," she said.

Kyle was only five, but Richard hated him for drawing her attention.

Napkins and paper plates were jumbled in Kyle's hands and in a heap on the floor. Just as the doorbell rang. Julie gave the delivery person the twenty. The pizza was $15.51.

The pepperoni pizza was nothing more than cheese and crust stuck to the grease-soaked cardboard box after about ten minutes. Richard took it outside. When he returned, Kyle had already picked a movie. This made Richard a little upset at first, and then he saw the title and laughed.

"No," Julie said sympathetically, and trying not to laugh. "We'll watch *Basic Instinct* in twelve or thirteen years, okay?"

"Okay," he replied.

How could you not agree with someone like Julie when everything about her was so hypnotic?

She leaned over to the movies under the television stand. As she did this, Richard's eyes were pulled to her stomach. It was not the abdominal muscles revealed by her tank top, which gravity held open to view; it wasn't even the tight curves of her butt, thighs, and legs, revealed by the silky running pants that clung to her skin like plastic wrap; it was the tattoo.

It drew his attention like a magnet. He stared at it as if his eyes would burst if he blinked or moved them away.

"Let's see," she said, and held up a movie. "How about *Spirit?* You want to watch the one about the horses?"

She looked to Kyle for approval, and then turned to Richard and discovered his stare. Another smile.

"This one all right?" she asked.

Richard nodded, his eyes never leaving the tattoo he was trying to decipher.

Julie turned back to the television and put in the movie. She set the remote down, flipped off her boots, and sat between them.

Richard noticed her toenails were painted dark blue.

His curious stare turned into an empty stare at the screen as his mind tried bringing shape to the tattoo on Julie's stomach.

Was it a bird? A flower? Why would a flower be black, stupid? Birds could be black, but a flower?

"You want to see?" Julie asked.

It came from nowhere.

Richard's heart skipped, and then beat wildly.

His felt warm and confused, all at once.

And light-headed.

He nodded, dumbfounded.

Julie bent toward him and away from Kyle, who was watching the moving unblinkingly, and slid down the couch, with her legs straightened. She untied the elastic tie around her waist, folded the band of her pants down a couple times. A section of tattoo appeared, and the first two inches of her black underwear.

Richard's heart fluttered again, for it was the most he had ever seen of a girl.

He had seen panties and bras on mannequins at the stores, but never before had he seen them worn by a real woman. A shoelace-like strap encircled her hips ... his eyes moving to her stomach and belly button as one set of fingers held the folds of her pants down while the other moved her tank top up to the bottom part of her bra. It, too, was black. There were so many curves, and everything looked soft and smooth, including the tattoo.

The top half of a black dragon.

Its head was sharp, as were its teeth, and its snout touched the outer rim of her belly button, which was pierced with a silver hoop. The body of the dragon was strong and scaly, with a jagged spine like a dinosaur. Claws reached to the lowest abdominal muscles and the little hairs below them, both powerful and frightening. The rest of the body was cut off by Julie's underwear line. The tail traveled to far depths, the tip coming back up from her underwear in a curve and a point on the other side of her lower abdominal muscles.

There was no color in the dragon—only black, lots of it.

Richard had never seen anything so amazing in his entire life. What he said next sounded wrong the moment it left his mouth.

"How far down does it go?"

"As far as it *can*, and then back. You're not old enough to see the rest of it, though. Your parents wouldn't let me back again and I'd probably go to prison."

His heart dropped.

"Does it hurt?"

"Not anymore."

Richard wondered if it felt scaly at all, and then she told him, as if reading his mind.

"You can feel it if you want. It only feels like skin. It hurt when I first got it, and peeled."

Richard brushed the dragon with the back of his finger. It felt like skin, not bumpy or like anything he'd expected.

Kyle was out like a light. Richard looked to the ceiling, wide awake and thinking of dragons. He had always been a fan of dragons and loved stories about them. He especially loved *The Eyes of the Dragon*, a book he had read one summer. The placement of Julie's dragon and the skin nearest her navel, the mysterious depths below … it had him in a dither. He imagined the rest of the dragon, wondered about the tail and how long it might be, and where it ended. He couldn't sway his thoughts from the thick black lines that outlined the dragon's body, and the sharp points ending in claws and teeth and wingtips.

His eyes were heavy and closing when he heard bathwater running down the hall. It perked his eyelids open.

Julie's voice, sweet and soft.

She must have had someone on the phone.

He eavesdropped.

(Isn't it?)

Richard had to focus all his attention in order to hear.

(With those kinds of hours, definitely.)

A silent moment.

(No, I'll stay at the club a while longer. Until this thing is a sure deal … Yeah. I'll quit and work for there full-time. The money's not as good, but—)

The water running into the tub ceased. What followed were splashes. Splashing meant only one thing: the door was open; otherwise, the splashes would sound muddled.

His stare at the ceiling widened. He got out of bed and put his ear to the open crack of his bedroom door.

(The benefits, mostly. I'll have to pay most of it from my paycheck, but at least I'll have benefits. Club doesn't offer anything like ... no, I can't afford anything like that.)

The buttons from her pants hit the tile floor.

Richard pushed his door open slowly, so it wouldn't squeak, and tiptoed down the hall. His bedroom door faced the bathroom door, but the doors weren't perfectly aligned.

Richard's heart raced as it had when she had first shown him the tattoo. He got almost all the way down the hall when he heard the soft whisper of something else hitting the floor.

The door crack revealed Julie, facing the opposite way, her left elbow angled on her hip.

Richard could see most of the room.

It felt wrong.

One eye peered through the crack; the other directly at the face of the door, creating a fuzzy, transparent view. He blinked heavily and quickly, as if closing his eyes for too long would cause the beauty he was seeing to go away.

Julie stood with a hand on her waist, the other holding a cell to her ear, and a foot resting on the edge of the tub. All she wore was the black bra and black panties he had glimpsed earlier.

His heart wanted to burst from his chest.

Julie leaned down to test the temperature of the water and her body transformed into a curvy L-shape. When her hand came back, it was covered in white foamy bubbles that she shook into the tub. A six-inch layer of the same substance blanketed the water surface, like cloud cover.

Richard knew it was wrong to stare in at her like this, but that idea was lost somewhere in a dream.

Julie unsnapped a magical latch; her bra fell to a crumpled

black lump next to the rest of her clothing on the floor, revealing her smooth, toned back.

She walked out of his line of sight.

His heart sank as a second lump flew across the room, landed on the floor, and his heart would *burst*, he knew, spilling blood everywhere and turning the white walls red.

Julie, still on the phone.

Richard, too distracted to hear the words.

Suddenly, her voice intensified; not because she was speaking louder, but because she was drawing nearer to the bathroom door.

Richard backed against the adjacent wall. His eyes mashed shut until Julie's voice stopped. He had no clue where in the room she might be, and waited for what seemed lifetimes before he heard the sounds of water again.

By the time he gathered enough courage to spy again, Julie was neck-deep in bubbles, a single knee exposed. She stretched that leg out and wiggled her toes, put her leg back in, and the knee rose to a polished point.

He stared through the crack for what seemed like half an hour, never blinking, and never looking away. He knew at some point she would eventually get out of the tub. A towel was folded neatly on the toilet seat a few steps away.

Julie added hot water once or twice, but her body never rose above the bubbles. The phone call didn't last as long as the bath—just a couple minutes. Julie lay back in the tub, tiny bubbles popping like Rice Krispies in milk. They must have been expensive bubbles because they lasted so long. He stared endlessly at Julie, at the bubbles, at the pile of clothing on the floor.

And then she rose from the water and showed him the

dragon. Its tail plunged deeper than he had imagined, working its way back from the abyss to her navel, with the top of the tail edging the bare skin above God's greatest creation in sharp black.

Soap bubbles streamed down her body, racing along her skin and to the dragon tail. Water glistened, reflected and shimmered light from the smooth curves of her body.

Richard's pulse slowed, and his breathing relaxed.

He was in bed not long after, thinking of the dragon. He never thought of his lifelong desire, to see a naked woman in the flesh, as having been fulfilled. All he remembered was the dragon, and how it had drawn his attention to it alone. He tried with all his might to remember a glimpse of breast, or *any* part of her, but all he could see was the image of the dragon.

As if it were protecting her.

Richard thought of only one other thing that night. Like some kind of inspiration born from seeing Julie's tattoo.

They had to stop Ray from becoming a monster.

They had to promise never to tell anyone.

They had to make a pact.

The dragon had shown him this.

Richard made a list of things they would need, and met with his friends the following morning in Canford Park.

6

THE KEY / MICHAEL

Michael Farley returned from the park after he and Billy nailed a few more pieces of wood to the tree. It had been a much safer time without Ray showing up with his fireworks. His absence allowed them to complete the final wall of the fort. The only thing left was to dam up the creek on Saturday morning.

"Absolutely not," his mother said. "What makes you think you can spend all day gallivanting around the park when you were there most of today? Look how dirty—"

He looked down at his once-blue jeans.

"I *have* to go," Michael said. "I'll do the dishes and take out the trash and clean my room and mow the lawn."

He wouldn't do any of those things, but it was worth a shot. *Please*, his expression pleaded.

"Tomorrow you're helping your father with the shed."

"I thought we were doing that Sunday."

"We *were* going to work on it Sunday, but the forecast is calling for rain, so now we're doing it tomorrow."

"Why not next weekend?"

"No," she said, and walked away.

Michael followed her and helped clean as she cleaned.

"I have to be there. I have to bring—" He almost said *the key to the mortuary*, but instead said, "rocks, to help with the dam."

"You have to *bring* rocks to the creek?"

"Yeah."

"Aren't there any rocks *at* the creek?"

"Not any good ones."

"And how will you be bringing these rocks?"

She was just full of questions.

"Allie Hart has a wagon."

She gave him a strange look. She could always tell when he was lying, as if lying turned him bright pink.

"We're going to be lugging loads from her house and Billy's house all day. That's why I'll be out all day … and home late. It's a lot of work. *Please?*"

"No."

His dad entered the room, kicked off his shoes and sat at the table. He appeared tired from embalming bodies.

"What's all this about?" he asked.

"Whether or not I can go to the park tomorrow and help my friends dam the creek, like I *promised*. Mom says we have to work on the stupid shed in the backyard."

"I thought we were doing that Sunday," he said.

"It's supposed to *rain* Sunday. I thought the two of you could work on it tomorrow instead," she said, and then added to her son, "If you finish early, you can go to the park to help with the bridge."

"Dam," Michael corrected.

He actually meant *damn*, and got away with it.

"That sounds like a plan," his father said.

"Can't we do it next weekend?"

"Your mother said no, Michael."

He watched his father loosen his tie and sort through a stack of mail on the kitchen counter.

Michael looked one last time to his mother.

"No," she said.

By the fourth or fifth *no, Michael*, he gave up.

He would just have to get the keys to Richard or someone else in the morning and not go. He'd be breaking the pact, but so what? The pact was stupid. It wasn't even a pact, really, as Richard kept calling it; it was more like a prank. What *was* a pact was that no one could ever talk about the prank.

He could still play a part, though, so he made it his plan to get the key to Richard in the morning and help his dad break down the stupid shed in the stupid backyard to make his stupid mom happy. He'd never tell another soul; he would get it back from Richard later in the day. No one would ever know.

Long after his parents were busy counting sheep, Michael crept downstairs in the dark to the key rack hanging by the front door. With as little sound as possible, he snatched the key ring from the third hook. He held it up to what little light gleamed in through the window. The skeleton key was easy to find.

It unlocked the town mortuary where his father worked.

Michael removed the key and placed the key ring back onto the third hook. As he did this, his luck changed.

It started to rain.

7

THE PRANK / THE PACT

Rain from the previous night left the ground wet, the air cleansed. What remained from the storm was a sky full of nimbus clouds broken apart by segments of blue canopy, floating buoyantly like battleships through a sky starting to break apart.

Richard got to Canford Park first. He inspected the fort, both to assure himself that it had remained undisturbed overnight and to verify the work of Michael and Billy the evening prior. Besides the black marks left by Ray's ambush, the fort was near completion.

It was a patchwork affair.

While he waited for the others, Richard attached a rope he had brought to the trapdoor underneath the floor—it would serve as a swing and also to aid in quick getaways, should the need arise.

He also brought a bat, which he placed on the hooks above the entrance door, the way one might display a rifle over a fireplace. He adjusted it so the words 'Louisville Slugger' faced outward.

Richard was knotting the rope in a couple places when Allie arrived. Like Richard, she rode in on her bike, and parked it against the base of the tree.

"Everyone coming?" she asked.

Richard concentrated on his knots.

"Billy's not, but he's too much of a risk. He would find a way to tell someone. Steven is coming. He's bringing blankets."

"I thought he was bringing sheets," she said.

"That's what I meant. Hopefully they're clean, though.

Everyone says he still wets the bed."

"Rumors," she said, "probably started by Raymond. He doesn't really wet the bed anymore, you think?"

"If they smell like piss, just don't say anything—we'll still use them. It might even be better."

Allie laughed and climbed up the tree trunk ladder. She leaned out the window with her elbows resting on the sills. She looked to Richard with her schoolgirl crush as he finished the last of his knots and started for the creek.

"I didn't think Michael was coming. He said he wouldn't have been able to, if not for the rain last night."

Richard stacked the rocks that had fallen back in their pyramid piles.

"But he's coming and bringing the key. If *he* weren't coming, we would've had to call the whole thing off. We're lucky it rained. His parents were making him do something with their shed. Tear it down, I think."

Allie leaned farther out the window and said, "I guess it's okay to play in the mud, as long as you're not working in it, huh?"

"His backyard is all dirt, so it's probably really muddy. He told me they're getting ready to lay sod in the back and it takes a lot of prep work. A couple weeks or something."

Allie tested the exit by climbing down the rope.

"This is cool," she said, joining Richard at the water.

The flow of the creek was only inches deep.

"The rope was Billy's idea," Richard said. "He thought it'd be cool to have a swing, so I made it both that, and an escape hatch. Crap. I forgot the—"

"What?" Allie asked, putting a hand on his.

"I forgot to grab the tape from Billy. He left it out for me since he wasn't coming. I'll swing by later, I guess."

"That was nice of him to do that," she said, holding his hand in the elementary school "going together" way.

"Get a room!"

It was Michael, from the dirt path through the park. A moment later he was visible and walking toward them.

They released hands and stood.

Richard cleared his throat. "Glad you could make it."

"You guys break-in the tree fort?"

"No," both answered.

Michael pulled the skeleton key from his pocket, and it looked tarnished and oily from use in the old locks of the mortuary.

"My dad would kill me if he knew. Everyone coming?"

"Everyone but Billy, so far," Richard said.

Allie kept a friendly distance away from Richard, no longer in a flirting mode. Now she was just one of the guys.

"Do you wanna start on the dam?" Michael asked. "We'll have to start over, I guess. Ray tore most of it down."

What they had started on was in ruins.

Richard said, "Nah, let's wait for Steven; he should be here any minute. I called before I left. Said he'd be right over. You want to check out the fort? I just tied the rope underneath."

Richard and Allie worked their way up the ladder as Michael inspected the rope.

"You tie a good knot?" Michael asked from below, and gave the rope a couple hard yanks.

Richard was on the last rung of the ladder when he answered, "It'll hold *your* skinny ass. You guys use good wood up here?" He stepped into the fort, Allie following.

"Clove hitch or square knot?"

"It's an I-don't-give-a-crap knot," Richard said.

Michael climbed the rope clumsily and inspected the mess of a knot at the top. It held; that was all that really mattered. With much effort, Michael made it through the hole in the floor.

"Next time I'll use the ladder."

"Mostly for going down," Richard said, "or swinging."

All three sat in the tree for a while, not saying anything, but not needing to. They looked at the black marks left by Ray's fireworks bombardment, and smiled at one another.

"What if he throws more," Allie asked, "while we're here, or even if we're not here at all?"

Her question was left hanging as a fourth rustled the leaves at the clearing's edge. Their first reaction was that it was Ray showing up early to spoil everything.

"Stevie," Richard said.

"Hey, *Steven*," Allie corrected.

Steven pedaled like mad as he approached the tree. He jumped off and to the side of his bike and let it crash. He ran the rest of the way, out of breath.

"I got here as fast as I could."

He panted and skipped steps as he climbed the ladder.

"No hurry," Richard said. "Ray's at summer school."

"If he shows up at all, it won't be until later," Allie said.

They all knew he'd show.

"I hope he gets held back another year, Steven said with heavy breaths. "Someday he'll be in the same grade as us and we can pick on *him* for a change."

"The sheets," Steven said. He threw his pack to the opposite side of the fort and glanced around at his friends.

"My mom made sandwiches," Allie said to break the awkward silence. "I think peanut butter and jelly."

They stared at one another with blank faces, all contemplating whether or not they were really going to pull this off.

Richard headed for the rope and said, "I don't know about you two, but I want to build a new dam."

Moments later he was on the ground.

They followed, each grabbing an armful of wood from behind the tree, and carried the loads to the water.

They were able to get the water a foot deep. At one edge of the creek lay horizontally arranged boards, supported by rock and mud. Water ran through the various places not yet patched. Above it was a growing pond, already three feet across in some places.

All four of them had their pant legs rolled above the knees and their backsides wet from bending into the water.

Hours later, they had a respectable-sized pond.

They took a break to eat sandwiches and to discuss and finalize the pact / prank. All four agreed they'd never talk about it afterward, to anyone, and for the rest of their lives, except within the tree fort. They sealed the pact by cutting their palms with a pocket-knife, and notarized it by shaking bloody hands.

Water ran over the top of the dam, no longer through it. They were each soaked to the waistline and a little cold from the water, with fingers and toes shriveled like raisins.

While Allie, Michael, and Steven patched the last few gaps, Richard raced over to Billy's house to get the tape.

Allie told him to hurry.

Richard rode like the wind down Mulberry Street. Billy lived on Newman Court on the southern side of town. As he cut the corner between Mulberry and Newman, he thought of the dragon, the black, sharp-edged lines and curved wings, the sharp points of the claws and teeth ...

As Richard flew across the middle of the road, a Lincoln nearly hit him. The man in the car cursed and looked down to his lap and then to the boy he had almost killed.

Richard overcorrected his bike and swerved aimlessly. Without another thought of the near tragedy, he cycled to the sidewalk and continued down the court.

He slid to a stop at Billy's, leaving parallel black tire marks on the driveway. He looked through the windows for Billy, but no one was home. On the porch was the gray roll of duct tape. Attached to it was a note, with *Be careful* scrawled on it. Before he left, Richard ripped thin strips of tape from the roll and stuck them to the porch to spell THANX. He jumped on his bike and pedaled like hell.

Ray Duschenne managed to show at the park before Richard made it back. Michael and Steven sat at the far side of the pond, their feet dangling in the water. Allie was knee-deep in the pond. When they saw Ray, they looked at each other as if to ask, "What should we do? Where's Richard? He should be back by now."

With no obvious answer, they watched as he approached.

"So, this must be your new bathing hole, huh girls?"

Ray's red hair was oily like his skin—the look of a high school student who had flipped burgers and worked the fry cooker a little too long. His pockets bulged with fireworks and mischief. He wore battered jeans more brown than blue.

"You just gonna sit there looking stupid?" he said to the boys. "What about you, Allie? You here to watch these two wash each other's backs and make out?"

Richard approached on his bike; all three saw him and averted their eyes. He rode slowly, not really pedaling, but coasting closer. He stopped a ways away, parked along the dirt path, and sauntered to the clearing behind the oak tree.

Ray continued with his insults.

"That's a nice pond you've got here," he said.

Ray picked up a river rock the size of a bowling ball with both hands and held it in his arms for a while as one might hold a small child, hefting its weight as he bobbed it up and down.

"Please don't," Allie said. "We've been working on it all day."

In the background, Richard climbed the rope.

"If you don't break anything, you can use the pond when we're not using it," she said. "Don't break it. *Please?*"

Michael and Steven looked at each other.

Steven spoke first.

"No way! There's no way this jerk's gonna use our pond. *We* built the dam. *We* worked our butts off. *We* get to use it. This creep can find his own part of the creek to dam. This is ours."

"Yeah, get bent, Ray," Michael said.

Ray heaved the rock into the water. It landed a small distance from Michael and Steven. Brown, mucky water exploded over the boys in a wave, engulfing them.

Steven spit some of it from his mouth.

Michael peeled a leaf from his face.

A rock like a gray gumball bounced off Ray's chest and landed at his feet. He looked to Allie and saw that she held a bigger rock.

Ray laughed a goofy laugh and picked up a similar rock.

"Do it, and I'll bury this into your face, you cunt."

Allie threw her rock, hitting him in the crotch. She smiled and looked to Michael and Steven, who sprang to their feet.

Ray doubled over, held his crotch while they laughed.

Michael held his side.

Steven pointed as Allie joined in.

Just as Allie turned back to her target, the rock Ray had been holding nailed her in the temple. She cried out, fell to her knees. Blood from her face dripped between her fingers.

Steven ran to her side, pulled hair away from her eyes.

Michael followed and kneeled next to her.

She was crying.

It was too late; Ray Duschenne was already a monster.

The Louisville Slugger made an awful sound as it cracked over the back of the monster's head, the monster eyes losing focus as its body collapsed to the ground, the monster face plunging into the soil.

Richard let the bat fall and joined his friends. He carefully brushed away the hairs around Allie's wound to reveal a V-shape cut. It wasn't deep but would swell and bruise badly. He helped her to her feet and asked if she was okay.

"I'll be fine," she said, sobbing, not really fine.

She had blood on her hand and smeared it over her face when she tried to rub away the tears.

Ray Duschenne lay face down in the dirt. Unmoving.

"He's not dead, you think?" Steven asked.

Michael walked to the lump and poked with his foot, leaned in closer for further inspection.

"He's still breathing. Look, you can see his—"
Smack!

Allie bludgeoned Ray's head a second time with the bat, hard enough to have knocked him out again, and then spat.

"That's for calling me the C-word, asshole!"

They turned Ray over and dragged him to the clearing.

8

THE MORTUARY / THE COFFIN

They fastened his hands and feet with duct tape and placed a strip over his mouth in case he happened to wake up en route. They had Ray wrapped in the bed sheets with tape around his legs and feet. Allie wheeled out her red wagon from the clearing and, combining their strength, they were able to lift Ray onto it. They propped him so his knees rose higher than his slumped-over head, stuffed pieces of wood around his body, and fluffed the sheets a little, making it appear as if anything could be under there.

And then wheeled him three miles.

A cop drove by slowly, but only threw them a tender smile. It probably looked cute seeing four kids carting junk in a wagon— that's what kids did during the summertime.

When they got to the mortuary, it was close to eight. They had less than an hour before dark.

The building had an antique look, as if it properly belonged in the 1800s. Granite blocks made the exterior walls. The roof peaked in several places like a castle. Everything around the building was dead: grass, trees, and shrubs—lifeless and dry. The only surviving tree on the lot had spidery branches which seemed to want to grab for the passing children. Farther back was an equally old cemetery with broken headstones scattered around.

Everything was dead, except for the roses. Crimson rose-bushes bled with color, the flower petals outlined in black, as if burnt.

Michael pulled the skeleton key from his Velcro pocket,

and struggled with the lock, which clunked mechanically as it turned. The old door rubbed against newer wood on the floor. Moments later, they were inside and gaping at the line of coffins. One would expect embalmed bodies to rise out of them.

Light through stained-glass windows brought an eerie, hazy orange-brown glow to the place, with dust streams filling the musty air.

The coffin that called to them was black and made of oak, with an exterior polished like a grand piano. The interior was a light blue satin. It was displayed on a raised platform surrounded by red velvet barriers of the sort once used in movie theaters.

It took all of their effort to lift his body into the coffin.

They uncovered Ray Duschenne and removed the tape around his wrists, ankles, and mouth, arranged his body in funeral fashion with his arms crossing his chest.

What would it feel like to wake in such a condition?

Smiles widened on this shared thought.

9

THE DEAD FIELD / THE END

They remained silent the entire trek homeward, trailing the wagon behind with the wood, bat, tape, and bed sheets. Fluffy clouds had turned vanilla. They stopped to watch the sky slowly darken to red. Far in the distance, a melodic rock song blared from a stereo and then faded to nothing. The sun was about to set when they reached the wheat field.

It was the field they had always crossed when returning home from Canford Park, the golden grain dry and ready for harvesting. The owner would soon cut it down using his giant combine, which was rumored years ago to have harvested a child who had used the shortcut—this was a favorite scary story told by parents in an effort to stop kids from cutting though the field. Walking through it left a flat, trampled trail where the brittle stems snapped underfoot. The red wagon made an even wider path as Allie dragged it along.

Soft wind hummed through the stalks, making wavy patterns as the grain tops shifted back and forth—a dry, golden ocean.

Shoelaces and socks filled with burrs, attracted to the children's feet like moths to light. Every once in a while, a sharp tip of a grain head would reach out and prick the child passing by, as if to upbraid them for their trespassing.

Richard stumbled over something and fell forward.

Michael tripped over Richard's feet, fell next to him. His hand landed in what he guessed was a cow patty, or the decaying carcass of a dead animal, warm and wet under his fingers, coated in a mix of raspberry jelly and melted marshmallow.

Richard's shirtsleeves were covered in the same vile- smelling ooze. He was speechless. Red everywhere.

Red ... and *white* ...

Steven bent down to see what they had tripped over. He gave a couple dry heaves before vomiting up bile and half-digested peanut butter and jelly.

Allie covered her nose and joined the boys at their discovery. She hysterically laughed and cried in an awkward combination of emotions. She dropped the wagon handle, gagged, and ran with her face buried in her hands. Her body disappeared into the dead field, leaving behind a tunnel.

Steven threw up a second time and bolted ahead with a rope of mucus hanging from his lips.

Michael wiped his hands onto his pants, then realized the marshmallow stuff was moving—a mass of plump maggots.

The body lay face-up, skin bloated and semitransparent.

The horrid face: a melted visage with a smile cut from ear to ear. All that remained of the eyes were black sockets. The crown of the skull was missing as well. Inside the head was a hallow cavern being scraped clean. The head, more than anything, looked like a jack-o'-lantern.

The two remaining boys ran. They caught up with Allie and Steven at the edge of the field, panting with their heads hung low and arms resting on their thighs.

No one could speak.

They had to tell someone ... call the police ... do something—anything—as soon as humanly possible. Each pair of eyes revealed the horror. Each small body shook with fear, trembling lips unable to construct words.

Richard wanted to offer an idea, but his mouth wouldn't move. His tongue constricted, so he pointed a trembling finger to a house in the distance.

The address of the place: 196, the six leaning slightly.

It was weathered and old, possibly deserted, with weeds covering the yard and shingles missing from the rooftop. The entire house slanted like a parallelogram.

Each step of the porch creaked as they approached, the boards ready to break through in many places and at any time. Nail heads stuck like thumbtacks above the rotting wood. The awning above the bewildered children drooped heavily, as if from an unbearable fatigue.

On the porch, in a flowerpot, bloomed a single black-edged crimson rose, like those surrounding the mortuary, the only offering of color to balance the gray sadness.

Richard knocked on the door and they waited.

The children had a sickening story to tell, one so twisted and unbelievable ...

A woman answered, holding a pumpkin carving knife.

Behind them, the sky bled.

Michael Bailey is a multi-award-winning author, editor and publisher, and the recipient of over two dozen literary accolades, including the Bram Stoker Award, Benjamin Franklin Award, Eric Hoffer Book Award, Independent Publisher Book Award, the Indie Book Award, the International Book Award, and others. His novels include *Palindrome Hannah*, *Phoenix Rose* and *Psychotropic Dragon*, and he has published two short story and poetry collections, *Scales and Petals*, and *Inkblots and Blood Spots* (illustrated by Daniele Serra, with an introduction by Douglas E. Winter).

He is also the founder of the small press Written Backwards, where he has created psychological horror anthologies such as *Pellucid Lunacy*, *The Library of the Dead*, four volumes of *Chiral Mad* (the fourth co-edited by Lucy A. Snyder), and a few dark science fiction anthologies such as *Qualia Nous* and *You, Human*. He also served as the co-editor of both *Adam's Ladder* and *Prisms* (with Darren Speegle). Most recent publications include *Oversight*, a collection of novelettes including *Darkroom* and *SAD Face*, and the standalone novelette *Our Children, Our Teachers*. He lives in forever-burning California.

You can follow him on social media at twitter.com/nettirw, facebook.com/nettirw, or online at www.nettirw.com.